## Just Jimmy

Richmal Crompton, the creator of *Just William*, was born in 1890. Her first William story was published in 1919, and she went on to write 38 collections of stories about William, many books of short stories, and several novels for adults before her death in 1969.

Much less famous than William but no less charming, her stories about *Jimmy* first appeared in the *Star* newspaper in February 1947, and this collection was first published in book form in 1949. It has been unavailable for decades. *Just Jimmy* introduces this rediscovered classic to a new generation of readers.

*Just Jimmy Again* follows soon.

JIMMY PUT HIS HANDS ON HIS HIPS AND PLANTED
HIS LEGS FIRMLY APART.

*(see page 130)*

RICHMAL CROMPTON

# *Just Jimmy*

*Illustrated by Thomas Henry*

MACMILLAN
CHILDREN'S BOOKS

First published 1949

This edition published 1998 by Macmillan Children's Books
a division of Macmillan Publishers Limited
25 Eccleston Place, London SW1W 9NF
and Basingstoke

Associated companies throughout the world

ISBN 0 333 71230 7

1 3 5 7 9 8 6 4 2

A CIP catalogue record for this book is available from
the British Library.

Typeset by SX Composing DTP, Essex
Printed and bound in Great Britain by Mackays of Chatham plc, Kent

# Contents

# Chapter 1

# *Jimmy Turns the Tables*

He had been christened James, but he was always known as Jimmy, except when he was unpopular or in disgrace. When he was unpopular he became Jim and when he was in disgrace he became James or simply "that boy". He was seven and three-quarters – sturdy and rather stocky, with an expression of solemnity that was apt to mislead people, and a deep voice that was apt to break into a slight stammer when he was excited.

He was plodding along the road now behind Roger, his eleven-year-old brother, and Roger's two friends, Charles and Bill – an inseparable trio whose nickname of the "Three Musketeers" had originally been given them by Jimmy's father. To an ordinary observer they were just three scruffy little boys – noisy, untidy, inadequately washed – but to Jimmy they were heroic beings from the legendary world of adventure and romance. His greatest joy in life was to be allowed to tag along with them, and, even when he wasn't allowed to tag along with them, he generally managed to do so. He knew that this morning they had been particularly anxious to avoid his company, so he kept a good twenty yards behind, and, whenever they turned round to see if he was still there, pretended to be absorbed in the hedge at the side of the road. He had gathered that something more exciting than usual was afoot today, and he wanted to take a part in it, however inglorious.

A group of boys was waiting for them at the crossroads – the other members of Roger's gang. They carried a motley assortment of weapons – pistols, airguns, bows and arrows, catapults, sticks. One boy carried a rolling-pin, another a potato masher (both commandeered without authority from their mothers' kitchen drawers), while another had a dustbin lid for a shield and a poker for a spear.

They gathered round Roger, their leader, and began to talk, scuffling about as they did so in the manner of small boys everywhere, pushing each other into the ditch, starting vague and inconclusive fights that ended as suddenly as they began, testing their weapons on each other, tweaking each other's hair and ears. In spite of these incidental activities, it was clear that the matter they were discussing was a serious one.

"We've declared war on the Mouldies," said Roger in his generalissimo voice, "an' it starts today, so we can't waste any time."

Jimmy gave a gasp of excitement. The Mouldies were the rival gang, whose leader was Archie Mould – a fox-like boy, red-haired, long-nosed, of formidable cunning and strength. It was a larger gang than Roger's and composed for the most part of older boys, which, in the eyes of Roger's gang, lent the warfare a zest it might otherwise have lacked.

"Does anyone know where they are?" said Roger.

As he spoke, he took his binoculars from his pocket with a slightly self-conscious air and scanned the horizon. He had made the binoculars only a few days before out of the tops of two pilchard tins rolled into cylindrical shapes and attached to a pair of spectacles discarded by his father. The tins still smelt of pilchards and the spectacles imparted an effect of astigmatism to the landscape, but Roger was willing to put up with these drawbacks for the sake of the air of importance that he imagined they gave him. The gang watched him in a respectful silence that was finally broken by a boy known as "Toothy".

"No one's seen 'em," he said. "I've asked everyone."

"Well, then," said Roger, "me an' Charles an' Bill will go to headquarters." He lowered his voice to a conspiratorial note. "Headquarters is the kitchen of the blitzed house in Barret Lane an' you've none of you gotter give away that secret even under the mos' deadly torcher." He abandoned the conspiratorial note and continued in his generalissimo voice: "The rest of you mus' go an' reconnoitre an' bring in your reports an' then we'll start the attack."

A small boy raised a cheer and was promptly extinguished by the dustbin lid.

"Stop messin' about and wastin' time," said Roger sternly. "Now we've all gotter remember what Nelson said at the battle of Waterloo. 'England expects that every man will finish the game an' beat the Armada.'"

"I think you've got that a bit mixed up," said Toothy. "I think the Black Prince said that at the battle of Agincourt."

"It doesn't matter who said it first," said Roger crushingly. "I'm sayin' it now."

Jimmy, on the outskirts of the group, was listening eagerly, his eyes alight with the lust of adventure, his heart swelling with pride in Roger, the leader, the hero, the superman. Suddenly he noticed that they were all looking at him in stern disapproval.

JIMMY, ON THE OUTSKIRTS
OF THE GROUP, LISTENED TO
ALL THIS ENTHRALLED, HIS EYES
ALIGHT WITH THE SPIRIT OF
ADVENTURE.

"We're not takin' that kid along," said Toothy in a tone of finality.

Jimmy stretched up his neck and tried to look taller than he was.

"I'm not a kid," he said stoutly. "I'm" – there was a note of appeal in his voice – "I'm seven and three-quarters and four d-days and a n-night."

Jimmy was so anxious to be eight that he always knew almost to a minute, how far off he was.

"You're a kid," said Toothy, "an' we don't want kids. Send him home, Roger."

Roger looked at Jimmy. He knew that the one thing you couldn't do with Jimmy was to send him home. At least, you could send him there, but he always came back.

"You leave it to me," he said.

He glanced round. A rickety signpost with half-obliterated lettering stood at the cross-roads.

"Guard that signpost, Jim," he said, "an' don't leave it till you're relieved."

"A'right," said Jimmy, deeply gratified by the trust reposed in him.

He stood – a small, stocky figure – at the foot of his signpost and watched the gang of noisy scuffling boys disappear down the road. Then he took a twig from the hedge and, holding it in his hand as if it were a pistol, shot down wave upon wave of attackers till the ground was piled high with the bodies of his foes. It was while he was thus engaged that he felt a hand on his shoulder and, turning round with a start, found himself looking up into the dreaded fox-like face of Archie Mould.

"Bit o' luck, taking Roger's young brother prisoner," grinned Archie. "You'll make a jolly useful hostage."

Jimmy freed his shoulder with a sudden jerk and was making a dash for liberty, when Archie grabbed him again, giving his arm a twist that brought a yell of pain from him despite himself.

Archie laughed. "I'm going to have a bit of fun with you, young James," he said. "Come on. Quick march. Across that field."

There was nothing for Jimmy to do but accompany his captor. Humiliation blazed within him – humiliation both for himself and Roger. He was Roger's brother, and he had let himself be taken prisoner. So terrible was the disgrace that, he felt, however long he lived and to whatever heights of fame he climbed, he would be branded by it for ever. Then suddenly a plan occurred to him – a plan so stupendous that for a moment it took away his breath.

"What are you goin' to d-do with me?" he said.

"Imprison you, of course," said Archie.

"Where?"

"In our coal cellar," said Archie, giving his arm another twist.

"Good!" said Jimmy, drawing quite a convincing breath of relief.

Archie looked taken aback.

"What d'you mean, good?"

"I like coal cellars," said Jimmy. "I'm always wantin' to play in ours, but my mother'll never let me."

"Oh," said Archie, thoughtfully.

"Yes," said Jimmy. "D'you know —" He stopped.

"Yes?" said Archie, his curiosity aroused.

"Well," Jimmy continued, as if reluctantly, "jus' for a minute I was afraid you were goin' to 'prison me in the kitchen of that blitzed house. There's rats there, an' I'm more scared of r-rats than of anythin' else in the world."

"Oh," said Archie again, and a slow smile spread over his fox-like face. "Well, come on! Quick march! No, the other way."

As they neared the blitzed house, Jimmy began to display signs of terror. They would not have deceived an acute observer, but Archie was not an acute observer and they deceived him.

In at the gate of the tangled garden, through the ramshackle door, across the grass-grown hall towards the kitchen – the only room left standing with four walls and a ceiling . . . Archie flung open the kitchen door and entered, dragging Jimmy by the arm. Then he stood petrified by amazement, for there, sitting round a packing case, covered by maps, were the Three Musketeers – an impressive sight if you did not know that, though Roger's was a rough-drawn map of the district, Charles's map was a map of the theatres and garages of London, and Bill's was a map of Uganda.

Archie started back with a gasp of horror, but Jimmy had turned the rusty key in the rusty lock.

He advanced to the packing case and spoke nonchalantly. Only his stammer betrayed his emotion.

"I've b-brought you a p-prisoner, Roger," he said.

## Chapter 2

# Miss Pettigrew's Parrot

"Won't you reconsider it, dear?" said Mrs Manning.

"No, I won't," said Mr Manning, ramming his hat on his head and snatching up his attaché case. "I've had a basinful from that kid this week, and this is the last straw."

With that he strode angrily down the path, out of the gate and off towards the bus stop.

"That kid" was Roger, and the "basinful" was a broken window on Monday, a cascade of water down the stairs on Tuesday, a campfire on the lawn on Wednesday, a tightrope exhibition, resulting in two broken clothes props, on Thursday and a lion hunt in the lounge on Friday. Today was Saturday, and the "last straw" was a letter, received by the morning's post from a neighbour, Miss Pettigrew, informing him that a football, kicked by Roger in the lane outside her cottage, had gone through her open window and overturned her parrot's cage, freeing the catch, so that the parrot had escaped and had not been seen since. At this, Mr Manning, displaying the natural fury of the male parent goaded beyond endurance, had decreed that Roger was not to go to the circus with the rest of the family in the afternoon.

Gloom pervaded the household. It was Jimmy who

showed most the open signs of it. Life for Jimmy was always overcast when Roger was in disgrace, and the thought of Roger's being left at home while the rest of them went to the circus was unendurable. Roger himself behaved with a stoical fortitude that increased Jimmy's always fervent hero-worship of him. He went about pale but composed.

"I suppose there'll be other circuses," he said nonchalantly, adding, with a generosity that staggered Jimmy: "The old chap's right from his point of view, of course. One can't really blame him."

But this carefully sustained attitude could not hide from Jimmy the blackness of despair that engulfed Roger's spirit.

And Jimmy determined to do something about it.

He met Bobby Peaslake in the shed at the bottom of the garden. Bobby Peaslake was the little boy who lived opposite. He was the same age as Jimmy but incredibly tall, with arms and legs that never looked adequately clothed, despite his mother's frantic efforts to keep up with them. He always wore on one bony wrist an enormous wrist-watch of antique design without works or fingers, which, he fondly imagined, gave him an air of maturity, and he cultivated a man-of-the-world manner that was apt to desert him in times of crisis. The two had already spent several precious hours in a fruitless search for Miss Pettigrew's parrot over the neighbouring countryside.

"Well, if we can't find her old parrot," said Jimmy, "we've gotter find her something that'll do instead, so that she'll say it's all right an' let Roger go to the circus. What does she want a rotten ole parrot for, anyway?"

"She says it's comp'ny," said Bobby.

"Well, so is anythin' else," said Jimmy. He was silent for a few moments, waging a secret battle with himself, then went on: "If it's comp'ny she wants, Henry's comp'ny. I wouldn't mind giving her Henry. Henry's jolly good comp'ny."

Henry was Jimmy's tortoise, a much-prized possession, which Jimmy considered to be endowed with almost superhuman intelligence and charm.

"It's not coloured, like a parrot," objected Bobby. "They're coloured red an' green, are parrots."

"Well, we could colour it," said Jimmy, determined not to be turned back by such a slight obstacle as that. "There's green paint in the garage an' there's a pot of red 'namel in the kitchen cupboard."

Bobby shook his head.

"It's not as easy as that," he said. "They talk, do parrots."

"Miss Pettigrew's doesn't."

"Yes, it does. It says 'Miaow!' It's all it can say, but it says it."

"Well, then —" A light broke suddenly over Jimmy's face. "I t-tell you what!"

"Yes?"

"Those kittens of yours!"

Bobby's family cat had, a few weeks ago, given birth to a litter of kittens, for which his mother was still trying to find homes.

"What've they got to do with it?" said Bobby.

"Well, she wants somethin' coloured for comp'ny that says 'Miaow,' so we'll paint Henry an' give him to her for – for sort of c-coloured comp'ny, an' we'll given her one of your k-kittens to say 'Miaow'."

Bobby looked at his friend admiringly.

"Gosh! That's a jolly good idea," he said.

"An' I bet she'll be so pleased she'll ring up Daddy an' he'll let Roger go to the circus," said Jimmy.

Then, with the air of one who has solved a difficult problem to the satisfaction of all concerned, he arose from his seat on the wheelbarrow and, accompanied by Bobby, went over to the greenhouse, where Henry, regardless of his doom, was sunning himself among the plant pots. Carried to the garage and thickly coated with red and green paint, Henry proved tractable enough, though there was a dispirited air about him as he stood dripping red and green paint on to the garage shelf.

"He looks jolly fine," said Jimmy, eyeing his handiwork with approval.

"He doesn't look like a parrot," objected Bobby.

"Well, he's not meant to," said Jimmy. "He's meant to be jus' a bit of coloured comp'ny *same* as a parrot. He looks *better* than a parrot to me. If I had to choose between Henry all painted up like this an' a parrot, I'd choose Henry any day. I bet she won't want that ole parrot back at all, once she's got Henry . . . Come on. We've got to hurry. We'll call for one of your kittens on the way to her cottage."

"We'll take Demon," said Bobby. "It can go on miaowing longer than any of the others. My mother says it's got a voice like a" – he paused for a moment, knitting his brows, then ended uncertainly – "syphon."

"A syphon hasn't got a voice," said Jimmy.

"This one had," said Bobby. "Someone told me about her once. She was a witch an' a man in hist'ry didn't want to listen to her singin', so she tied him to a pole an' made him."

"I don't think much of that tale," said Jimmy after

consideration. "I'd sooner have Robin Hood or Boadicea any day . . . Oh, *come* on!"

They went down the road, Jimmy carrying the still dripping Henry as best he could, and called at Bobby's house for Demon. Demon, a ball of grey fur, allowed himself to be put under Bobby's coat, and they proceeded to Miss Pettigrew's cottage.

Fate seemed to be on their side.

The cottage was empty, the drawing-room window open. The two climbed in at the window, and Jimmy placed Henry in the parrot's cage, while Bobby, on a sudden inspiration, put Demon into Miss Pettigrew's workbox.

"She won't see him at first," he said, "an' it'll be a nice surprise for her when he starts miaowing."

"Yes, that's a jolly good idea," agreed Jimmy. "We want it to be a surprise. She'll enjoy it more if it's a surprise."

It had been arranged that Jimmy should have lunch at Bobby's house, joining his own family in time to go to the circus with them. At Bobby's house, therefore, he ate an ample meal (for anxiety never impaired his appetite), removed as much red and green paint from his person as possible, and hurried home, to find the family all ready to set out. Roger was with them, obviously one of the party.

"Is Roger coming?" said Jimmy, breathless with eagerness.

"Yes, dear," said Mrs Manning.

"D-did Miss Pettigrew ring up?"

"No, dear. Why should she?" said Mrs Manning. "No . . . Your father reconsidered the matter."

She smiled to herself as she remembered the telephone conversation she had had with her husband half-way through the morning.

"I don't think for a moment that I was in the wrong," he had said with dignity. "I'm reconsidering the matter simply because the thought of the kid's not going to the circus is putting me off my work. I've lost *pounds'* worth of business through it already, and I can't afford to go on. Don't say anything to him. I intend," he had ended in an impressive, almost magisterial tone of voice, "to have a serious talk with him as soon as I get home."

Mr Manning had begun his "serious talk" with Roger as soon as he got home, but, after reaching a compromise consisting of the docking of Roger's pocket money, by which the honour of both was satisfied, it degenerated with deplorably rapidity into a discussion on circuses in general and a description of every circus that Mr Manning had ever seen.

"Daddy decided to let him go, after all," said Mrs Manning.

"Oh!" said Jimmy.

He was very thoughtful on his way to the circus . . . He was still very thoughtful as he took his seat. He was more thoughtful than ever, as fragments of a conversation carried on by two women in the row behind reached him.

"Poor Miss Pettigrew . . . the room a *shambles*! . . a horrible tortoise in the cage *dripping* red and green paint on to her carpet . . . a frightful cat that had *wrecked* her work-basket and scratched the legs of that lovely table and torn her muslin curtains to shreds . . ."

"What about the parrot?"

"Oh, that came back early this morning, but it seemed nervous of its cage and the drawing-room, so she left it loose in her bedroom . . . She says she's going round to every house in the village tomorrow to find out which boy played that wretched trick on her."

Jimmy glanced at his father, who was explaining to Roger how a flying trapeze worked. Oh, well, thought Jimmy, the worst that could happen was soon over. And Roger was at the circus, which was all that really mattered. And tomorrow was a long way off . . . Meantime a little cart was entering the ring, drawn by two dogs and driven by a monkey, who took off his hat with a flourish. Behind came a clown, tripping up at every step . . .

Abandoning himself to the pleasure of the moment, Jimmy gave a yell of delight.

*Chapter 3*

# *The Mousse*

Jimmy awoke with a vague feeling that something exciting was going to happen today. Then, quite suddenly, he remembered what it was. It was Sally's birthday party . . . There on his chest of drawers was the paintbox that he had bought for her birthday present. It had cost two-and-sixpence and he had been saving up his pocket money for five weeks to buy it. The week his father had stopped his pocket money for putting the mincing machine out of order (he'd been experimenting on the best way of making sawdust from firewood) he had sold his tame beetle to Bobby Peaslake for twopence three farthings. (Later they'd had a fight about it, because Bobby said it bit him and demanded a penny back, but they had compromised by sharing Jimmy's ice cream.) Anyway, there it was, wrapped up somewhat bulkily and inelegantly in the middle page of his last week's comic and tied by a piece of picture cord because Jimmy thought it looked more important than string. He had "borrowed" a luggage label from his mother's writing desk and written "Do not krush perrishubble" on one side in red crayon and on the other side in blue crayon "Menny hapy retterns from Jimmy Manning." Underneath that he had drawn a little house because that was the only thing he could draw that didn't look like something else.

He had fastened this to the picture cord by a safety pin and was completely satisfied with the result. It was, he felt, good enough even for Sally . . .

Roger was going to the party, too, but Roger had resolutely refused to buy a present.

"I'm not buying a present for that soppy girl," he had said contemptuously.

Sally was the little girl next door. She was nine years old, with blue eyes, ash-blond curls and a rare but entrancing smile. Her nine years made her look on Jimmy as a baby and Roger as a hero, so that the situation was a difficult one.

Jimmy was looking forward to the party, not only because of Sally, but because of the games and cakes and jellies. He was a sociable little boy and always enjoyed parties.

"It's Sally's party today," said his mother at breakfast.

"Gosh, yes!" said Jimmy, trying to imitate Roger's voice, torn between his longing to be like Roger in everything and his admiration of Sally.

"*Need* I go, Mother?" said Roger.

"Of course you must, dear," said Mrs Manning.

Jimmy resisted a temptation to ask if he need go, in case his mother said he needn't. Mrs Manning glanced out of the window.

"Sally's in the garden now," she said. "Would you like to take her your present, Jimmy?"

"S'pose I'd better," said Jimmy, trying not to rise from his seat too eagerly.

He took his paintbox down to the bottom of the garden. Sally was standing near the hole in the hedge through which most of their communications took place.

"Many happy returns of the day," said Jimmy.

"Thank you," said Sally politely.

He thrust the package through the hedge into her hands.

"I've brought you this," he said. "It's a paintbox."

"Thank you," said Sally without enthusiasm. "I have three of them already."

"B-but you said you w-wanted one," said Jimmy.

"That was weeks ago," said Sally. "I've had three given me since then."

"I'm sorry," said Jimmy.

"It doesn't matter in the least," said Sally. "It's very kind of you."

Then Roger came into the garden, with Charles and Bill, who always called for him on Saturday mornings, and at once Sally's air of boredom vanished.

"We're having ice cream for the party," she said in a high-pitched eager voice.

Roger passed by without looking at her.

"Hello, Roger," she called ingratiatingly.

"'lo," muttered Roger gruffly, still without looking at her, and then, without troubling to lower his voice, continued: "Come on. Let's get out of here. Away from soppy girls."

The three walked with an air of lordly magnificence out of the garden gate into the lane. Sally stood there for a few moments, then went away. It wasn't any use standing there any longer. She'd forgotten all about Jimmy. Jimmy, too, walked slowly away, wondering what he could give Sally for her birthday present to make up for the paintbox that she didn't want.

He was still pondering over the problem when he sat in the hall, clean and shining and ready for the party, waiting for his mother (who was going to help at the

ROGER PASSED BY WITHOUT
LOOKING AT SALLY.

party) and Roger. He would have liked to give her one of
his own treasures, but somehow he didn't think she'd
like his ball of putty or his robin's egg or the thing he used
for taking imaginary stones out of his imaginary horse's
hooves.

"Jimmy," called Mrs Manning from upstairs, "I'm not
sure whether we're supposed to be there at half-past
three or four. Will you look at that note that Sally's
mother sent round this morning? It's on the bureau."

Jimmy went to look at the note on the bureau.

*You'll all be here by three-thirty, won't you? I've been
making cakes and what-nots nearly all night, and I've
used up every grain of my rations. Sally wanted a
mousse, but I simply couldn't manage it.*

Jimmy stood staring at the note. So that was what Sally

wanted. A mouse. He saw nothing unusual in spelling it with two s's. That was the way he would have spelt it himself. Nor did he see anything unusual in her wanting a mouse. He'd always liked mice. He'd had a white mouse once, but it had died as a result of a difference of opinion with Bobby Peaslake's piebald rat, into whose cage it had been introduced for the sake of companionship. A great resolution was forming in his breast. He'd get Sally a mouse for her birthday present. He didn't know how he was going to get one, but he was determined to get one at all costs.

"Jimmy!" called Mrs Manning impatiently.

Jimmy tore himself from an intoxicating vision of Sally, bright-eyed with gratitude, saying, "Oh, Jimmy! A mouse! Just what I wanted!"

"Half-past three," he said absently.

"I shall never be ready in time," said Mrs Manning. "It's nearly that now. Look, Jimmy. Will you go to the post with those letters that are on the hall chest? You needn't come back. You can go straight on to the party."

Jimmy took up the letters, and, his small face set in lines of grim resolve, started out in quest of his mouse.

He was still in quest of it a quarter of an hour later. He had looked in ditches, in barns, in outhouses, even in the blitzed house. His face was streaked with mud from the banks of the stream where he had vainly pursued a water rat (thinking hopefully that perhaps Sally wouldn't know the difference), his hair stood up wildly from being pushed through hedges, his coat was torn by barbed wire, his shoes bore the marks of every pond and ditch and even midden heap into which his search had led him. And still he hadn't found his mouse . . . And then he met the woman.

She was just an ordinary woman walking along the road with a shopping basket. It wasn't until Jimmy had almost passed her that he noticed that her basket contained a mousetrap and that the mousetrap contained a mouse. His gasp of amazement was so arresting that the women was arrested by it. She stopped.

"Yes, it's a mouse," she said as if in apology. "You see, I'm simply run-over by them, so I catch them in traps – the sort that don't hurt them."

"And what do you do with them?" said Jimmy.

"Well," said the woman still more apologetically, "I can't bear to kill them, so I take them about a mile out of the village, where I hope it's too far for them to find their way back, and let them out. It wastes a lot of my time, but—"

She sighed and left the sentence unfinished. She had a kind vague, bewildered sort of face, and ordinarily Jimmy would have been interested in her, but just now he wasn't interested in anything but mice.

"Shall I t-take if for you?" he said breathlessly.

"Oh, if you would!" said the woman. "There are a million-and-one things I ought to be doing. You won't hurt it, will you?"

"No," said Jimmy. "What about the t-trap?"

"It doesn't matter about the trap," said the woman. "You can have it. I really don't think I'll try to catch any more. It's more trouble than it's worth."

"Thank you," said Jimmy. "Goodbye."

Then, a seraphic smile on his mud-streaked face, he set off quickly down the road to Sally's.

The party was just like other parties. Groups of little girls stood together chattering self-consciously. Groups of little boys stood together eyeing each other warily, ill-at-ease in their best suits, resentful of the social convention that forced them to behave politely to friend and foe alike. Enemies who would rather have been punching each other's heads smiled at each other glassily and passed each other the chocolate biscuits. Friends who would rather have been rampaging together over the country-side were constrained to make futile conversation with each other or answer imbecile questions from each other's aunts about their growth and progress at school. Grown-ups hovered about them, plying them with food, trying to break the ice, but with secret apprehension at their hearts, for one never quite knows what will come out of the ice of a children's party, once it's well and truly broken.

"I wonder what's happened to Jimmy," said Mrs Manning.

And then Jimmy arrived, tattered, bedraggled, tousled, his face beaming with triumph, holding his mouse-trap in both hands.

"Look, Sally!" he said.

He never quite knew what made him open the mouse-trap, but in a moment all was pandemonium. Little girls screamed. Little boys shouted. They plunged over the house, some running away from the mouse, some run-ning after it. An aunt of Sally's had hysterics. A little girl with ferrety eyes and rabbity teeth said that she'd had enough of this party and went home before anyone could stop her. At last the mouse vanished under the garden door, making a bolt for home and freedom, and the tumult ceased. But not for Jimmy. Angry faces and voices surrounded him on all sides.

"You naughty boy!"

"But I th-thought—" he kept beginning, and no one

ever let him get any further.

"I'll never speak to you again, you hateful boy!" said Sally.

"But I th-thought—" began Jimmy again, and again someone cut him short.

"I'm ashamed of you, James," said his mother. "I don't know what your father will say when he hears of it."

Then, because they didn't know what else to do with him, they left him alone, and he stood there, slouched, scowling, hands in pockets – an outcast, a pariah, the boy who had let a mouse loose at a little girl's party . . . They went on talking to each other as if he were not there.

"What a delicious mousse!" said someone to Sally's mother.

"Yes," said Sally's mother. "Sally adores mousse, so I managed to make one, after all."

Jimmy glared balefully at the vapid-looking pink shape. So *that* was what she'd wanted – a rotten ole blancmange! Why couldn't she have said so? Well, he had finished with girls. He never wanted to look at another girl as long as he lived. Nor at a mouse. Nor at a blancmange.

Roger came up to him grinning.

"Jolly good show, Jimmy!" he said. "I've often wanted to do it myself."

For a moment Jimmy almost believed that he had let the mouse loose in a spirit of pure devilry. He felt himself rapt up into the world of adventure in which Roger, his hero, lived. Then he came down to earth.

"Well, axshully—" he began, and ended morosely, "They don't seem to know the diff'rence between mice and blancmange, girls don't."

"Girls!" echoed Roger scornfully. "They don't know

anythin', they're jus' soppy idiots. I wouldn't have anythin' to do with any ole girl – not for a million pounds."

Jimmy thrust his hands into his pockets with a swagger. This moment of man-to-man intimacy with Roger
would compensate, he felt, for whatever fate held in store
for him.

Suddenly Sally was there, looking adorable in a white
frock with a blue ribbon in her hair. She turned her
shoulder on Jimmy as if to exclude him from the entire
universe and, gazing up at Roger with her blue eyes,
smiled her rare entrancing smile.

"We're going to dance, Roger," she said. "Will you
dance with me?"

Sheepishly, self-consciously, avoiding Jimmy's eye,
muttering "Thank you" so gruffly that it sounded like a
bark, Roger followed her into the next room, where dancing had begun, leaving Jimmy alone with his disgrace and
the remains of the tea.

The remains of the tea . . . The party had displayed the
finest flower of its party manners. It had refused second
helpings. It had only had as much of anything as polite-
ness enjoined. Platefuls of sandwiches were left . . .
chocolate biscuits . . . iced cakes . . . fruit salad . . . Half the
strawberry mousse stood intact, leaning a little drunkenly
over its dish. Jimmy stood looking at it. Retribution
awaited him at home; Roger, the superman, had betrayed
an all too human weakness; Sally was never going to
speak to him again; but a life that held a spread like this
was still eminently worth living. That thing he'd thought
was a mouse looked jolly good. It had wrecked his afternoon, but he bore it no malice. Hungrily, zestfully, with
scientific thoroughness, he set to work upon it.

## Chapter 4

# Jimmy, Detective

The Three Musketeers sat in the tool shed at the bottom of the garden – Roger and Charles in the wheelbarrow and Bill, somewhat precariously, on the mowing machine – and discussed the affair.

"Well, it was certainly stolen," said Roger, "an' we've gotter find out who did it."

"How?" said Bill simply.

"Well," said Roger, hedging a little, "they do in books. They're always findin' out who did things in books."

"Yes, but how?" persisted Bill.

"Clues," said Roger. "Cigarette-ends an' bloodstains an' things."

"I don't see how there can be bloodstains," said Charles. "It's only a brooch that was stolen."

"That's all it seems like," admitted Roger, "but you never know what'll come to light once you start 'vestigatin' crime. An' we've gotter be disguised."

"Why?" said Bill.

Bill had a simple direct enquiring nature, and there were times when Roger found him rather irritating.

" 'Cause they *do*," he said shortly. " 'Cause they want people to think they're someone else." He saw another "Why?" hovering on Bill's lips and went on hastily: "All detectives disguise themselves an' we've gotter do it prop'ly, so stop arguin'."

The "crime" was the loss of a brooch that Sally's aunt had been wearing when she came to tea the day before. She was wearing it when she arrived, and when she reached home she hadn't got it on. She had rung up Mrs Manning to tell her so, adding that it didn't really matter, as it wasn't of any value. Mrs Manning had looked for it without success, and, if it hadn't been for Roger, that would have been the end of the affair. But Roger had recently read a story in which a detective had brought a gang of international jewel thieves to justice, and he had felt all the time he was reading it that he could have done it just as well.

"We oughter have a bloodhound or two," he said reflectively.

They considered the matter in silence.

"Our cat's jolly intelligent an' jolly fierce," said Charles at last. "I don't see why they shouldn't have bloodcats as well as bloodhounds."

"Well, they don't," said Roger firmly. "You'll be wantin' to start bloodmice nex'!"

"I'll pretend to be one if you like," said Charles. "I can growl a jolly sight better than any dog I know."

"No," said Roger. "If we haven't got a bloodhound, we'll jus' have to do without one."

"I say, Sally ought to be jolly grateful to us for findin' her aunt's brooch," said Charles.

"We haven't found it yet," said Roger.

"I don't s'pose she will," said Bill, "'cause she doesn't like her aunt. She wishes she'd go away. She's been stayin' there for three weeks and Sally's sick of her."

"Are we talkin' about soppy girls or 'vestigatin' a

crime?" said Roger sternly. "We've not got any time to waste. The person that took it must have been one of those people that came to tea yesterday, an' I bet they took it when they all went down to the greenhouse after tea to look at the carnations. They were all crowded up together, so they easily could, so we've gotter go down to the greenhouse now an' look for clues. It's the gardener's afternoon off, so it's all right. We'd better be armed, 'cause they're generally desperate, are crim'nals, an' they always return to the scene of the crime."

"Why?" said Bill.

"Oh, shut up," said Roger.

It was then that they noticed Jimmy, standing in the doorway listening, open-mouthed with interest.

"Go away, Jim," said Roger. "We don't want kids."

"C-can't I be a d-detective, too?" said Jimmy.

"GO AWAY JIM," SAID ROGER. "WE DON'T WANT KIDS."

"No," said Roger sternly.

"C-can I be a bloodhound, then?" said Jimmy. "I can bite jolly hard."

"*No.* Go away."

Jimmy went away and crossed the road to Bobby Peaslake's house. Bobby joined him in answer to the owl call that was their summons and they went down to the tool shed, where they generally held their conferences. There Jimmy told him about the loss of Sally's aunt's brooch and the plans the Three Musketeers were making for catching the criminal.

"An' they won't let us help them, 'cause I've asked them," he said despondently. Then suddenly his despondency vanished and he drew a deep breath.

"I s-s-say!" he said.

"Yes?" said Bobby.

"Why shouldn't we s-set up as detectives ourselves, if they w-won't let us join them?"

Bobby considered the plan with a judicial frown.

"Yes," he said at last; "that's one of the best ideas you've ever had. Axshully, I don't think that Roger's undauntable enough to make a good detective."

"Oh, yes, he is," said Jimmy, who would never admit to any flaw in Roger's perfection.

"No," said Bobby. "It needs someone cool an' – an' unflinchable like" – he coughed modestly – "well, like you an' me."

Bobby was fond of long words, but didn't always get them right.

"Oh," said Jimmy, a little taken aback by this unexpected aspect of his character.

"Well, we'd better make our plans," said Bobby. "Tell me everything you heard them say."

Jimmy told him. Bobby nodded sagaciously. "Let's go an' see what they're doin' now," he said.

The three were already at work in the greenhouse. They wore their disguises with an air of mingled gratification and self-consciousness. Roger's was a heavy black moustache that his father had once used for amateur theatricals and that kept falling off into whatever he was doing. Charles's was a tweed fishing hat adorned with flies that he mistakenly imagined made him look like Sherlock Holmes, and Bill's was a pair of sun spectacles that his mother had once sat on by accident, cracking both lenses so badly that Bill had to take them off whenever he wanted to see anything.

Their arms lay ready to hand – a rusty saw found in the tool shed by Roger, a bow and arrow brought by Charles and a toy pistol that Bill considered to look exactly like a real one.

They were engaged in collecting clues in a tin box. They had already found twenty cigarette ends (the gardener was a heavy smoker) a bus ticket, a half-filled-in football pool form, a broken bootlace, and a letter from the gardener's mother, hoping that it found him as it left her and that he hadn't stopped wearing his winter vests yet, as the weather was still a bit chancy. All these clues, they thought, were important, but the two that seemed most important were a label with the word "Insecticide" written on it in pencil and a bill from Hammet's, the local ironmonger, for a three-pronged weed fork. Charles was most impressed by the "insecticide" clue.

"It's a foreign word," he said. "I 'spect it's a sort of password. I shouldn't be surprised if we've stumbled on somethin' big. Somethin' international, I mean. An' we've got to be jolly careful 'cause they stick at nothin', don't international gangs."

Roger favoured the three-pronged weed fork.

"I bet it's the instrument he used to snatch the brooch off her when she wasn't lookin'."

Bill was inclined to discount both clues, but his objections were overruled.

"Now come on," said Roger. "We'll go down to Hammet's first of all an' find out who bought that fork. An' we'll put on our disguises 'cause we don't want the crim'nals to know we're on their track."

Moustachioed, tweed-hatted, spectacled, the three detectives slunk furtively out of the garden gate and set off towards the village.

Jimmy and Bobby emerged from the bushes by the greenhouse door, where they had been hiding.

"Well, now we know what they're doin'," said Jimmy, "we've gotter do somethin' different, an' I b-bet we catch the crim'nal first."

"What'll we do?" said Bobby.

"Well," said Jimmy, "I've been thinkin' . . . There were a lot of prickles runnin' into my head in that bush an' they m-made me think quicker than I do ordin'ry. Roger said that a crim'nal always returns to the scene of the crime, so this crim'nal'll come back to the greenhouse, an' I bet he'll come the same time he did the crime, an' that was jus' after tea – about five o'clock – an' it's nearly that now, so we've gotter be there to catch him."

"How?" said Bobby.

"Well, it won't be easy," admitted Jimmy. "We're jolly strong, of course, but crim'nals have the strength of ten men."

"I know that," said Bobby, who never liked to admit himself deficient in any branch of knowledge.

"We'll have to lay a trap for him an' then overpower him," said Jimmy.

"What sort of trap?" said Bobby.

"I've thought of that, too," said Jimmy with an air of modest pride. "I thought of it when those prickles were stickin' into my brain. There's a bucket of spraying stuff in the greenhouse an' I bet we can fit it up over the door so's it'll fall on the crim'nal an' then we can overpower him."

"It's goin' to be jolly difficult," said Bobby doubtfully.

But it was less difficult than they expected. With the help of the garden ladder the bucket was hoisted up, fixed precariously on top of the half-open door and concealed by a branch of a tree that overhung the greenhouse. Bobby was stationed once more in the bush to watch events, and Jimmy went indoors to the boxroom, where all the junk of the family had accumulated for years, to find some substitute for handcuffs by which the criminal could be secured. The search took him longer than he had thought it would. Grown-up voices from the hall reached him faintly, but he paid no heed to them. When at last he had found a length of chain and a rusty meat hook that he thought would work, if only the victim would keep still long enough for him to fix it on, he descended the staircase to find his mother in the hall.

"Sally's aunt has just been, dear," she said. "She's found her brooch. It had got caught in her scarf."

"Oh," said Jimmy blankly.

"She was talking about the carnations in the greenhouse, and I told her to go down and take as many as she liked."

"She's g-gone down to the greenhouse now?" stammered Jimmy.

"Yes, dear," said his mother and turned back into the sitting-room.

Jimmy ran breathlessly down to the greenhouse, where Bobby, pale with horror, was waiting for him.

"It went all over her," he said. "She was as mad as mad."

"Gosh! Where is she?"

"She went out of the back gate an' in at Sally's back gate, carrying on like a – like a volcano."

And then Sally appeared at the gap in the hedge.

"Did you throw a bucket of lime wash over Auntie?" she said to Jimmy.

"Well, I d-did in a s-sort of way," said Jimmy miserably, "b-but—"

"Oh, it was *wonderful* of you, Jimmy," said Sally, her eyes alight with gratitude and admiration. "Roger was *hateful*. He kept fussing on about that wretched brooch, as if it *mattered*, and you did this wonderful thing to make her go away because you knew I was sick of her staying with us and bossing me about. She's packing now. She says she won't stay another minute after this."

For a moment Jimmy was too much bewildered to do anything but blink. Then quickly he rallied his forces. He could see the three detectives slinking back down the lane and he wanted to consolidate his position before they arrived. He thrust his hands into his pockets with a swagger.

"That's all right," he said. "A little thing like that's n-nothin' to me."

## Chapter 5

## *Setting the Stage*

"It's a c-c-crisis, Bobby," said Jimmy, stammering a little more than usual in his eagerness, "an' we've gotter *do* something about it."

The two were perched precariously on the rain tub at the bottom of Bobby's garden, discussing the situation – breaking off occasionally in order to drink in turns out of a bottle of fizzy lemonade brought by Jimmy, or to eat pieces of a cake that Bobby's mother had given them because it had sat down in the middle and so was considered unfit to be offered to the visitors for whom it had been intended. Neither Jimmy nor Bobby could understand why people ever made cakes that stood up in the middle.

The situation they were discussing was certainly a grave one. Miss Pettigrew's nephew had come to stay with her for a few days, and Miss Pettigrew's nephew was a national hero – a VC and an explorer – whose exploits had passed into legend. Everyone wanted to meet him, but it turned out that he didn't want to meet anyone. Jimmy had been bitterly disappointed by this – not on his own account but on Roger's, for he knew that Roger had cherished a passionate admiration of Major Pettigrew ever since he had read of his adventures in a boys' magazine.

He had been interested to hear Miss Pettigrew explaining the Major's attitude in the village shop when he bought his lemonade.

"He hates being lionised," she had said. "Articles in the paper and people trying to take his photograph and that sort of thing infuriate him."

Jimmy was now recounting this conversation to Bobby to the best of his ability.

"She said he didn't like being" – he hunted an elusive word in his memory, lost track of it, and finally brought out – "tigered."

"What d'you mean, tigered?" said Bobby.

"It's a word," explained Jimmy.

"But what does it mean?"

"It means paper articles an' havin' your photograph taken," said Jimmy.

There was a pause during which Bobby rallied his forces.

"I knew that," he said at last. "I was jus' seein' if you did."

"If only she'd let Roger jus' go an' *look* at him," said Jimmy wistfully.

"Someone told me she'd asked Archie Mould to tea," said Bobby.

"Gosh!" said Jimmy, choking over his lemonade bottle from sheer horror. "That's serious, t-that is."

It was indeed serious, and yet Jimmy was not really surprised. Though mean and treacherous, Archie had charm when he chose to exert it. With the help of his smile and beautiful manners, he could easily have wheedled the invitation out of Miss Pettigrew. And Jimmy knew that he had done it simply in order to triumph over Roger. Heroes as heroes meant nothing to

Archie. The only hero Archie worshipped was Archie himself.

The news that Miss Pettigrew had extended the invitation to Roger ought to have relieved Jimmy's anxiety, but somehow it hadn't. He wanted Roger to impress the hero and outshine Archie, and he couldn't see him doing it. Roger, intrepid leader of his contemporaries, was shy and tongue-tied with strangers. His "company manners" comprised an imbecile woodenness of expression, a gruffness of manner and a ferocious scowl that, Jimmy had to admit, would stand little chance beside Archie's charm.

"Roger's brave, all right," he said to Bobby, "but he can't show off like Archie. We've got to fix somethin' brave for him to do."

"What sort of thing?" said Bobby.

"Well, it's no good me gettin' into danger, 'cause I'm his brother an' he'd think I was a nuisance, but if you got into some deadly danger jus' outside the window when they're havin' tea, I know Roger would dash out an' save you, an' then this man would know how brave he is."

"What sort of deadly danger?" said Bobby without enthusiasm.

"Well, you could climb one of those trees by the pond in her garden an' fall out of it into the water."

There was a marked coldness in Bobby's manner as he replied:

"If you think I'm goin' to risk death jus' so's Roger can show he's brave, I'm jolly well not."

"I think you're very selfish," said Jimmy. "A bit of water couldn't hurt you. You could spit it out afterwards. I should have thought you'd have w-wanted to do a little thing like that for me."

"Well, I don't," said Bobby, "an' anyway, I'm goin' to that conjurin' show on Saturday, an' I'm not riskin' death for anyone before then."

"All right," said Jimmy. "I s'pose I'll have to do it myself." And they parted without rancour on either side.

Jimmy started out to Miss Pettigrew's about half an hour after Roger and set to work on his tree as soon as he arrived. The lower part was easy enough, but the middle part was more difficult. From half-way up he could see right into Miss Pettigrew's drawing room and he paused there for a moment or two to survey the scene. It was as he had feared. Roger was sitting with a fixed glassy stare and an aggressive scowl, answering in monosyllables when addressed, contributing nothing to the conversation. Archie was chatting easily and naturally, waiting on Miss Pettigrew with that air of deferential courtesy that elderly ladies always find so irresistible. The hero was looking bored. Oh, well, thought Jimmy, he'd soon change all that. He had noticed with relief that Roger was sitting near the french window. At the sound of a splash he could leap out into the garden and arrive first at the pond. He swung himself higher up . . . on to the next branch . . . then on to the next . . . And then something happened that can happen to the most expert climber. He got stuck. He couldn't get up and he couldn't get down. He couldn't move. He clung there, paralysed, panic-stricken, in nightmare helplessness. And then something happened even worse than that. Looking down into the window of the drawing room, he met Roger's eye and saw Roger's face stiffen into a mask of horror – a horror not unmixed with fury and the promise of vengeance to come. One would have thought that that was the worst

LOOKING
DOWN, HE MET
ROGER'S EYE . . .

that could possibly happen, but it wasn't. For Archie's gaze followed Roger's and a slow crafty smile overspread his fox-like face. Archie had seen him, too. And all Jimmy could do was to cling precariously to his branch, praying unavailingly for the end of the world.

Inside Miss Pettigrew's drawing room the atmosphere was becoming more and more strained beneath a surface ripple of polite conversation. Archie was playing with Roger as a cat plays with a mouse, letting him think one moment that he was going to say nothing about Jimmy's presence in the tree, pretending the next moment to be on the point of denouncing the intruder. Archie was enjoying himself. He had been waiting to get his own back on Roger and Jimmy every since Jimmy had delivered him as a prisoner into Roger's hands in the blitzed house. And now fate had put them in his power. When he had extracted as much satisfaction from the situation as the situation was capable of affording, he looked out of the window as if noticing Jimmy for the first time and said:

"There's a boy climbing trees in your garden, Miss Pettigrew."

"Good gracious!" cried Miss Pettigrew indignantly, and the whole party rose, went out of the french window and crossed the lawn to the pond. There they stood at the foot of Jimmy's tree, looking up at him. Suddenly Miss Pettigrew gave a scream.

"Oh, the brave little boy!" she said. "Look! He's gone to help Sooty."

Glancing up, Jimmy noticed for the first time on the branch just above his head the evil-looking mossy-coated cat (euphemistically known as a "half-Persian") that was the mainstay of Miss Pettigrew's existence.

"Can you manage it, dear?" she said anxiously.

With a courage born of despair, he reached up a hand, took the cat ungently by its neck, let go his hold on the branch, shutting his eyes as he abandoned himself to the void, caught hold of the next branch by a miracle . . . caught hold of the next . . . got down to the easy part and landed on his feet on the lawn, still holding Sooty.

"Oh, I *am* grateful to you, Jimmy," said Miss Pettigrew. "He'd never have got down by himself."

"It was a pretty neat piece of climbing," said the Major.

"It could have got down by itself quite easily," said Archie. "It always goes up trees when you throw stones at it."

Miss Pettigrew turned on him a look of dark suspicion.

"*Does* it?" she said icily.

"I don't mean I—" he began hastily, but she interrupted him.

"You've said quite enough, Archie. I think it's time you went home."

Archie, who knew when he was beaten, went off muttering down the drive.

"And now come in, the rest of you, and finish tea," said Miss Pettigrew, still fondling the mossy-coated wanderer.

But the Major stayed outside for a minute with Jimmy.

"Did you see the cat from the road?" he said curiously.

"Well, axshully—" began Jimmy, and poured out the whole story.

The Major threw back his head and laughed.

"That's great!" he said. "Come on in. We must follow it up."

Jimmy went with him into the drawing room, where a magnificent chocolate cake, almost untouched, stood in the middle of the table. Miss Pettigrew was engaged in making soothing noises at a wholly unperturbed Sooty. Roger was gaping bewilderedly.

"I say, old chap," said the Major to Roger, "I'm going to Twickenham tomorrow to see the match against Scotland. Would you care to come along with me?"

Roger went white, then red. He blinked and gulped.

"I say!" he gasped. "Thanks *awfully*!"

It was a moment too sacred to be intruded upon by a third person.

Jimmy turned tactfully away and gave his undivided attention to the chocolate cake.

## Chapter 6

# *The Smuggler Hunt*

The Three Musketeers sat in the kitchen of the blitzed house, cooking one of their special mixtures. The fireplace had been blown across the room and still lay – in a heap of scrap iron and broken tiles – in a corner, but in the space it had occupied a sulky fire of damp twigs smouldered fitfully, and Roger, his face blackened by smoke and set in lines of earnest concentration, was stirring the mixture in the soup tin that they used as a saucepan with the stick that they used as a spoon. The actual composition of the mixture mattered little, for the flavour of smoke generally predominated, so that little else could be tasted, but today's mixture consisted of cold porridge and cheese-rind contributed by Roger, cold potato contributed by Charles, and half a sardine, together with the scrapings of a pot of jam, contributed by Bill – the whole moistened by a little water from a puddle (it had been raining hard since early morning) and stirred vigorously with the stick. Charles and Bill, their faces as black as Roger's, were pushing damp twigs under the soup tin to feed the smouldering "fire", while Jimmy, ignored by the other three, was hovering in the background and trying to look as if he wasn't there. He had taken advantage of the shower of rain to slip into the kitchen, giving away the fact that he had followed them there and had been hanging about to follow them home. It thrilled him to be with his heroes in the head-quarters of the gang, secure in the knowledge that, though they didn't want him, they couldn't turn him out into the rain.

"I think it's done," said Roger at last judicially, and the three divided the contents in a somewhat primitive fashion and ate them with an enjoyment that was as incredible as it was unfeigned.

"You can lick that, if you like, Jim," said Roger, hand-ing him the stick.

"T-thanks," said Jim.

He licked the stick in contented silence. To him, as to the others, it was not a nauseous, smoke-blackened mess. It was the food of the gods.

"That was a jolly good feast," said Charles, scraping the last morsel from the soup tin.

"I nearly brought some mint sauce," said Bill, "but my mother stopped me."

"Yes, that would have been another taste," said Roger, adding, with the air of a connoisseur, "I always think that the more tastes you have in them, the better."

"I liked the one we had on Sat'day," said Bill. "The one with the salad oil in."

"Y-yes," agreed Charles meditatively, "but my mother made an awful fuss when she found I'd taken it."

"I once drank some vinegar in mistake for g-ginger beer," said Jimmy, who was a bit above himself through having been allowed to lick the twig.

"Shut up, Jim," said Roger, putting him back into his proper place.

"All r-right," said Jimmy.

Bill glanced out of the window. It was still raining.

"What are we goin' to do this afternoon if it rains?" he asked.

"I'm goin' on with that book of mine about smugglers," said Roger. "Gosh! I wish I lived in the days when there was somethin' excitin' goin' on. There's *nothin'* excitin' in these days. No pirates or smugglers or highwaymen or anythin'."

"There's atomic bombs an' rations," said Bill. "They're excitin' in a way."

"No they're not," said Charles. "You can't carry an atomic bomb about with you, same as you could a sword, an' rations are only excitin' when there's chocolate biscuits."

"Or j-jelly," said Jimmy.

"Shut up or go home, Jim," said Roger sternly.

"All r-right," said Jimmy again deprecatingly.

"You know, I bet there's still smugglers today," said Charles. "I've heard people talkin' about 'em. They bring things over same as they used to an' hide 'em up in caves an' things same as they used to. Stands to reason there's still smugglers when you come to think of it."

" 'Course it does," agreed the other two, and Jimmy ventured to slip in a " 'C-course it does," but so cautiously that they didn't hear him.

"I expect there's smugglers' hideouts all over the country if only we knew where they were," said Charles. "I'll bet there's some round here. Well, we're on the road to the coast, so there mus' be."

" 'Course there mus' be," said the other two.

Jimmy got as far as " 'C-course—" but they looked at him, so he turned it into a cough.

"I *say*!" said Roger. "That ole quarry's full of caves. There's caves all along the sides, where they used to blast

it. It's all grown over with bushes an' things now, an' that
makes it all the easier for smugglers to hide things in . . .
*Tell* you what!"

"Yes?" said the other two, so excited that they forgot to
snub Jimmy for saying "Yes?" too.

"We'll go an' explore there this afternoon. I *bet* we'll
catch a smuggler."

"A gang of them, prob'ly," said Charles. "An' we'd
better take weapons. They're sure to be desp'rate."

"Yes," said Roger. "Well, it's stopped rainin' now,
so let's go home to lunch, an' we'll start off d'rectly
after." He turned a stern gaze upon Jimmy. "An' you're
not comin' with us, Jim. You're too young to catch
smugglers."

"All r-right," said Jimmy with disarming humility.

They assembled outside Roger's house immediately
after lunch and inspected each other's weapons. Charles
had brought his bow and arrow, Bill his pistol and Roger
a penknife that had once contained two blades and a
corkscrew and that now only contained a corkscrew.

"Dunno what good you think a corkscrew's goin' to
be," said Charles.

"It's like a native spear with twists at the end," said
Roger. "If you got it in anyone he'd find it jolly difficult to
get it out."

"Yes, but you'd have a job gettin' it in," said Charles.

"I'd have to act quick, of course," admitted Roger.
"Anyhow, that bow an' arrow of yours'll be no use when
it comes to hand-to-hand fightin'."

"It's a jolly good weapon, is a bow an' arrow," said
Charles with spirit. "Think of that man in hist'ry that shot
William Tell for puttin' an apple on his head. He used a
bow an' arrow."

"You've got that mixed," said Bill. "It was the *apples* he shot as they were falling on William Tell's head, an' that's how gravity was discovered . . . Or was it steam?" he added uncertainly.

"Oh, shut up showing off," said Roger.

They started out down the road. Turning round at the corner, they saw Jimmy following them. They stopped and waited for him.

"We told you not to come with us," said Roger sternly.

"I'm not c-coming with you," said Jimmy. "I'm jus' walkin' along the road."

They looked at him, nonplussed. They couldn't, after all, stop him walking along the road.

"Oh, come on," said Roger to the others. "We'll take no notice of him."

At the top of the large pit that was the disused quarry they stopped and waited for him again.

"Now look here, Jim," said Roger. "You're not coming with us down the quarry. Do you understand?"

"C-can I be on guard, then?" pleaded Jimmy.

"Yes," agreed Roger after consideration. "You can stay up here on guard. It might be useful if we're overpowered by smugglers. You could fetch help."

Jimmy's small stocky form quivered with eagerness.

"C-can I have a whistle?" he said.

The Three Musketeers each had a whistle which they used to send messages to each other when playing Red Indians or Commandos. The system of messages was perhaps unnecessarily complicated, but the two simplest ones were – one blast for "safe" and two for "in danger."

"Yes," conceded Roger again, "you can borrow Bill's whistle. An' when we've been down there a bit you can blow it an' if we blow once back it means we're safe an' if we blow twice we're in danger."

"C-can I come down an' r-rescue you if you blow twice?" said Jimmy.

"'Course not," said Roger indignantly. "You're too young to rescue anyone. You must fetch help if we blow twice."

"All r-right," said Jimmy.

The three clambered down the steep sides of the old quarry and were soon lost to sight. Jimmy imagined them exploring the overgrown "caves" perhaps even now engaged in desperate fights with smugglers. Perhaps – he thought of the pond of stagnant water that lay in the bend formed by one of the jutting sides of the pit. Suppose they fell into it . . . Raising the whistle to his lips, he blew a loud blast. Two distinct blasts answered him.

Jimmy's heart almost stopped beating. They were in danger . . . He must get help at once. Araminta Palmer, a fat little girl with blue eyes and an adenoidal expression, was coming down the road. He accosted her stammeringly but imperiously.

"Go to the p-police station," he said, "an' tell the police to c-come to at once to the old quarry to arrest a smuggler. T-tell them it's a matter of life an' d-death."

Araminta gaped at him, and her expression became, if possible, more adenoidal than before.

Araminta was not usually a docile child, but today was evidently one of her better days.

"All right," she said at last. "I will if you wad be to," and trotted off obediently towards the village.

Jimmy stood listening intently. There was no sound of shouting or fighting from below. It must be the pond.

And he must do something at once. At that moment a car came quickly down the road, took the bend at full speed, skidded along the greasy surface, collided with a telegraph pole and rocked to a stop. The driver got out to inspect the damage. He was a small rat-like man with a grey face that became distorted by some strong emotion as he surveyed the broken wing deeply embedded in the tyre. Jimmy hailed him as a heaven-sent deliverer.

"P-please could you c-come down to the quarry an' help my brother," he said. "He's in deadly d-danger."

The man wheeled round and poured out a stream of curses.

"And tell me where the nearest garage is," he ended, "or I'll wring your neck."

"It's there," said Jimmy pointing. "N-next the post office. But *p-please* come an' help my brother first. I think he's d-drowning."

"Get out of my way," said the man, and, pushing Jimmy aside, set off at a run down the road.

Jimmy was left by the abandoned car. A sudden memory flashed into his mind. He had once read a story in which someone had been saved from drowning by using a motor tyre as a lifebelt. He'd forgotten exactly how it had been done, but he knew it had been. He looked at the car. It was the same make as his father's. You got the spare tyre out by unfastening a catch at the back. Coming to a sudden decision, he undid the catch and lifted down the tyre. Araminta was trotting back down the road.

"I told deb," she said.

"All right," said Jimmy with a touch of the masculine arrogance that feminine compliance is always apt to call forth. "Now you can stay by this car an', when the man comes back, tell him I've b-borrowed his spare tyre an' it's down in the quarry. Can you remember that?"

"Yes, I cad rebebber that," said Araminta.

Jimmy wheeled the tyre to the edge of the pit and sent it hurtling down. It crashed over boulders and bushes, then vanished. Jimmy followed it, scrambling down the precipice-like sides to the bottom. There stood Roger, Charles and Bill, staring mystified at the tyre that had descended upon them, apparently of its own volition, out of the void.

"Are you all r-right?" said Jimmy anxiously.

"Course we are," said Roger.

"But you d-did two whistles."

"We didn't," said Roger. "We only did one."

"We did one each," Charles reminded him. "It may've sounded like two."

"ARE YOU ALL RIGHT?"
ASKED JIMMY ANXIOUSLY.

And then the policeman came, climbing down the steep slope behind them. He had received Jimmy's message and had come prepared to give those young devils a lesson they wouldn't forget in a hurry.

"I want your names and addresses," he said, taking out his note-book, "and I'm going round to see your fathers about this straightaway."

Then he saw the tyre and lifted it up to inspect it.

"Where did you get this?" he said sternly.

They looked at Jimmy.

"I b-b-b-borrowed it," said Jimmy.

And then the rat-faced man appeared, sliding rather than climbing down the quarry side. His face was set in lines of fury that changed to resignation as his eyes fell upon the policeman holding the tyre.

"All right," he said. "It's a fair cop. Anyway, I couldn't get up out of this blasted pit if I tried." He nodded at the tyre. "Yes, the stuff's in there. I suppose you know that or you wouldn't be here."

The policeman was a reader of sensation fiction. He thought and acted quickly. Taking a monster penknife from his pocket, he ripped open the tyre and from it drew yards on yard of sacking. But not only sacking. From the folds of the sacking flowed a stream of small shining watches, littering the grass around them.

It was Jimmy, after all, who had caught a smuggler.

## Chapter 7

# Sandy Makes his Entrance

Jimmy plodded slowly along the road, his hands thrust into his pockets, his brows drawn into a frown.

It was Roger's birthday tomorrow, and Jimmy, knowing that he wanted a specific penknife, had saved up his money to buy one. It had seemed to Jimmy a quite superlative penknife till Uncle Matthew arrived yesterday, breezy and hearty, in an enormous Daimler, fresh from a visit from the United States.

"Can't stay more than a minute," he had said in his loud, re-echoing voice. "Just popped in on my way to London. Remembered it was your birthday this week, Roger, old chap, so I've brought you this."

"This" was a penknife – so large, so magnificent, so superbly equipped with blades and gadgets of every kind that for a moment they could hardly believe it was real. And all at once Jimmy saw his own penknife as the paltry thing it was. He couldn't give it to Roger now. And he hadn't anything else to give him. He'd spent all his money on it. He was just wondering whether he could find someone to buy the seagull's skull that he had found last year at the seaside and that, elaborately labelled, formed the sole exhibit of his "museum", when he noticed the little brown dog wandering disconsolately by the roadside.

"Hello, boy!" said Jimmy.

The little brown dog leapt up at him ecstatically, then, as if all its problems were solved, began to trot happily along behind him. Mingled delight and apprehension filled Jimmy's heart – delight at this glorious make-believe of dog ownership, apprehension because the encouragement of stray dogs was forbidden by his parents. Well, I didn't do anythin' but speak to it, Jimmy assured himself. It's only p'lite to speak to people. Well, I can't help him walkin' along the road. It's a *free* road, isn't it?

Occasionally the dog would stop to carry on investigations in the ditch, and then Jimmy would slow his pace and whistle as if absently, not turning round but waiting anxiously till from the corner of his eye he saw the small brown form emerge from the ditch and take its place again at his heels. Well, I can't help it, he assured himself again. They never told me not to whistle. I didn't stop or turn round. Well, not *right* round . . . His apprehension increased as he entered the garden gate, still followed by his new friend, but fortunately only Roger was there, and Roger welcomed the newcomer as eagerly as Jimmy had done. The newcomer made himself completely at home, racing round the garden after sticks and stones, jumping up at Roger and Jimmy, following them into the house as if he had lived there all his life, his plume-like tail waving joyfully. So entranced was Jimmy that he almost forgot about Roger's penknife. Almost, but not quite. It was there – a faint dark cloud over his happiness.

"What shall we call him?" said Jimmy.

Roger considered.

"Let's call him Sandy," he said at last.

Then the garden gate opened, and Mrs Manning came

in with her shopping-basket. Sandy leaped up at her in frenzied welcome.

"Whose dog is that?" said Mrs Manning, putting down her shopping-basket, which Sandy promptly knocked over.

"N-nobody's," said Jimmy, picking up the parcels.

"He came home with Jimmy," explained Roger.

"Did you encourage him, Jimmy?" said Mrs Manning.

"N-no," said Jimmy doubtfully. "N-not axshully *encourage* him!"

"Can we keep him if he's lost?" said Roger.

Mrs Manning looked down at the three beseeching faces. Sandy had joined the other two and was looking up at her, head on one side, teeth bared in an ingratiating smile.

"I'll ask Daddy," she said, "but I'm afraid he'll say 'no'. I believe that's his key in the lock now."

She went indoors to ask him, and Mr Manning, disposing of hat, umbrella and attaché case in the hall said "No" firmly and definitely.

"I've told those kids a dozen times," he said, "that I'm having no animal in this house while food rationing lasts. And I mean it. I'll go out and send the wretched creature away."

He went out to send the wretched creature away. The wretched creature was crouching on the lawn, its front paws wide apart, guarding a stick, its hind legs erect, ready to spring, challenging the whole world to throw its stick for it. Before Mr Manning quite realised what he was doing he had thrown the stick. He threw it again. And again. He found an old ball that they both liked better than the stick. After that they had a sham battle with an old gardening glove, Sandy uttering soft little growls of mock ferocity. It was while Mr Manning was ringing up the police, half an hour later, to ask whether, if no one claimed the dog, they might keep him, that the fish-faced woman arrived. She came in by the garden gate and turned her expressionless gaze on Sandy who was still worrying the gardening glove.

"That's our dog," she said.

Jimmy went brick red.

"*P-p-p-p-prove* it," he said furiously.

"Jimmy!" said Mrs Manning in mild reproof.

The woman explained that her sister was giving up her house and letting her have the dog to guard her poultry farm. The sister had brought the dog over that afternoon, and, shortly after her departure, it had disappeared. A child in the village had told her that she had seen it following Jimmy, and she had come to claim it.

" 'Is name's 'Ector," she said and, raising her voice, called shrilly, "'*Ector!*"

Sandy's tail moved in a deprecating unhappy fashion.

Mr Manning had now brought his telephone conversation with the police to an abrupt conclusion and had joined the group in the garden.

"Of course you must take the dog, if he's yours," he said a little testily. "There's no question about it at all. In any case I couldn't possibly consider keeping an animal here with the food situation as it is."

He looked at the ball and the gardening glove and gave an aloof sort of cough as if dissociating himself from them.

"I'll swop my tortoise for it," said Jimmy desperately.

"Don't be silly, Jimmy," said Mrs Manning and the fish-faced woman looked at him in dispassionate contempt.

So Sandy was handed over to the fish-faced woman,
and she tied a piece of rope round his collar and dragged
him off. He went reluctantly, feet splayed out in protest,
tail between his legs, still looking round in piteous appeal
as he vanished from sight. Blackness closed over Jimmy's
spirit, and he went away quickly from the others lest they
should see how near he was to tears.

The evening dragged slowly to an end. Roger sat over
a book, but, Jimmy noticed, did not turn the pages, and
even Mr Manning seemed depressed and irritable. Mrs
Manning did her best to lighten the atmosphere by opening a tin of peaches for supper, but its effect was only
temporary.

Just before he went to bed, Jimmy made his way down
to the cottage where the woman had said she lived. At
first there seemed to be no signs of Sandy; then he saw

SO SANDY WAS HANDED
OVER TO HER.

him, tied to a tree by a piece of rope in the darkening field at the back of the cottage, surrounded by ramshackle chicken houses – cowering, shivering, tail between his legs. A fish-faced child who stood just inside the gate, eating a slice of bread and jam, stared vacantly at Jimmy.

"Where's he going to s-sleep?" said Jimmy.

The fish-faced child spat out a plum stone and said: " 'Oo?"

"The d-dog," said Jimmy.

"Where 'e is," said the child. " 'E's to guard the chickens, that's wot 'e's for. 'E's a watch-dog not a pet, mum says."

"Oh," said Jimmy and went miserably home.

He awoke next morning to a vague but heavy weight of depression that gradually resolved itself under two separate heads – Sandy's departure and Roger's birthday present. Sandy's departure was, if possible, the heavier weight of the two. He got up and leant out of the window, trying to see round the bend of the road to where Sandy lived. He couldn't see round the bend, but he saw a motorcycle with a sidecar attached speeding along the road. The sidecar seemed to be packed with a conglomeration of junk, and, just as it passed the house, a bundle fell from it and rolled to the side of the road.

"Hi!" shouted Jimmy, "you've d-dropped somethin'."

The driver turned round, looked at Jimmy, then at the bundle, and sped on without stopping . . . Jimmy dressed and went down into the road. Yes, the bundle was still there. He picked it up and unfolded it . . . a shabby motor-rug, lined with patchy moth-eaten fur. He thought of Sandy shivering at the end of his rope in the damp field, and an idea suddenly occurred to him. The rug was now his property. He had called the man's attention to it, and the man had gone on without picking it up. He would take it to the poultry farm for Sandy to sleep on. Surely they couldn't object to that. He ran down the road to the cottage, the rug over his arm. And there at the gate was the fish-faced woman with several of her neighbours. The fish-faced child stood in the background sucking an orange.

"Took me best coal bucket," one woman was saying.

"Took me washin' off the line," said another. "Wringin' wet las' night, it was, so I left it out."

"Took me Grandmother Buzzard's fur rug," wailed the fish-faced woman, "what she left me in 'er will. Reel fur, it was. Orf an animal."

Jimmy gathered from their conversation that the man with the motorcycle was a sneak thief who had passed through the village in the early morning, picking up such unconsidered trifles as came his way.

"Took it orf the car through the garage winder," went on the fish-faced woman. "We'd locked the door, but the winder catch is broken. Jus' pushed 'is 'and through an' nabbed it, 'e did . . . an' *'im*" – she turned and pointed indignantly at Sandy, who could be seen shivering miserably at the end of his rope, in the field behind the house – "never as much as a bark or a whine from 'im. Nice sort of watch dog *'e* is!"

Sandy, aware that their eyes were turned on him in disapproval, gave a faint apologetic flicker of his tail.

Suddenly the woman noticed Jimmy standing in the background with the rug over his arm. She gave a cry of delight.

"Why, there it is!" she said. "'E's brought it back. Me Grandmother Buzzard's fur rug. How did you find it, ducks?"

Jimmy told them how he had found it.

"Well, I never!" said the fish-faced woman. "If that isn't providence, I don't know what is! I'd never have knowed a moment's peace, I wouldn't, if I'd lost me Grandmother Buzzard's fur rug. Thank you ever so, ducks. Would you like an apple?"

Jimmy shook his head.

"No, th-thanks."

"A nice bit o' cake?"

"No, th-thanks."

Again Jimmy shook his head.

"A bit o' choc'late?"

"No, th-thanks."

"Well, wot would you like?"

Jimmy was silent for a few moments, summoning all his courage, then:

"C-can I have the d-dog?" he blurted out.

" '*Im*?" said the woman. " 'Im what let this 'ere thief come right up to the garage an' never so much as raised a bark? You can 'ave 'im an' welcome. I can tell whether a dawg's goin' to be worth 'is keep an' when 'e isn't, and '*e* isn't. No matter 'ow long we keep 'im. 'E won't be. 'E's not the sort of dawg I could take to, any-ways" – she turned to the fish-faced child – "could you, love?"

The fish-faced child spat out a shower of orange pips and said "Naw."

So Jimmy and Sandy set off down the road again, Sandy leaping up with short sharp barks of delight, his plume-like tail waving exultantly.

The family was just starting breakfast when they entered the dining-room.

"M-many happy returns of the day, Roger," said

Jimmy. "The woman's given me Sandy an' I'm givin' you him for a b-birthday present."

Sandy jumped up at Roger, covering his face with what were evidently meant to be birthday greetings.

"Thanks," said Roger, bending down to Sandy. "We – we'll share him, Jimmy."

Jimmy's heart overflowed with joy. To share Sandy with Roger! But he remembered in time that Roger hated fuss.

"Th-thanks," he said gruffly and sat down to eat his porridge.

## Chapter 8

# A Not So Clean Sweep

"I dunno what to do about it," said Toothy gloomily. "It's like one of those insolvable problems you see in the newspapers – same as fuel an' the cost of living."

"You were an awful chump, Toothy," said Roger. "You ought to know what Archie is by now."

"I know," groaned Toothy, "but that doesn't help."

The Three Musketeers were in the kitchen of the blitzed house – engaged in cooking a mixture of cold porridge, cocoa, fish paste and ice cream, the whole moistened by generous lashings of orangeade, over a smouldering fire in the wrecked hearth, and Toothy had dropped in to tell them his troubles. Jimmy, who had been deputed to fetch twigs from the garden to feed the reluctant flames, hung about on the outskirts of the group, listening, appalled, to Toothy's recital. And Toothy's recital was enough to appal anyone. Some weeks ago he had, in a moment of folly and financial stress, borrowed one-and-sixpence from Archie Mould. On offering to pay it back this morning, he had discovered that, at the rate of interest agreed to by him without question or comprehension at the time of the transaction, the loan now amounted to ten shillings. (Till enlightened by this incident, Toothy had thought that interest was something his parents said he ought to take in his school work and didn't.) And that wasn't all. Archie had demanded security and had refused to consider as such either the cocoon that Toothy thought was going to turn into a Red Admiral, or his collection of sevenpenny bus tickets. He had demanded, instead, the gold tiepin in the shape of a horse's head, that Toothy's godmother had given him last Christmas. This was not an ordinary tiepin. It had belonged to Toothy's godmother's father and had been handed on to Toothy as a sort of sacred trust. He only wore it for his godmother's visits, and there had seemed no danger in giving it to Archie as security. But now he had heard that his godmother was coming over tomorrow, and, if the tiepin was not forthcoming, there would be, as Toothy put it, "the most awful bust-up there's been for years."

"Let's kidnap Archie an' make him give it back to you," said Charles. "We could keep him prisoner till he does."

"No," said Toothy. "That wouldn't be honest. It's a debt of honour. The sort people shoot themselves for in books. I'd be disgraced for ever if I did that. No, I've gotter give him that ten shillings or be cut off for ever by my godmother and get into the most frightful row of my life with my father."

"Ten shillings!" echoed Roger helplessly. "*No* one's got ten shillings!"

"How much pocket money do you have?" said Bill.

"None," said Toothy simply. "I broke my brace again, taking the top off a lemonade bottle, an' they've stopped my pocket money till it's paid for. I'd saved up the one-an'-six for Archie before they stopped it, but it's no use now."

He had been nicknamed "Toothy" because he possessed a set of teeth so wildly irregular that they seemed to be doing a sort of complicated war dance among themselves. They were usually enclosed by a gold brace – usually but not always, for Toothy was in the habit of detaching his brace in order to use it for various unauthorised purposes such as cleaning his airgun or taking the tops off bottles or even, with certain adjustments, providing spare parts for his toy motor launch. When not lost or out of action, it was generally as wildly irregular as the teeth it enclosed.

"Have you told Archie about your godmother coming?" said Bill.

"Yes," said Toothy, "but that's not the worst. He soaped up to her when she was here last – you know how he can" – they nodded – "and she asked my mother to ask him to tea tomorrow, and he says he'd going to come wearing my tiepin, so that I can't say I've lost it. And he's going to tell her that I sold it to him."

"Gosh!" said Roger aghast.

"It's a s-shame," said Jimmy.

They realised for the first time that he was listening.

"We don't want you here, Jim," said Roger loftily. "You've got enough sticks. You'd better go now."

"All r-right," said Jimmy, and went in search of Bobby Peasdale.

He found Bobby in his back garden, sitting by the jam jar that formed his aquarium, holding the lifeless form of a tadpole in his hand and fanning it with a grimy handkerchief.

"It's fainted," he explained. "I'm trying to bring it round. It's the one that's called Moses."

"Never mind that now," said Jimmy. "We've got more important things to think of than tadpoles."

"It's a jolly important tadpole," said Bobby, a little hurt.

"It's the biggest I've ever had. An' the most intelligent. It was jus' gettin' to know me."

"Well, listen," said Jimmy, and proceeded to tell him about Toothy and Archie Mould.

"So you see," he ended, "we've got to find some way of gettin' ten shillings for Toothy."

"There isn't any way," said Bobby, putting the tadpole back into the jam jar. "It might be jus' sort of tired an' sleepin' it off. Or it might have got mercerised an' gone into a trance . . . There isn't any way. Not all that money."

"There must be," said Jimmy, "or there wouldn't be any millionaires. We've gotter think hard. So stop botherin' about Moses an' think hard."

Obediently dismissing Moses from his mind, Bobby thought hard, scowling fiercely into vacancy and twisting his watch round and round his wrist, a process that always accompanied his deeper mental processes. Then slowly a light dawned on his small freckled countenance.

"I *know*!" he said. "My mother had a sweep last week an' I saw her give him five shillings."

"Corks!" said Jimmy. "We could make ten shillings with jus' sweeping two chimneys, then."

"But we couldn't do it," objected Bobby. "We're not big enough."

"We are," said Jimmy. "They used to have boy chimney sweeps in the old days. I heard someone talkin' about it, an' I thought it was a jolly mean shame they stopped it. It must have been wizard goin' up chimneys."

"We haven't any brushes."

That nonplussed Jimmy, but only for a moment.

"You don't need brushes. Our gard'ner was tellin' me how they used to push holly branches up the chimney to clean it when he was a boy. There's a holly bush in the garden . . . I say!"

"Yes?"

"Let's start right away on our chimney. It'll be sort of practice, an', if we do it right, p'raps they'll give us five shillings, then we'll only have to do one more to make ten. There isn't a fire in our sitting room, 'cause my mother's out an' she wasn't goin' to light it till she came back. Let's get the saw an' cut down a holly branch now."

At the end of the afternoon, the two surveyed the results of their labours despondently. The saw, its every tooth twisted by the cutting of the holly bush, was only a minor casualty. The hearth-rug was buried in soot, for the chimney was of the wide open variety and had given the amateur sweeps plenty of scope, and the holly branch

SURVEYING THE RESULTS OF THEIR LABOURS — DESPONDENTLY.

was firmly wedged up the chimney, for they had been able to get it – and themselves – so far and no further. At long last and despite all their efforts, they had had to admit defeat.

"I b'lieve it's a specially d-difficult sort of chimney," panted Jimmy.

"Well, I think I'll be goin' home now," said Bobby, whose courage was apt to desert him in moments of crisis.

"All right," said Jimmy, and turned his attention to his own immediate problems.

The first thing to be done, he considered, in order to lessen the inevitable shock to his mother on her return, was to clean up his person. He did this to the best of his ability, washing himself and his hair and leaving a trail of glutinous black slime all over the bathroom. Then he saw Roger with Charles and Bill in the garden and went out to them.

"I say, Roger," he said, "about T-Toothy's—"

"Oh, that's all right," interrupted Roger. "They got a letter by this afternoon's post to say that she isn't coming till next month. She sent Toothy ten shillings to make up for the disappointment, and he's taken it round to Archie and got his tiepin back. And, anyway," he went on, hastening to reassert his dignity after this moment of confidence, "it isn't your business."

"No," said Jimmy and went slowly indoors.

Mrs Manning had returned while Jimmy was in the garden and was standing in the middle of the sitting room, surveying the scene of desolation.

"Who on *earth* has done this?" she said.

"M-me," admitted Jimmy. "I'm s-sorry about it."

"Whatever possessed you, James?" said Mrs Manning.

"I was t-trying to be a ch-chimney sweep," explained Jimmy.

"But *why*?" said Mrs Manning helplessly.

Jimmy wondered whether to tell her about Toothy and decided not to. It was a long story and grown-ups never understood. Moreover, it might get round to Toothy's father and that would mean more trouble for Toothy.

"I jus' was," he said vaguely and added again, "I'm s-sorry."

"I should hope you are," said Mrs Manning. "I don't know what your father will say about it. Or," she added ominously, "do about it."

Jimmy, who could make a pretty good guess, thrust his hands into his pockets and grunted thoughtfully.

"I think I'll go to b-bed," he said. "I'm a b-bit tired."

"Very well," sighed Mrs Manning. "It's nearly your bedtime, anyway."

Mr Manning returned home almost immediately after Jimmy had gone upstairs, and his wife pointed out to him (though they needed little pointing out) the flagrant proofs of Jimmy's guilt.

"And we can't light the fire," she ended, "because there's half a holly bush up the chimney."

"All right," said Mr Manning, setting his jaw squarely. "The kid's asked for a darn good hiding and he's going to get it. Where is he?"

"He's gone to bed."

"That won't help him," said Mr Manning firmly, taking the stairs three at a time and entering Jimmy's bedroom, followed by his wife.

Jimmy was in bed, his face half-buried between pillow and eiderdown, his eyes closed, his cheeks flushed as if with sleep. Jimmy could lay no claim to beauty, but there is something vaguely affecting in the sight of any sleeping child. Only Mrs Manning noticed the slight twitching of his eyelids that showed the effort it cost him to keep them shut and, on the chair by his bed, the folded pyjamas that he had not had time to put on; and she did not draw her husband's attention to these details.

"You can't wake him, dear," was all she said.

"No," frowned Mr Manning, annoyed to find his anger slipping away from him as he looked down at his son. "I – I'll speak to him very seriously in the morning."

Jimmy, beneath the bedclothes, drew a deep sigh of relief.

## Chapter 9

# *The Punitive Expedition*

"An' we've gotter have a punitive expedition," said Roger.

"What's that?" said Bill.

"It's an expedition to punish someone," said Roger, "an' we've gotter punish Archie Mould for takin' that ten shillings from Toothy."

"How'll we punish him?" said Charles.

"We'll duck him," said Roger. "We'll send him a challenge first, of course, an' then we'll duck him."

"Where?" said Bill.

"Anywhere. There's a lot of ponds about. We'll send him a challenge an' then we'll call the gang together an' then we'll hunt him till we find him an' then we'll duck him."

"Let's sign the challenge in our blood, shall we?" said Charles, who liked to extract the last ounce of drama from any situation.

"All right," agreed Roger.

"My blood's jolly hard to get out," said Bill. "Would red ink do instead?"

"No," said Roger and Charles firmly.

The challenge was written and signed by the three of them. It read:

*You are a cheet and a swindler and we the undercined*

*intend to duk you in the neerest pond. Undercined in our*
*blud:–*

The signatures followed. Roger's signature, obtained by digging the point of his mother's nail scissors into the tip of his finger, was fairly legible. Charles, slashing magnificently at his wrist with his penknife, produced such a copious flow that only the C could be distinguished. Bill's signature was a thin brownish scrawl, for Bill, on pricking his finger gingerly with a pin, had immediately applied so much iodine that little else could be seen. Charles even accused him of drawing no blood at all and dipping his nib into one of his, Charles's, blobs, but time was too precious to be wasted on private quarrels, and the finished document was so impressive that pride in it swamped every other feeling. Jimmy pleaded to be allowed to add his signature, running a corkscrew into his arm to prove his fitness for the honour, but Roger refused.

"We don't want kid's blood," he said.

So Jimmy had to be content with drawing a picture in blood of Archie hanging from a gibbet inside the cover of his history book and was kept in the next day by the history master, who – not unreasonably, considering the relations between them – thought the picture was meant to represent himself.

Only Bill had slight doubts about the spelling of the challenge and said that perhaps they ought to have looked out the words in a dictionary, but Roger said that he was pretty sure it was spelt right, and, anyway, probably the Mouldies couldn't spell either. He was evidently right, for the answer to the challenge arrived a few hours later and consisted of the words:

*Hule duk huƧ Wate and sea.*

Actually Archie was an excellent speller, but he had employed Georgie Tallow to write the note, and spelling was the one weak spot in Georgie's armour. Generally Archie corrected his spelling, but on this occasion time was pressing, and he merely reminded him to put a question-mark at the end of the first sentence, which Georgie had done to the best of his ability.

It was an understood thing that battles between the two gangs should take place on Saturday afternoon, so on Saturday afternoon Roger, Toothy (who as *casus belli* was admitted to their councils), Charles and Bill met immediately after lunch in their headquarters. Roger had chosen as their headquarters one of the overgrown caves in the old quarry, beside the pond of stagnant water, which could not be seen from the road, and there the four of them took up their position round an improvised table consisting of a jagged boulder on which were Roger's home-made binoculars, a pair of handcuffs made out of the metal rings from the tops of four potted meat jars, and the map of Uganda that was one of Bill's most prized possessions and without which he considered no head-quarters complete. The rest of the gang had been sent off to reconnoitre.

"C-can I reconnoitre, too, Roger?" Jimmy had pleaded.

"We need every man we can get," said Charles to Roger, seeing the familiar refusal forming itself on Roger's lips. "The Mouldies are out in full strength."

"Very well," agreed Roger, "you can reconnoitre, Jim, but for heaven's sake, don't get taken prisoner."

Jimmy scrambled up the side of the quarry and set off to reconnoitre. He wandered along the road, keeping in the shelter of the hedge, ready always to take to flight across country at the first sight of a Mouldy, but in imagination capturing the whole gang, single-handed, and leading them proudly down the quarry side to Roger . . . It was just as he was turning the bend in the road that he overtook a little boy wheeling a guy in a push-chair. He had never seen the little boy before, but it was the guy that attracted his attention. The head lolled somewhat to one side, but the mask was large and rubicund, adorned by a handsome moustache, while wisps of straw between head and broad-brimmed hat represented a luxuriant growth of hair. Straw, too, protruded from the cuffs of the old coat, and a rug of sacking concealed whatever might be amiss in the workmanship of the lower limbs. It was a most magnificent guy. Jimmy stood staring at it, open-mouthed. The little boy stopped.

"Hello," he said.

"Hello," said Jimmy. "What are you doin' with that guy?"

"I've made it for my uncle for a surprise," said the boy. "I'm takin' it to him now."

"But it's not the fifth of November," objected Jimmy. "It's the third of March."

"It's the fifth of November in Australia," said the boy, "an' my uncle's an Australian. That's why I've made it for him."

Jimmy considered. He knew Australia to be a country whose inhabitants clung precariously upside-down (by what means he had never been able to fathom) to the opposite side of the globe. He had been told that they had picnics there on Christmas Day, and he saw no reason at all why, in that unaccountable country, it should not be the fifth of November on the third of March.

"It's a jolly good guy," he said.

"It's not bad," admitted the boy. The two began to

walk along the road together. "I say," said the boy suddenly, "d'you belong to Roger Manning's gang?"

"Yes," said Jimmy guardedly.

"You're going to duck Archie Mould, aren't you?"

"Yes."

"D'you think Roger'd let me join his gang?"

Jimmy remembered Charles's "We need every man we can get."

"I think so," he said.

"I want to join it, 'cause I hate Archie Mould," said the boy. "Look here! Will you show me where their headquarters is, an' then I'll take this guy as quick as I can to my uncle's an' come straight back an' enlist. I want to do something to get Archie Mould ducked. He's a sneak and a bully and a beastly cheat."

It was such a tiny, ghost-like, quickly smothered chuckle that for a second Jimmy thought he must have imagined it. But he knew he hadn't. It had come from the guy. And it was Archie's chuckle – familiar, malicious, mocking. And in a flash the whole plot became clear to him. Archie had discovered this boy, a stranger to the neighbourhood, and induced him, probably by bribery, to join his gang. Archie, of course, was the guy, beneath the disguise of straw and mask and broad-brimmed hat. And Archie hoped by this means to discover Roger's headquarters and, having done so, lay his plan of campaign accordingly and bring up his whole gang to capture it . . .

"Jus' show me where it is," said the boy again, "an' I'll be back there to enlist, soon as I've taken this ole guy to my uncle."

Jimmy realised suddenly that they were walking along the road just above the old quarry. Immediately below them, invisible from the road, was the stagnant pool and the cave that was the headquarters of the Three Musketeers. He came to a sudden decision.

"All right," he said. Then: "I say! C-can I p-push the ch-chair for a b-bit?"

Anyone who knew Jimmy would have guessed his excitement from his stammer, but fortunately the boy did not know Jimmy. He hesitated, however, and the guy gave an almost imperceptible shake of its head, but, without waiting for permission, Jimmy seized the handles of the chair, ran with it over the wide grass verge, and, before either Archie or the boy knew what was happening, had tipped Archie out into the quarry. Archie rolled down the grass-covered slope and fell plop into the pond.

The Three Musketeers came out of their cave and gazed, paralysed by amazement, at the strange sight of Archie floundering in the pond, his mask and hat floating

HE CAME TO A SUDDEN DECISION. SEIZING THE HANDLE OF THE PUSH-CHAIR, HE RAN WITH IT OVER THE GRASS VERGE.

beside him. But their paralysis did not last long. As he emerged, dripping and slime-covered, they were there at the edge to meet him. Toothy and Roger took a leg each, and Charles and Bill an arm each.

"We'll duck him ten times," said Roger. "One for each shilling."

Small, horror-struck faces peered over the edge of the quarry as Archie's bodyguard, who had been creeping along in the ditch behind him, saw their leader, dripping with slime, howling for mercy, receive his ducking. They had vanished long before the tenth was reached. The battle was over. Archie had been ducked. Home was the safest place, for Archie, defeated, was not a pleasant companion.

At last the victim was released and began to clamber up the sides of the quarry. Threats of vengeance bubbled out of his mouth, together with the water he had swallowed. He reached the top and, still howling, still bubbling threats of vengeance, set off for home.

The Three Musketeers looked at Jimmy, who had watched the scene from halfway up the slope.

"Who pushed him down?" said Roger.

Jimmy was silent for a moment. Thinking over what had happened, he couldn't believe that he had really tipped Archie Mould into the quarry. It seemed too fantastic to be true. But still . . .

"I th-think it was m-me," he said uncertainly.

## Chapter 10

# The Fancy Dress Costume

Despite his seven years and resolute cult of toughness, Jimmy had a secret weakness that he tried to hide from everyone around him. Furtively, guiltily, he still read the book of fairy stories that someone had given him on his fourth birthday – and still half believed in them. Only half, but quite half. He liked to see himself as Jack the Giant Killer and Dick Whittington, and he fully intended to marry a princess when he grew up. And, whenever he thought of the princess, she turned into Sally, the little girl next door. He often indulged in day-dreams in which Sally set him seemingly impossible tasks, which he performed with the ease and fearlessness of his fairy tale heroes, and at the end Sally's father offered him Sally's hand and half his kingdom. Sally's father's kingdom was not, of course, an extensive one, but Jimmy had decided to choose the half next to the fence that took in the poplar tree, so that he could keep Poplar Hawk moths.

This morning he had awakened early and reread "The Goose Girl". The goose girl, of course, had been Sally and he had been the prince. He had put the book back in the bookshelves reluctantly, when the breakfast bell rang (hiding it behind *Hereward the Wake*, so that no one would guess he had been reading it), and ate his breakfast in such a bemused state that he poured his spoonful of syrup into his tea instead of onto his porridge.

After breakfast he wandered down into the garden with Sandy.

Sally was standing by the hole in the hedge that formed the unofficial communicating door between the two gardens. She looked as pretty as ever, but unusually disconsolate. She did not smile even when Sandy began his never-ending attempts to fraternise with Henry, who was sunning himself on the lawn. Ever since Sandy had joined the household he had been trying to make Henry out. Sometimes the creature seemed to have a head, but, when you went nearer to investigate, suddenly it hadn't got one any longer. Sandy was sniffing the edge of the shell, trying to fathom the mystery.

"Hello, Sally," said Jimmy.

"Hello," said Sally.

She sighed deeply as she spoke. Something in her tone told Jimmy that she was not unwilling to be questioned as to the cause of her grief.

"W-what's the matter, Sally?" he ventured to say.

"Haven't you heard about Peggy Bolton's fancy dress party?"

"No," said Jimmy.

Sally sighed again, refusing to be amused even by the sight of Sandy, sitting in front of Henry, watching him with his head on one side, his ears cocked and a comical look of bewilderment on his brown face.

"Well, she hasn't sent out the invitations yet," said Sally, "but she's going to have a fancy dress party on her birthday and" – tears invaded Sally's voice – "Mother won't let me have a new fancy dress costume."

"Oh," said Jimmy, feeling that some comment was needed and not knowing what else to say.

"I shall have to wear that rotten old Dutch Girl costume again, and everybody's seen it."

"Oh," said Jimmy again, trying to sound less puzzled than he felt by this incomprehensible reason for distress.

"And that's not the worst," said Sally.

"What's the worst?" said Jimmy.

"Georgie and Patsy Tallow have got lovely new costumes as Pierrot and Pierrette. They'll simply *laugh* at me for going in that old thing."

Jimmy was silent, considering the situation. Georgie Tallow was a golden-haired little boy of angelic appearance but obnoxious disposition, who lived next door to Archie Mould and was one of his chief supporters.

"I'd give *anything*," went on Sally, "to have a new fancy dress costume."

Suddenly Jimmy realised that the moment he had been dreaming of for years had come. Sally, his princess, had set him a task. He reacted almost automatically to the situation.

"I'll get you one, Sally," he said.

She gazed at him in surprise, but so decided was his voice, so resolute his small round countenance that she was almost convinced.

"Oh, Jimmy, if you *could*!" she said.

Her eager supplicating expression went to his head. He gave a short amused laugh and said:

" 'Course I can."

"When?" she asked.

Even that didn't bring him to his senses. He thrust his hands into his pockets and said nonchalantly:

"When would you like it?"

"Today," said Sally.

"Oh," said Jimmy. "Well, I'd b-better go an' see about it."

He turned on his heel and went indoors with a swagger that gradually deserted him as he realised the magnitude of the task he had undertaken. By the time he reached the kitchen, where his mother was mixing a pudding, he looked less like the hero of a fairy tale than a rather worried small boy.

"Will you do an errand for me, dear?" said his mother.

"Yes," said Jimmy, uncertain whether to consider the request a welcome diversion or a tiresome interruption to his heroic enterprise.

"Just run down to Miss Pepple's and fetch the skirt she's been altering for me. It won't take you a minute. She'll have it ready."

"All right," said Jimmy.

He called Sandy, who was now rolling Henry over on the grass, and the two set off for Miss Pepple's cottage.

Miss Pepple opened the door. She was a small mouse-like woman, who wore a black dress covered by pins and bits of cotton, with a tape measure round her neck and a pair of enormous steel spectacles on her nose.

"I've come for mother's skirt, please," said Jimmy.

"Oh yes, dear," said Miss Pepple. "Come upstairs. *Not* dogs, please, if you don't mind. I'm always afraid that they'll swallow pins."

Jimmy left Sandy outside and followed Miss Pepple upstairs to her workroom. It was a tiny room, its space almost completely occupied by a monumental sewing-machine and an equally monumental dressmaker's dummy. The dresses she was making or altering hung from the picture rail all round the room.

Jimmy gazed absently about him, his mind still busy with his problem, while Miss Pepple made the skirt into a parcel . . . and suddenly his eyes nearly started out of his head.

"Is that a f-fancy dress costume?" he stammered eagerly.

"Yes, dear," said Miss Pepple, looking at the costume to which he was pointing. "A little girl's fancy dress costume. Miss Hook of Holland. Isn't it pretty? I'm altering it for one of my clients."

It was, Jimmy considered, the prettiest costume that he had ever seen. Sally would look lovely in it.

"Here's the skirt, dear," went on Miss Pepple. "I've pinned the paper together, so carry it carefully."

"Th-thanks," said Jimmy, taking the parcel so absent-mindedly that one pin ran into his finger and another into his chin.

He walked home slowly and thoughtfully, ignoring Sandy's attempts to lure him into hunting for water rats in the ditch. The plan that was forming in his mind seemed at first too daring to be attempted, but the spell of the fairy tale still hung over him, and nothing was too daring to be attempted in a fairy tale.

He dumped the parcel down on the hall chest and took Sandy round to his kennel.

"I'll be back soon, Sandy," he said, as he fastened the chain to Sandy's collar. "I'm sorry I can't take you, but they d-didn't take dogs."

Then he went out into the road again, where Bobby Peaslake was hanging about, waiting for him.

"I say, Jimmy," he said, "will you come fishing in that stream where we caught those tiddlers yesterday?"

"No, I can't," said Jimmy. "I'm busy. I'm doin' something for Sally."

He had decided to exclude Bobby as well as Sandy from his adventure. The princes in the fairy tales always did things by themselves, and Bobby had never understood his feelings for Sally.

"Sally!" echoed Bobby, adopting a cynical world-weary air. "Fancy wastin' your time on a soppy girl!"

"She's d-different, is Sally," said Jimmy.

"None of them's different," said Bobby, turning his watch round his wrist. "They're all mean an' soppy an' – an' irreliable."

"N-not Sally," said Jimmy and went on down the road, leaving Bobby gazing after him morosely.

Reaching Miss Pepple's cottage, he hung about uncertainly, realising that the heroes of the fairy tales had many unfair advantages. The cap of invisibility, for instance, would have been most useful. He could have simply walked into the cottage and taken the dress for Sally . . . Suddenly he saw Miss Pepple emerge from her front door, wearing her hat and coat (even her hat and coat had bits of cotton on them) and carrying a shopping basket.

"Hello, Jimmy," she said. "I hope the skirt was all right," and then went on down the road.

Jimmy waited until she had vanished round the corner, then turned his attention to the cottage. He had seen her lock the front door. Cautiously he went round to the back door and tried that. That, too, was locked. The downstairs windows were shut and fastened. Then he noticed that the window of the little workroom upstairs was open and that a drainpipe ran conveniently near it. The seven league boots, of course, would have taken him up to it in one stride. As it was, he must climb it and climb it through a particularly prickly sort of bush that seemed to cover the whole length.

He felt some slight stirrings of conscience at the thought of what he was about to do, but he smothered them without much difficulty. The heroes of his fairy tales were troubled by no such scruples. They just took what they wanted. Anyhow there was no time to waste in pondering the niceties of right and wrong. If Miss Pepple had only gone for her rations she might be back any minute . . .

He put his foot on the first joint of the drainpipe and hoisted himself up . . .

The ascent proved fully as difficult as it had looked. The bush scratched his face and hands, and a nail that stuck out of the wall tore his trousers and shirt. But he reached the top safely (feeling rather like Jack and the Beanstalk), swung himself over the window-sill into the little room, snatched the fancy dress costume from its dress hanger, bundled it under his coat and began the perilous downward climb. The bush and the nail seemed to have grown more ferocious in the interval. They tore a hole in the lace cap of the costume and took a bite out of the full gathered skirt. Again Jimmy envied the heroes of the fairy stories, who would, in these circumstances, have had some friendly fairy at hand to mend the rents by a wave of a wand. Reaching the ground, he bundled the costume more securely under his coat and ran down the road to Sally's. Sally was in the front garden. She gazed at him disapprovingly as he entered.

"You do look *awful*, Jimmy," she said.

Breathlessly, triumphantly, Jimmy drew out his prize.

"Look what I've brought you, Sally," he said. "It's got a bit torn, but I 'spect it'll m-mend all right."

Sally gazed at the dress in horror.

"LOOK WHAT I'VE BROUGHT YOU, SALLY," HE SAID.

"It's *mine*," she screamed. "It's that rotten old Dutch Girl costume."

"It can't be," said Jimmy. "It's Miss H-Hook of Holland. It was at Miss P-Pepple's."

"I *know* it was," said Sally furiously. "She was lengthening it because I'd grown out of it. And now it's *ruined*. Look at it!"

"B-but, Sally—" began Jimmy.

She interrupted him tearfully.

"You're a horrible, stupid, beastly little boy, Jimmy Manning, and I *hate* you. I'll tell my father the minute he comes home, and I hope he'll be *furious* with you."

Jimmy was silent, realising that, whatever Sally's father offered him now, it wouldn't be Sally's hand and half his kingdom.

And then Georgie Tallow came in at the front gate, golden hair brushed and shining, wearing an immaculate grey flannel suit.

"Oh, Sally," he said, "Patsy won't be at home for the fancy dress party, because she's been asked to stay with her godmother. Would you care to wear her pierrette costume and go with me?"

Sally's face shone. She smiled her most radiant smile.

"Oh, *Georgie*, I'd love to. Thank you *so* much. Do come in, Georgie, and I'll ask my mother if you can stay to lunch."

They went indoors together, ignoring Jimmy, except that Sally turned her head aside and twisted her face into a mask of fastidious disdain as she passed him.

Jimmy threw his fancy dress costume down on the garden seat and went out into the road again. Bobby was still hanging about disconsolately.

"L-let's go fishing, Bobby," said Jimmy.

Bobby brightened.

"Good!" he said. "I thought you didn't want to."

"Yes, I do," said Jimmy. "They – they're all those things you said they were."

"Who are?" said Bobby.

"G-g-g-g-girls," said Jimmy.

## Chapter 11

# The Party

Peggy Bolton's fancy dress party was in full swing. Bill had measles and couldn't come, but Roger was there as a pirate, wearing an eye-shade that, as he imagined, lent a sinister aspect to his otherwise innocent countenance. Charles was there as an Arab in a turban and a sheet that had been patched so often that his mother said it didn't matter what happened to it. Toothy, whose mother had been too busy to see to him till the last minute, was there as Night, wearing a pair of pyjamas with a gold paper moon fastened to the middle button of his jacket and gold paper stars stuck at random all over him. Bobby Peaslake was a Mexican in a hat that engulfed his face completely and rested insecurely on his short nose. Jimmy was a clown, the red and white on his face already dissolving into strange erratic patches, suggestive of a somewhat complicated map of an archipelago. The highlights of the whole affair, however, were Archie Mould, dressed in an elaborate cavalier costume, correct in every detail, and Georgie Tallow, in a pierrot costume of dazzling whiteness and newness, accompanied by Sally, who looked exquisite but a little wistful as a pierrette. It was quite obvious that the prizes would be awarded to them, but Peggy's great-grandmother, who was to judge the costumes, had not yet arrived, so the parade had been postponed. Sally had not looked wistful at the beginning of the party. She had looked carefree and radiant and extremely satisfied with herself. The wistfulness had appeared gradually during the course of the afternoon as she discovered one by one the disadvantages of being Georgie's partner. Moreover, she felt herself to be in the wrong camp. For, despite a surface amity, and the unremitting efforts of the grown-ups to "keep the children together," the company was beginning to split up into two groups. The Mouldies gathered round Archie, resplendent in wig and ruffles and feathered hat. Roger's gang gathered round Roger, sinister-looking with eye-patch and cutlass. They played games, danced and sat in rows to watch Peggy's father attempt some not very successful conjuring tricks with the book of instruction open on the table before him and the handkerchief that was half-red and half-white hanging out of his pocket . . . But, immediately these diversions were over, they gathered together into the two groups again, eyeing each other across the room warily, distrustfully, aggressively. Georgie, as Archie's henchman, stood next to Archie with Sally beside him, and Sally looked wistfully across the room at Roger and Jimmy. In the interval of a game she slipped across to Jimmy.

"Hello, Jimmy," she said.

"Hello," said Jimmy, overcome by confusion and delight at being thus singled out for her attention. "Are you enjoying it?"

Sally pouted.

"No, I'm not," she said. "I hate being with Georgie. He's greedy and rude and conceited. And he knows that he and Archie are going to get the prizes and he keeps boasting about it. But that's not what I came to say. Now listen, Jimmy."

"Y-yes?" said Jimmy eagerly.

"They're making a plot against Roger and Charles. I don't know what it is yet but I'm going to find out. And, Jimmy . . ."

"Yes?"

"I'm sorry I was beastly to you about that Dutch Girl costume."

"It's all r-r-right," said Jimmy. "I'm sorry I m-messed it up."

At this point Georgie approached them. A circle of chocolate round his mouth detracted a little from his air of elegance, but he still looked debonair and complacent.

"You must stay with me, Sally," he said imperiously. "Our costumes go together and people hardly notice mine when I'm alone. After all, I lent it you."

Reluctantly, dispiritedly, Sally accompanied him back to the Mouldie group.

In the next interval of the game she slipped across to Jimmy again.

"I've found out what the plot is," she said. "They've altered Roger's and Charles's clues in the Treasure Hunt so that Roger's takes him to the coal shed and Charles's to the boxroom right at the top of the house, and Archie's going to be hiding near the coal shed to lock Roger into it and Georgie's going to be hiding near the boxroom to lock Charles into it and they're going to keep them locked up for the rest of the party. We'd better warn Roger and Charles, hadn't we?"

Jimmy considered, his face wearing an expression of such deep thought that a whole fresh set of islands seemed to appear on his archipelago.

"No," he said at last. "We've gotter d-do something to get *them* into the boxroom an the coal shed an' lock them in. It's an awful risk to take, but you g-go back to them, Sally, an' find out where the Treasure Hunt clues are kept an' I'll go an' t-talk to Bobby."

He made his way over to where Bobby was standing at the buffet-table eating his seventh ice cream.

"Hello," said Bobby, leaning his head back as far as it would go in order to look at Jimmy from under the shade of his hat.

"You've got to stop eatin' ice cream," said Jimmy.

"Why?" said Bobby simply.

" 'Cause the Mouldies are makin' a plot against Roger an' Charles, an' we've got to stop 'em. Every minute's a matter of life an' death, so there's no time for ice creams. I'll tell you about it."

He told him about it.

"Corks, yes!" said Bobby, setting his hat at a businesslike angle, which it retained for a fleeting second before it settled on his nose again. "What are we goin' to do about it?"

Before Jimmy could answer, Sally flitted back to him.

"The clues are in the study on the bureau," she whispered, and then once more obeyed Georgie's imperious summons.

Jimmy outlined his plan to Bobby, then, choosing their moment carefully, when the party was engrossed in Blind Man's Buff, the two slipped from the room. Yes, there on the bureau in the study was the box containing the Treasure Hunt clues. Hastily they found the two that had Roger's and Charles's names on the outside. It was a Treasure Hunt of the simpler variety. Each guest had one clue, and the one clue led to a treasure. Roger's clue read:

> *Go out of doors, tread gently through the mire.*
> *You'll find me in the shed that feeds the fire.*

"That's jolly good po'try," said Jimmy judicially. "Now let's look at Charles's."

Charles's read:

> *Go up three flights of stairs, turn to the right.*
> *You'll find me when the boxes come in sight.*

"That's not bad po'try, either," said Jimmy. "Now what shall we put instead? We want to get them right out of the way so that the other Mouldies'll think the trick's worked."

"The pond!" said Bobby. "You know what they are. Once they get near a pond they stay there for hours."

"That's a jolly good idea," said Jimmy. "Now let's think of some po'try for it."

He wrinkled his brow in desperate thought for a few moments, then wrote:

"Go to the water underneath the trees" – then stopped, frowning thoughtfully. "What rhymes with 'trees'?"

"Sneeze," suggested Bobby.

"Yes, that's good," said Jimmy, and wrote:

" 'But don't get wet in it or else you'll sneeze.' Now we'll write two of it," he went on "and put Roger's name on one and Charles's name on the other and put them in the box 'stead of the ones about the coal shed an' the box-room. P'raps," hopefully, "they won't notice that they're diff'rent writing from the rest."

And, as it happened, they didn't. A harassed Bolton

*Just Jimmy*

aunt gave out the clues, and she was too busy trying to stop two little boys throwing cushions at each other to have time or energy for studying the handwriting on the slips of paper.

The party swarmed over the house in search of treasures, discovering them without much difficulty and with squeals of excitement. Two little girls, both dressed as Peace, with stuffed doves, wings, and white dresses, began to fight each other with silent ferocity for the possession of a doll's chair, and, though frequently parted, continued to fight till the end of the evening. Roger and Charles, only mildly surprised to find that they had the same clue, wandered down to the pond and, as Bobby had foreseen, became from that moment lost to everything but their immediate surroundings.

Bobby, Jimmy and Sally were holding a whispered consultation on the stairs.

"What's Georgie fondest of – to eat, I mean?" said Jimmy.

"Chocolate biscuits," said Sally bitterly. "He finished the whole plate an' then grumbled 'cause there weren't any more."

"And what about Archie?"

"Let's ask Toothy," suggested Bobby.

They found Toothy testing on the buffet tablecloth a printing outfit that had fallen to his lot in the Treasure Hunt. His pyjamas were beginning to look a little tumbled and his moon had dropped off, but a few stars still adhered to him.

"What d-does Archie like most?" said Jimmy.

"Money," said Toothy, simply, trying to rub out a blob of printers' ink from the tablecloth with his handkerchief.

There was another whispered consultation, then Bobby made his way up to the boxroom, where Georgie was waiting at his post, ready to fasten the door on Charles.

"I say, I'm sorry," said Bobby, trying to look guilty, but only succeeding in looking half-witted. "I was jus' comin' up to see if I could find any more of those chocolate biscuits."

Georgie's eyes gleamed.

"Where?" he said.

"In the boxroom," said Bobby. "They use it as a sort of storeroom, an' there's a tin—"

But Georgie had pushed him aside to enter the boxroom. In a second the door was slammed on him and the key turned in the lock.

At the same moment Jimmy was approaching Archie, who stood by the coal shed door.

"Oh, I'm s-sorry," said Jimmy. "I was jus' comin' to see if I'd d-dropped a half-crown in the coal shed when we were playin' here this morning an'—"

"You stay out there," said Archie with a sly smile. "I'll look for you."

He plunged into the coal shed. The door slammed on him and the key turned in the lock.

Bobby and Jimmy returned to the party. Musical Chairs was just beginning. From the distance came the sound of shouting and banging on doors, and the Mouldies exchanged triumphant smiles. Mrs Bolton might have noticed that two of her young guests were absent if she had not been busy trying to repress a little boy who was pretending to be a lion and biting everyone within reach.

The first rift in the satisfaction of the Mouldies appeared when Roger and Charles wandered in from the garden, obviously unaware of any plot against them. The second appeared when Archie burst into the room, bedraggled and coal-covered, his cavalier costume hardly recognisable after its passage through the coal shed window. He sat down on the nearest chair and pointed a black accusing finger at Jimmy.

"Jimmy Manning locked me in," he shouted.

But Mrs Bolton had nearly reached the limits of her endurance. She had discovered the youngest guest (aged two and a half) being sick on her Persian carpet, and now Archie was scattering coal dust over her new chair covers.

"You can surely protect yourself against a little boy like that," she said acidly. "Get up off that chair at once, Archie."

ARCHIE BURST INTO THE ROOM, BEDRAGGLED AND COAL-COVERED.

It was almost an anticlimax when Georgie came in, covered with dust and cobwebs, howling dismally, having been released by a passing maid. The Mouldies eyed each other in consternation, Roger and Charles stared at each other and everyone else in bewilderment, and the youngest guest began to be sick again.

And then Mrs Bolton's grandmother arrived. She was a forceful and incalculable old lady and insisted on pulling a cracker and putting a paper hat on her head before she got down to her job of judging the costumes.

Mrs Bolton led Archie and Georgie up to her.

"These are the best boys' costumes, Gran dear," she said, "though I'm afraid they've got a bit—"

"Grimy?" said the old lady. "They're in a shocking state. I should never dream of giving them the prizes." She raised her lorgnettes and surveyed the room. Then she pointed to Roger. "I award the first prize to Nelson."

"He isn't Nelson, Gran dear," said Mrs Bolton faintly.

"Of course, he's Nelson," said the old lady. "Don't you know that Nelson wore a patch over his eye? The costume may not be historically correct in every detail, but I like the idea. It's patriotic. I've always had a weakness for the Navy. Come and get your prize, little boy."

As Roger, too much bewildered to protest, went up to receive the aeroplane kit that was his prize, the old lady swept the room again with her lorgnettes.

"And I award the second prize to America," she said, pointing to Toothy.

"He isn't America," said Mrs Bolton still more faintly.

"Of course he's America," said the old lady tartly. "Don't you know that stars and stripes stand for America? I thought everyone knew that. It's not, of course, an elaborate costume, but it's a graceful compliment to our late allies, and I like to encourage anything that fosters good international relationship. Come here, dear boy."

So Toothy, gaping and goggling, went up to receive his penknife.

Mr Manning was driving Roger and Jimmy home in the car. He heard the news that Roger's costume had won the first prize with parental gratification tempered by a little natural mystification.

"And did you enjoy it, Jimmy?" he said after congratulating Roger.

"Yes, thanks," said Jimmy.

"What did you do there?"

"Oh, there were games and conjurin' and a Treasure Hunt."

"The usual sort of party, in fact?" said Mr Manning.

Jimmy was silent for a few moments then said:

"M-more or less."

## Chapter 12

# *The Treat*

Jimmy swaggered down the road, hands in pockets, surveying the landscape with a stern frown. He was a potentate who ruled not only England but half the inhabited world, and he was rapidly conquering the other half. He rode a magnificently accoutred black charger, and on either side of him rode his bodyguard, on slightly less magnificently accoutred chargers. Behind him troops of soldiers and war equipment filled the roads as far as one could see.

When he reached the crossroads his expression of stern authority gave way to one of surprise. The field where he had meant to hold a review of his army was already full of tents. A group of children hung about the gate, on which was a notice: "London Children's Holiday Camp". He strolled up to them.

"Hello," said a little girl with a mop of dark curls and blue eyes.

"Hello," said Jimmy rather distantly.

"D'you live here?"

"Yes," said Jimmy.

"D'you like it?"

"Yes," said Jimmy, considering the question for the first time.

"I don't. There ain't nuffin' to do."

"Yes, there is," said Jimmy.

"How old are you?"

"Seven an' three-quarters."

"Can I come to tea with you?"

"Yes," said Jimmy graciously.

After all, he had three castles and four palaces and armies of servants. There was no reason why he shouldn't have a little girl to tea.

"Can I?" . . . "Can I?" . . . "Can I?" choroused the other children.

"Yes," said Jimmy still graciously. After all, he was a world potentate. There was no reason why he shouldn't have hundreds of children to tea if he wanted to . . . but already the cold breath of reality was breaking up the roseate mists of his dream world, and there was a faint apprehension behind his graciousness.

"When?" they clamoured. "Tomorrow?"

"Y-yes," said Jimmy in rather a small voice.

"Where do you live?"

Sanity came in time to Jimmy's rescue.

"I'll f-fetch you from the c-crossroads," he said.

"What time? Half-past three?" they clamoured.

"Y-yes," said Jimmy and turned to retrace his steps homewards – no longer a world potentate, but a small boy aghast at the enormity of the crime he had committed. For the rest of the day, horror closed over him whenever he thought of it. He didn't even know how many children he'd asked. Sometimes he thought there had been ten, sometimes twenty, sometimes thirty. To invite one guest to tea without permission was a crime in his mother's eyes. He tried at intervals to summon up his courage to ask her permission. He rehearsed a careless, "May I ask a few friends to tea tomorrow, Mother?" but whenever he tried to say the words they refused to come. "Tomorrow, dear?" his mother would say in surprise. "How many?" and he'd have to reply, "I don't know . . . ten or twenty."

He went to bed with the problem still unsolved, the crime still unconfessed. As soon as he woke in the morning, the memory of it enveloped his consciousness like a thick black cloud. He was so silent and thoughtful at breakfast that his mother said:

"Do you feel all right, Jimmy?"

"Y-yes, thanks," said Jimmy with a deep sigh.

"It's those green apples he was eating yesterday," said his father. "I told him they'd give him collywobbles."

Jimmy said nothing. So much had happened since yesterday morning that it was difficult to remember how he had wandered happily about the orchard, munching windfalls. All the trouble in the world seemed to have fallen on him since then. He made a determined effort, counting thirty (which generally gave him courage) clearing his throat and beginning:

"M-mother, m-may I . . .?"

Then he stopped.

Mrs Manning looked at him enquiringly.

"Yes, dear?"

"M-may I have some more marmalade, please?" he ended feebly.

"Yes, dear," she said, passing him the jar.

By lunchtime, of course, he knew it was too late. One couldn't ask to ask people to tea as late as lunchtime. By quarter past three there was a feeling of constriction at the pit of his stomach, and he would have welcomed the onset of any incurable disease that would have rescued him from this plight. He was even tempted to ignore his guests, to leave them waiting at the crossroads. He hadn't told them where he lived. But he couldn't quite bring himself to do that. He had invited them. He was their host. At twenty-five past three he set out, his face pale and set and desperate, and walked slowly, very slowly, towards the crossroads. Yes, there they were – about fifteen of them – clean and tidy and wearing the happy expectant faces of children who are going to a party. A harassed-looking woman was watching from the field. She had evidently been a little uncertain about the invitation, but, when she saw Jimmy coming to collect his guests, her face cleared and she waved her hand to him. It was plain that she viewed the prospect of a few hours' respite from her charges with equanimity.

"We're ready," shrilled the children. "Where is it?"

Jimmy stretched his features in a glassy smile of greeting, then clutched frantically at the only chance he saw of postponing the catastrophe.

"It's this way," he said, pointing down a lane that led in the opposite direction from his home.

They waved goodbye to the harassed-looking woman and began to follow him. Down the lane, over the fields, through a wood, up a hill . . . They chattered happily at first, then gradually became silent, as doubt and weariness took possession of them. At their head walked Jimmy, in the grip of the worst nightmare he had ever known, walking on and on at random.

They had reached Eckton now – the village next to the one where Jimmy lived – and were passing Eckton Village Hall when Jimmy stopped short, gaping amazedly. For the door was wide open, revealing a long trestle table loaded with jellies, blancmanges, cakes, biscuits and sandwiches. Two women in overalls stood near the door.

AT THEIR HEAD
WALKED JIMMY . . .

"Come in, children," smiled one of the women, and Jimmy, too much bewildered even to wonder what was happening, led his flock into the room. The party brightened. Their weariness and depression fell from them. Laughing and talking gaily, they took their seats and set to work. The two women in overalls hovered about, handing them food. Jimmy sat near the head of the table and heard one woman talking to the other.

"Yes, I've been giving Cookery Lectures here all the Spring. I like to make a little social event of each lecture, and this morning's was a Children's Party. We got it ready before lunch, and I arranged that the children of the members of the cookery class should all come and have tea here this afternoon. Actually, they've arrived about an hour before I expected them, but that doesn't matter."

If Jimmy hadn't already plumbed the depth of horror, he would have plumbed it then, but, as it was, he abandoned himself with a sort of stony resignation to whatever further crisis the day might have in store.

The guests had just finished the last crumb on the last plate when the door opened and a woman entered, followed by some other women and a crowd of children, all carrying baskets. She swept the room with an indignant eye.

"What is the meaning of this?" she said, and, as nobody answered her, went on: "*Who* brought these children here?"

Jimmy gulped and blinked.

"M-m-me," he said.

The indignant eye held him fast. It seemed to go right through him and come out on the other side.

"And are you aware," said the woman, "that the shameful trick you have played on us has deprived poor children of a treat? We were going to take all this food down to the London Children's Holiday Camp. *How* can we take it down now?"

Again Jimmy gulped and blinked.

"It's all right," he said. "They've c-come up for it."

## Chapter 13

# *Righting a Wrong*

"It's j-jolly unfair," said Jimmy.

He and Bobby were sitting astride the roof of the tool shed at the bottom of Bobby's garden. The tool shed was a battleship, from which they had just shot down twenty enemy aeroplanes, sunk eleven enemy battleships and, by means of depth charges (consisting of an empty lemonade bottle lowered at the end of a string), blown to smithereens fifty enemy submarines. Sweeping the horizon in turn with the telescope (a rolling pin of Jimmy's mother's that had lost its handles) and finding no further signs of the enemy, they had fallen to discussing their immediate personal problems, and the foremost of these was Roger's dormouse. Roger's dormouse had been given to him last week by an aunt and had at once become his most precious possession. But it was his possession no longer. Bill had borrowed it for a night in order to put its cage next to his guinea pig's and see if they would fraternise. (The result had been negative, as, after the interchange of a few terse home truths, the two had settled down to ignore each other with the magnificence of a couple of rival film stars). But that had not been the end. Bill had brought the dormouse to school the next morning in order to return it to Roger and, arriving rather late, had slipped it into his desk, meaning to give it to

Roger at "break", but he could not resist the temptation to take it out during the history lesson to show it to his neighbours. And then the bomb had fallen. For Mr Robinson, the new history master, had confiscated the dormouse, cage and all, and had refused to restore it, even when Bill pointed out that it was not his property and that the confiscation amounted to theft. That had happened two days ago, and Roger was still dormouse-less. Protests by Charles, by Roger himself, had proved useless. Mr Robinson had refused even to discuss the matter and had cut short Charles's rather confused appeal to the Habeas Corpus Act by the threat of a hundred lines.

"It's stealin'," said Bobby indignantly. "I 'spect he's sold it to a hedge already."

"A hedge?" said Jimmy.

"That's what they call a man you sell things you've stole to," explained Bobby. "Don't you remember? We read it in a book."

"You mean fence," said Jimmy.

"It's the same thing," said Bobby a little distantly.

"Yes, p'raps it is," said Jimmy, who felt that the crisis was too urgent to allow for argument over unimportant details.

"Anyway, he's a thief," said Bobby, "an' it'd serve him right if someone stole *his* pet."

"I don't 'spose he's got one," said Jimmy.

"Yes, he has," said Bobby. "He's got a cat. He lives in rooms over at Eckton an' he's got a cat. He told Freddy Pelham so."

A look of grim resolve was slowly forming on Jimmy's face.

"All *right*," he said. "We'll t-t-take it."

Bobby stared at him.

"We can't do that," he said. "That *is* stealin'."

"No, it isn't," said Jimmy. "It's j-justice. We'll only keep it till he gives Roger back his dormouse."

"We'd better let him know that," said Bobby, turning his watch round nervously, "or we might get put in prison. It mus' be rotten in prison. I don't think they even let you out to get your sweet ration."

"Y-yes," agreed Jimmy. "We'll write a note tellin' him . . . Let's go'n' do it now."

He swept the horizon with his telescope, shot down a dozen more aeroplanes, sank two battleships, blew up ten submarines, then scrambled down the side of the shed, followed by Bobby. Together they went up to Bobby's bedroom to write the note. The composition took them some considerable time and involved much wrinkling of Jimmy's brow, much chewing of the pen and much turning of Bobby's watch; but, when finished, it seemed to them little short of a masterpiece. It ran: "We will keap your pett til the rong you did is rited."

"How'll we sign it?" said Jimmy. "We don't want him to think Roger wrote it, an' we don't want him to know we did."

"No," agreed Bobby. "My father once wrote a letter to the newspaper an' he signed it 'For the common weal.' He signed it like that for a sort of disguise, so they wouldn't know who'd done it."

"Weal?" said Jimmy. "There isn't a word 'weal'. There's 'weasle'."

"P'raps it was that," said Bobby vaguely.

"Let's try it an' see what it looks like," said Jimmy.

Slowly and laboriously he added to the note: "*Cined,* Two common weasles."

"Yes," he said, considering it approvingly. "It looks all right. It makes a jolly good disguise, too. Now we've got to go to Eckton with it an' bring back his cat."

They set out across the fields to Eckton, Jimmy holding the note tightly in a hot grubby hand, both wearing the set stern expressions of knights errant resolved to stamp out injustice from the universe.

On the outskirts of Eckton they stopped and stood irresolute, looking vaguely down a lane that branched off from the main road.

"I dunno where he lives, do you?" said Jimmy.

"No," said Bobby and added: "P'raps we'd better not go on with it, after all. It's a bit dangerous."

" 'Course we're goin' on with it," said Jimmy firmly.

A small boy was coming down the road, kicking a stone.

"D'you know where Mr Robinson lives?" Jimmy asked him.

"Straight on an' first on right," said the small boy as he vanished into the ditch after his stone.

The first house on the right was a picturesque cottage with honeysuckle growing over the porch. Slowly, a little apprehensively, they approached it. It appeared to be empty. Going round to the back, they saw, through the open window, a grey Siamese cat asleep on a chair. The window was unlatched, the distance from the ground to windowsill inconsiderable, the theft almost incredibly easy of accomplishment. A few minutes later the chair was unoccupied except for a grubby crumpled note, and two small boys, one of whom seemed to be carrying a miniature tornado under his coat, were hurrying as best they could across the fields.

"What'll we do with it?" said Bobby, as they entered

the gate of Jimmy's back garden.

"We'll put it in the coal shed jus' for n-now," panted Jimmy, who was still struggling with his burden and only just beginning to realise the difficulties that beset the situation, "an' I'll be jolly glad to get it there. It's gettin' madder every minute."

Inside the coal shed the cat seemed to lose the last vestige of its sanity. It tore up and down the heap of coal, it burrowed in the coal dust, it tried to climb the walls, it brought down a whole pile of "slack" upon its head, imperilling every one of its nine lives, it turned in a few minutes from a smoke-grey Siamese into a coal-black Siamese.

"Corks!" said Jimmy, as he closed the door. "I dunno what we're goin' to do with it. He's jolly lucky only havin' a d-dormouse."

IT TURNED INTO
A COAL-BLACK
SIAMESE.

Slowly the two went indoors and into the sitting room. And there they stood stock-still, staring at amazement at the scene before them. For on the hearthrug was Roger's dormouse in a new cage – a super cage-de-luxe, twice as large as the old one, with a little wheel in one of the two compartments. Roger sat by it, looking down at it, his face shining with joy and pride. In the armchair by the fire sat Mr Robinson, smoking a pipe. In front of the fire stood Jimmy's father, also smoking a pipe. For one wild moment Jimmy thought that Mr Robinson must have gone home, found the note, and come here to offer his surrender, then he realised that there wouldn't have been time.

Mr Robinson was watching Roger with a twinkle. He seemed younger and more human than he seemed in school.

"I thought a little lesson wouldn't do you any harm, young man," he was saying. "You *have* tried to play me up once or twice, haven't you?" Roger grinned and nodded. "But the real reason why I kept it was that the cage was far too small. I knew that – somewhere or other at home – I still had the cage I'd kept a dormouse in when I was a boy, so I went home yesterday and had a look for it, and here it is."

"It's *awfully* good of you, sir," said Roger.

"More than you deserve, evidently," said Mr Manning, but there was a twinkle in his eye too.

"Almost makes me want to keep a dormouse again myself," said Mr Robinson. "All I've got in the way of a pet now is a rather moth-eaten ginger cat."

Jimmy gave a gasp.

"You can have a look at it," said Roger, pushing the cage towards Jimmy and Bobby, but they could only look at Mr Robinson with horror-stricken faces.

"It carries on a perpetual warfare with my next-door neighbours' cat," went on Mr Robinson. "Oddly enough, my neighbours' name is the same as mine. Their cat is a prize Siamese called Purkins – the apple of their eye. It's going to a show tomorrow and they've spent all day cleaning and brushing and grooming it. It's a beautiful creature. Smoke grey."

Jimmy thought of the prize Siamese in the coal shed only a few yards away, and the thought brought a strange feeling to the pit of his stomach.

And then a frantic little woman entered the room. She ignored everyone else and addressed herself to Mr Robinson.

"Oh, forgive me for coming, sir," she said. "I don't know where my husband is, an' someone said they had seen you come here, an' I thought that, with knowin' about cats, you could tell me what to do. Oh dear! Oh dear!"

They made soothing noises at her, and Mr Manning asked her to sit down.

"I couldn't," she said. "Oh, I'm in such a state. I've run all the way. I've been out shoppin' and I come home to find the kitchen boiler burst. The kitchen's *wrecked*, but that doesn't matter. It's Purky. He's been blown to nothin', sir. To *nothin'*. He was in the chair by the fire an' there's nothin' of him left. It mus' be this atomic power you read about in the newspapers. I can't find so much as a whisker."

She burst into tears and sat down weakly in the chair that Mr Manning had drawn forward for her. "Oh Purky, my pet," she moaned, "where *are* you?"

And then Jimmy found his voice. It was a very small voice and seemed to come from a long way off.

"He's in the c-coal shed," he said.

*Chapter 14*

# *The Criminal*

"I think he'll make a jolly fine bloodhound," said Jimmy, looking down proudly at the mixture-of-all-breeds that was Sandy.

Sandy gazed up at him, waving his retriever tail, cocking his fox terrier ears, smiling his foolish collie smile in agreement.

"Yes, he's jolly clever," said Bobby. "He only needs a bit of training."

After reading a more than usually exciting detective story in a boys' magazine, the two had once more decided to become detectives, and, not wishing to leave Sandy out of it, had decided to train him as a bloodhound. The training was proving a somewhat slow business owing to Sandy's unconquerable belief in human nature. He welcomed complete strangers as if they were his dearest friends. The shabbier, the more furtive-looking the stranger, the more eager was Sandy's welcome. As a watchdog he was, of course, useless, but Jimmy's and Bobby's hopes of turning him into a bloodhound were still undamped.

"It's a good thing, really, he's so friendly," said Jimmy. "It'll sort of put crim'nals off their guard."

"But we've got to teach him to be fierce when he's axshully *catchin'* 'em,' said Bobby. "You can't axshully *catch* a crim'nal without fierceness."

The only thing that seemed able to rouse any "fierceness" in Sandy was a bedroom slipper. Bedroom slippers seemed to release some dark force of destruction in his dog soul. He worried them furiously and could reduce them to their component parts in a few seconds. So Jimmy was building his training on this foundation. He hid his bedroom slippers in old sacks and newspapers and egged Sandy on to the attack, rescuing his slippers just in time.

"The nex' thing," he explained to Bobby, "is to teach him to c'nect slippers with crim'nals, and then sort of get him to know crim'nals without slippers."

"Yes," agreed Bobby and added meditatively, "Pity there aren't any crim'nals round here for him to practise on."

"I bet there are crim'nals round here," said Jimmy earnestly. "There's crim'nals everywhere, if we knew where to look for 'em. Why, in that book we read there were hundreds of 'em in that one gang, an' the detective only caught the ringleaders. You remember he caught 'em single-handed in the underground cellar – all ten of 'em and shot 'em or stunned 'em one after the other. He must have been jolly brave. That's the sort I'm goin' to be."

"Yes, but what about Sandy?" said Bobby, bringing him back to the matter in hand. "How do we start findin' a crim'nal for him to practise on?"

"We – we jus' go out an' look for one," said Jimmy a little vaguely. "I bet I can tell a crim'nal when I see one."

"All right," said Bobby.

He felt less sure on the point than Jimmy, but he was accustomed to follow Jimmy's leadership without question, and to accept without resentment any consequences it might entail.

The two sallied out into the village street. Jimmy had put his slipper into his pocket, and Sandy, unaware of the important role assigned to him, was leaping up at it light-heartedly. Suddenly Georgie Tallow appeared, strolling down the street towards them. Jimmy would have ignored him, but Sandy – a dog, as even Jimmy had reluctantly to admit, of little discrimination – flung himself upon him in an ecstasy of delight. Georgie aimed a kick at him, but, being a poor kicker, missed him by several inches.

"Call your wretched mongrel off," he said to Jimmy. "I don't want his filthy dirty paws all over my suit."

"If you say he's a m-mongrel again . . ." said Jimmy threateningly.

Georgie smiled his superior smile.

"What is he, then?"

"He's bloodhound."

"A what?"

"A b-bloodhound," said Jimmy. "He catches c-crim'nals."

Georgie laughed his superior laugh.

"I'd like to see him doing it."

"All right," said Jimmy doggedly. "You w-wait. You w-will."

"Really?" sneered Georgie and passed on down the street, disappearing into the Post Office.

The two looked about them. The street was quite empty.

"Well, I don't see any crim'nals," said Bobby.

"I 'spect they're all havin' tea or somethin'," said Jimmy. "It's about tea time. Let's go 'n' have a look at the Ole Tudor Café."

The Old Tudor Café was a picturesque half-timbered

building that stood at the end of the village street. Its interior was dark and draughty, and its "home-made cakes", advertised in the window, were chiefly famous for their solidity and dryness, but it was much patronised by visitors who came to view the beauty spots of the neighbourhood.

Jimmy and Bobby approached it and stood pressing their noses against the small window panes. Only two of the tables were occupied, and at each of them a man was having tea alone. Jimmy's eyes opened wide with excitement.

"L-look," he said. "*He's* a crim'nal, all right."

Certainly the man having tea at the table nearest the window was the most sinister-looking object either of them had every seen. One eye-lid drooped so much that only the narrow glint of an eye was visible, the nose had a villainous twist half-way down, and the mouth was a long thin slit across the face. Even the clothes had something sinister about them. They were drab and dun-coloured, as if anxious to escape notice. Then their eyes wandered to the other occupant of the café – a tall, good-looking, open-faced young man in a garish check suit.

"He's a *good* man, you can tell that by lookin' at him," said Jimmy with a judicial air. "I bet he's a detective doggin' the other one. He'll be jolly grateful to us for helpin' to catch him."

"Yes, but how do we start catchin' him?" said Bobby.

"We've got to think a bit," said Jimmy. "It takes a bit of thinkin'."

Bobby waited trustfully, while Jimmy, thrusting his hands into his pockets and ravelling his brow into a complicated pattern, abandoned himself to the process of thought.

"I've *got* it," he said at last. "We must put the bedroom slipper into the crim'nal's pocket, an' then Sandy'll attack him, an' then after that, when he's caught a real crim'nal, p'raps he won't need bedroom slippers any more, an' we'll be able to hire him out to the p'lice as a b-blood-hound."

"How'll we get it in his pocket?" said Bobby.

"I've got an idea about that, too," said Jimmy with modest pride. "Have you still got that threepence your mother gave you for not playing your mouth organ while your grandmother was staying with you?"

"Yes," said Bobby, taking three pennies from his pocket, and carefully counting them. "I've got the whole lot."

"Well, look," said Jimmy. "They've hung up their overcoats by the door, haven't they?"

"Yes," said Bobby, pressing his nose once more against the window-pane.

"Well, we'll go in, an' you can go to the counter an' ask for an ice cream, an' while you're doin' it I'll put the slipper in the crim'nal's pocket, an' then, when he comes out, Sandy'll jump at him, an' we'll sort of over-power him an' – well, then we'll have c-caught him, won't we?"

"Yes," said Bobby, a little uncertainly.

They entered the café, and Bobby approached the vague, short-sighted, middle-aged woman who presided over the establishment, while Jimmy busied himself unobtrusively with the overcoats by the door. One was drab and dun-coloured, the other bright and checked. There seemed no doubt which belonged to the criminal. With a quick movement, Jimmy thrust the slip-per into the pocket of the dun-coloured one, then joined

JIMMY THRUST
THE SLIPPER INTO
THE POCKET.

Bobby at the counter. A hasty glance round showed that no one had noticed him. The vague proprietress was explaining that she was sold out of ices, the two customers were engaged on their teas.

"Well, *that's* all right," said Jimmy when they had regained the safety of the street. "I bet no one in Scotland Yard could have done it better. Now all we've got to do is to wait till the crim'nal comes out an' set Sandy loose on him."

"An' what happens after that?" said Bobby.

Jimmy's imagination had not taken him beyond that glorious moment. He considered the question for the first time.

"We ought to have a p'liceman near to arrest him," he finally decided. "Of course we ought to be workin' *with* the p'lice really. I 'spect we shall be soon when we've caught a few crim'nals."

"*Look!*" said Bobby.

As if in answer to their wish, a policeman had appeared at the end of the street.

"Go an' ask him the t-time," said Jimmy. "Keep on askin' him the time so's he won't go away."

"A'right," said Bobby, trotting off obediently.

Then Georgie Tallow came out of the Post Office and sauntered slowly towards Jimmy.

"Caught your criminal yet?" he said with an unpleasant snigger.

Before Jimmy had time to answer, the door of the café opened, and the sinister-looking man came out. Jimmy stared at him open-mouthed, for, over his dun-coloured suit, he wore the checked overcoat. He got into a car that stood by the kerb and drove off.

Two women were passing.

"That's Dr Helsham from Eckton," he heard one of them say as they watched the departing car. "They all think the world of him over there."

"Gosh!" said Jimmy in dismay.

Bobby came trotting back from the policeman.

"I've asked him the time four times," he said, "an' he's gettin' mad."

The policeman was glaring at them from the end of the street. He considered that one small boy spelt possible trouble, two small boys probable trouble and three small boys certain trouble, and he had decided not to let the little devils out of his sight as long as they stayed there.

Then the door of the café opened again, and the young man, wearing the dun-coloured overcoat, came out and

bent over a motorcycle that stood by the kerb. At once
Sandy sprang at him, barking wildly, jumping frantically
up to the pocket that contained Jimmy's bedroom slipper.
The attack took the young man by surprise. He lost his
balance and fell on to the pavement. A woman screamed.
The policeman came running up. At first he seemed
interested only in the young man, and then, quite suddenly, he became interested in the motorcycle. He examined it carefully.

"Well, I'll be blowed!" he said. "If this ain't the one
we've just 'ad particulars of. Stole from over Barsham
way, it was. I'll trouble you to come along to the police
station with me, young man."

"No trouble at all, Sergeant," said the young man
politely, as he picked himself up and brushed the dust
from his clothes. "I was a fool to stop for tea."

The policeman set off, pushing the motorcycle, the
young man accompanying him with a swagger.

Jimmy, now holding Sandy firmly by the collar, turned
to Georgie.

"You see?" he said nonchalantly. "He knows a
crim'nal jus' by lookin' at him. Good ole Sandy!"

Georgie was gaping amazedly. All his bounce and
arrogance left him. He was like a pricked balloon. Then
he made a supreme effort to recover himself.

"But the policeman caught him," he said.

"Oh yes," said Jimmy airily, "we work with the p'lice.
We have to have the p'lice here to arrest them," and
Georgie collapsed again.

But an uncomfortable thought had just struck Jimmy.
A missing bedroom slipper would cause trouble even in
the home of a budding detective.

"One m-minute," he said, still retaining his airy

manner. "I've g-got to go an' fix up with the p-p'liceman about our next job."

He ran down the street after the departing figures of the policeman and the young man.

"I s-say!" he panted.

The policeman turned round.

"If you've come to ask the time—" he said threateningly.

"N-no," said Jimmy, "it's n-not that. It's – p-please can I have my b-bedroom slipper? It's in his p-p-pocket."

## Chapter 15

# The Hostage

The Three Musketeers were making their way along the road towards the old quarry, looking round occasionally to make sure that Jimmy was not following them.

"He's not coming," said Roger. "I told him not to, so I knew he wouldn't."

They were going to the old quarry for no other reason than that it was a fine Saturday afternoon and they thought they might as well spend it at the old quarry as anywhere. Charles had a theory that they would find hidden treasure there; Roger wanted to practise mountaineering up the steep boulder-strewn sides; Bill had brought his fishing rod, consisting of a bent pin on a string at the end of a stick, together with some bait, consisting of a bag of potato peelings, and had come prepared to fish in the pool of stagnant water that had collected in a corner of the quarry. No one had ever seen a fish of any kind in it, but Bill did not allow his hopes of catching a salmon, or at least a trout, to be damped by that fact.

"See if he's comin', Bill," said Roger, feeling that it was inconsistent with his dignity to look round again.

Bill turned to survey the empty road.

"No, he's not comin'," he reported.

"I've knocked some sense into his head at last," said Roger with satisfaction.

"Toothy's comin' out with us, isn't he?" said Charles.

"Yes . . . I 'spect he'll be waiting for us at the quarry," said Bill.

And the next bend in the road showed them Toothy, waiting by the side of the road at the point from which they usually made their precarious descent into the quarry. But he was not alone. He stood, looking pale and harassed, beside a perambulator containing a baby. The dismay on his face was reflected on the faces of the Three Musketeers as they approached him.

"You can't bring *that*," said Roger sternly.

"I'm sorry," said Toothy with almost desperate humility. His large irregular teeth seemed to be trying to hide behind each other in abasement, as he spoke. "She said I'd got to." (She, in Toothy's vocabulary, always meant his mother.) "She had to go out, and the woman that comes to look after it's away. She said I'd either got to stay in the garden with it or take it out with me." The silence of the Three Musketeers told him plainly that he had made the wrong choice, but he went on plaintively, almost tearfully: "I couldn't help it. Honestly, I couldn't. I told her I felt too ill to look after it, but she said I'd got to. It's asleep now. It's all right when it's asleep."

They gazed down at all that could seen of Toothy's two-year-old sister – a tuft of dark hair between pillow and coverlet.

"Well, we can't take it down the quarry," said Roger.

And then they saw Jimmy and Bobby, scrambling through the hedge that separated the road from the field, and realised that the two had been following them all the time, eluding their vigilance by keeping on the other side of the hedge.

Roger looked at them sternly, but his sternness gradually faded into thoughtfulness as an idea occurred to him.

"I say!" he said. "Those two could stay here and guard it while we go down."

"Yes, that's a good idea," said Toothy, relieved, "but I think the Mouldies are out, Roger. I b'lieve I saw some of 'em in Archie's garden."

"Gosh!" said Roger. He'd forgotten the Mouldies. They certainly had a large score to wipe off, and it was natural they should choose this fine Saturday afternoon to do it. He took a battered toy pistol from his pocket. "Good thing I remembered to bring this."

"Crumbs!" said Bill in dismay. "I've not brought my map."

Bill considered his map of Uganda an indispensable part of any campaign.

Roger turned to Jimmy and addressed him in his commander-in-chief manner.

"You'd no business to come," he said, "but now you're here you can guard the pram an' keep a look out for the Mouldies."

"Yes, we'll d-do that," said Jimmy eagerly.

Any post that Roger assigned him in that particular voice seemed an important one to him.

The four disappeared down the sides of the quarry, and Jimmy and Bobby were left alone with the pram.

"Let's be sentries," suggested Jimmy.

Taking sticks from the hedge, they paced to and fro on opposite sides of the pram in martial fashion, stamping smartly as they turned at the end of their "beats". The baby continued to sleep peacefully. Suddenly Jimmy stopped short.

"I say!" he said. "I b'lieve I can see some boys over there on the edge of the wood. I bet they're Mouldies.

Let's go 'n' see. We'll leave the pram. It'll be all right. We won't be a minute."

They crept down the road by way of the ditch, and crossed the field to the wood, but no Mouldies were to be seen. They stayed to search a few possible hiding places, without success, then returned to their post . . . Their eyes widened in horror as they approached it. For the pram and its occupant had vanished, and on the spot where it had been was a piece of paper held in position by a stone. They bent down to read the words: "Thanks for hoztidge." The writing (and spelling) was that of Georgie Tallow, Archie's second-in-command.

"Corks!" gasped Bobby. "What'll we do now?"

"We've gotter get it back before Toothy finds out," said Jimmy. "Come on. Let's go to Archie's house."

Breathlessly they ran down the road to Archie's house and surveyed the garden from the cover of the hedge . . . Yes, there was the pram, under the chestnut tree at the end of the lawn. Except for the pram, the garden was empty. Summoning all their courage, they entered the gate, crossed the lawn, took the pram, and ran with it out of the garden and back along the road. They were only just in time. Toothy and the Three Musketeers were climbing up the sides.

"We needn't tell 'em," whispered Jimmy to Bobby.

But Toothy was gazing in consternation at the occupant of the pram, whose face was now plainly visible.

"Gosh!" he said faintly. "It's turned into a diff'rent one."

"It can't have," said Roger.

"P'raps it's a changeling," suggested Charles. "Same as Dr Jekyll and Mr Hyde."

"Its face is diff'rent," said Toothy wildly. "Its hair's

THEY WERE ONLY JUST IN TIME. TOOTHY AND THE THREE
MUSKETEERS WERE CLIMBING UP THE SIDE.

diff'rent. Its clothes are diff'rent. It's diff'rent altogether.
What – what's happened to it?"

Guiltily Jimmy and Bobby told them what had happened to it. Neither Toothy nor the Three Musketeers
wasted time in reproaches.

"It mus' be Archie's aunt's baby," said Bill. "I know
she's stayin' with them. Come on. Let's take it back."

The six of them set off, Toothy wheeling the pram and
staring in front of him with a fixed expression of anxiety
and gloom.

"She'll be mad if it's gone for good," he said apprehensively.

They approached the house with caution, but still no one seemed to be about. They opened the gate, and Jimmy took the pram back to where it had been, under the chestnut tree. Then after a hasty consultation they decided to search the garden for traces of the missing hostage. The discovery of the empty pram outside the garage revived Toothy's worst fears, and his teeth chattered together agitatedly.

"I'll get in a frightful row if they're torcherin' it," he said. "She thinks an awful lot of it."

A sudden sound from the garage attracted their attention, and silently, on tiptoe, they went nearer. There was a small window at the side, and through this they peered, craning their necks to see round each other's heads.

The Mouldy car was not in the garage, but Archie, Georgie and the hostage were. Archie was crawling round the garage on all fours with the hostage on his back, his face twisted into lines of anguish and exhaustion as the hostage tugged at his thick red hair.

"Gee-up!" shouted the hostage. "Gee-*up*!"

It was clear that Archie had had more than enough. With an air of hopelessness that showed it was not his first attempt, he tried to remove the hostage and rise to his feet, but the hostage uttered such a piercing scream that even the watchers outside blenched – all except Toothy, who, accustomed apparently to the phenomenon, merely murmured with a sort of modest pride, "That's nothin' to what it *can* do."

"Get down again, Archie," said Georgie anxiously. "She'll go on till someone comes if you don't."

That drew the hostage's attention to Georgie.

"Bow-wow!" she ordered.

Obediently Georgie dropped on his knees and began to bark.

"'Gain!" said the hostage, a smile of delight on her rosy face. "*'Gain!*"

And Georgie, evidently returning to a task from which he had had only a brief respite, went on crawling and barking while she guided her unwilling steed through the thickest pools of oil on the garage floor. The slightest signs of revolt were met and quelled by the ear-splitting scream.

"Well, you needn't have worried about *her* bein' torchered," whispered Roger to Toothy.

He took his pistol from his pocket and, followed by his band, went round to the door, flinging it open and covering the occupants with his weapon. "Hands up!" he said.

Archie and Georgie rose to their feet. Their faces, streaked with oil and perspiration and marked by scratches, evidently dealt by the hostage, showed relief rather than dismay.

"Will you surrender the hostage?" said Roger.

"Gosh, yes!" said Archie, and Georgie, who was too hoarse from barking to speak, nodded his head in fervent agreement.

There was a moment's silence. The hostage seemed to welcome the diversion. The circle wedged away uncomfortably. Then her chubby hand shot out towards Jimmy, and a smile of happy anticipation spread slowly over her face.

"Nice boy!" she said. "Gee-gee!"

# Chapter 16

# *The Dream*

Jimmy and Bobby were hanging over the kitchen table, watching Aggie, Bobby's family maid, making a cake. They always tried to be on hand when Aggie was making a cake. She was not an expert cake maker, but she was recklessly generous with the ingredients. "Go on," she would say. "'Ave a sultana or two. Yer ma'll never notice."

The "scrapings" of the cake bowl, too, were so lavish that they almost constituted a cake in themselves. And she allowed them to "help" – to weigh flour, mix and beat egg powder, mess about with the marge and lard, perform experiments with the grater, egg beater, even the mincing machine. "Yes, go on," she would encourage them. "'Ave a bit of fun. That's what kids are for."

Dusted with flour, spattered with reconstituted egg, they were now munching raw carrots, dipping the ends occasionally in a tin of syrup.

"Carrots and syrup taste jolly good together," said Jimmy with the air of a connoisseur.

"Let's try dates with it," suggested Bobby.

"Yes, go on," said Aggie, pushing towards them the dates that Bobby's mother had carefully doled out to her for the cake. "Yer ma'll never notice. Leave me one or two, that's all."

"Well, they're wasted in cakes," said Jimmy.

"Jus' what *I* think," said Aggie, stirring the cake mixture in a happy-go-lucky fashion. "'Ave a bit of sugar with it, too. Go on. Yer ma'll never notice."

The swift movement with which she pushed the carton of sugar towards them knocked a knife from the table to the floor. She stood gazing down at it.

"I can't pick it up meself," she said.

Jimmy jumped down to pick it up for her.

"Is *that* bad luck, too?" he said.

"Coo, yes!" said Aggie. "I once 'eard of a man what . . ."

For Aggie was superstitious. She had nerve-shattering stories of people who had walked under ladders, sat down thirteen at table, opened umbrellas indoors, used the third match. A magpie . . . a bird in the house . . . an owl hooting . . . a shoe on a table . . . all portended disaster, and disaster invariably followed.

"What would happen to you if you did pick it up?" said Jimmy.

"I don't 'ardly like to think," said Aggie with a shudder. "Why, even to dream of knives is bad. It means someone is plottin' against you."

Portents and omens were Aggie's chief interest in life. The drawer of the kitchen dresser in which she was supposed to keep her dusters and cleaning materials was a confused welter of dream books, fortune-telling books, palmistry books . . .

"Why does it?" said Bobby.

"It's Fate," said Aggie solemnly.

She threw the cake mixture into a tin in a hit-or-miss fashion, put the tin into the oven and passed the mixing bowl (in which she had left a large proportion of the mixture) to Jimmy and Bobby.

"You can scrape that out," she said.

"Gosh! Thanks," said the two, and set to work, burying their noses in the bowl.

Aggie sat down by the table with her dream book, turning the pages idly.

"To dream of vinegar means business worries . . . Funny thing I've never dreamed of vinegar . . . Footmen in livery means great wealth . . . Never dreamed o' them, neither . . . Jam's a good sign . . . Never dreamed o' jam, neither . . . Eels means success in a lawsuit . . . Funny thing I've never dreamed of eels, but I never 'ave . . . 'Am means a legacy. I once dreamed of somethin' that might 'ave been an 'am, but I never 'ad no legacy. Onions means 'ealth an' prosperity. Never dreamed of them, neither . . . Funny the number of things I 'aven't dreamed of . . . It's a bit dis'eartenin' when you've got a book what puts it all so plain . . . *Coo!*"

Jimmy and Bobby raised their faces from the mixing bowl and looked at her questioningly. They had reached the final stages of bowl-licking and each had blobs of cake mixture on chin, nose and forehead.

"What's the matter?"

"Listen . . . 'To dream of an 'edge'og means a proposal of marriage.' Now I b'lieve I *did* dream of an 'edge'og las' night. Leastways, I woke with a sort of pricklin' feelin' in me fingers, an' if that's not the same as dreamin' of an 'edge'og I don't know what is."

They looked at her earnestly. She was a small, thin, homely woman, with a pale freckled face and carroty hair, her homeliness redeemed by a pair of hazel eyes so bright that they made the little kitchen a cheerful place even on the dullest day.

"Do you want a proposal of marriage?" said Bobby.

"That'd be telling," said Aggie.

"Are you in love?" said Jimmy.

"I don't say 'yes', an' I don't say 'no'," said Aggie.

"Is it the milkman?" said Jimmy, licking the last spot of cake mixture from his wooden spoon. "You go out with him sometimes, don't you?"

"I bet it's the window cleaner," said Bobby, giving a final polish to the inside of the mixing bowl with his tongue. "You went to the fair with him."

"Least said, soonest mended," said Aggie. "Now I've got to clean up this mess an' you'd better run off an' leave it to me." She plunged a spoon recklessly into the syrup tin and handed it to them. "Lick that between you, then off you go."

Shining with syrup, plastered with cake mixture, the two set off down the road.

"I say!" said Jimmy thoughtfully. "I wish we could make that dream of Aggie's come true. It's r-rotten for her, them never comin' true."

"Well, we couldn't get her a proposal of marriage," said Bobby.

"I don't see why not," said Jimmy. "We could write one."

"We don't know how."

Jimmy frowned thoughtfully, then his brow cleared.

"There's an old letter book in our bookshelves at home," he said, "an' it's got love letters in, 'cause I looked at it once. It's a hundred years old, but I don't s'pose p-proposals change much."

"But who'll we write it from?"

"The m-milkman," said Jimmy.

"I think it's the window cleaner," said Bobby.

"It's more likely to be the milkman," said Jimmy. "The

milkman's got a horse an' the window cleaner's only got a ladder. You can have much more fun with a horse than with a ladder. Anyway, we'll write one from the milkman first an', if she doesn't seem to like it, we'll write one from the window cleaner."

They went to Jimmy's house and, sitting on the floor by the bookshelves, took down the book and studied it.

"This'll do," said Jimmy at last. " 'From a young man lately begun business to a young lady.' He's not been a m-milkman long."

They went to the writing desk, and, slowly and laboriously, copied the letter.

*Dear Madam,*

*I have long struggled with the most honourable and respectful passion that ever animated the heart of man, and I assure you that my happiness depends on the reception this letter meets with. I own a linen draper's shop in Fleet Street, and, though I have been hardly two years in trade, have a tolerable custom. If happily your inclinations are not engaged, I shall be proud of the honour of waiting on you and paying my addresses.*

*Your most humble servant.*

"What's the milkman's name?" said Jimmy.

"Tom Finder," said Bobby.

"Tom Finder," wrote Jimmy, at the end of the letter.

"But he isn't a linen draper," objected Bobby.

"Well, if we start alterin' it an' cuttin' bits out, it'll end by not being a proposal of marriage at all," said Jimmy. "It's all right. She knows he's a milkman really."

They took it to Bobby's house, but Aggie was not in the kitchen.

"I said she could go out as it was such a nice afternoon," said Bobby's mother. "She'd finished making the cake." She sighed. "It's so small you can hardly see it. I suppose you two boys were there?"

"Well, yes," admitted Jimmy.

They repaired to the garden to consider what to do about the letter.

"Let's leave it on the table," said Bobby.

"No," said Jimmy. "It might g-get thrown away. Let's wait till she comes in."

"We may have to wait ages," said Bobby, "an' if we take it with us, we'll be sure to lose it or get it messed up."

"Let's leave it in a safe place," said Jimmy.

"What safe place?"

"I know," said Jimmy excitedly. "Our charwoman says that when she's going out at night she leaves all her money in the d-dustbin, 'cause she says things are always safe in dustbins, 'cause no one would think of looking in them. L-let's leave it in the dustbin."

"All right," said Bobby, pleased by the originality of the idea.

They found a newspaper to protect the letter from the tea and cabbage leaves, and, placing it on the top of the bin, set off for an hour's "tracking" in the woods. Then they returned to Bobby's

THEY FOUND A NEWSPAPER TO PROTECT THE LETTER AND PLACED IT ON TOP.

house, stopping short in sudden dismay when it came into sight, for there in the middle of the road stood the dustcart.

"Gosh!" said Bobby. "I'd forgotten that today was the day they emptied it."

They hurried round to the dustbin. It was empty. They entered the kitchen. The kitchen was not empty. Nor were the dustman's arms. He stood clasping Aggie in his dustman's coat. Neither of them saw the two boys.

"You just 'ung round an' round an' never spoke," Aggie was murmuring. "I did all I could, short o' speakin' myself."

"I didn't dare speak," said the dustman, fondling Aggie's hair. "I thought I weren't good enough for you, Aggie. But when I found that letter from Tom Finder, tellin' you 'e'd got a linen draper's shop in Fleet Street, I 'ad to come in an' tell you 'e was a-deceivin' of you. Known 'im from a boy, I 'ave, an' 'e's never bin near Fleet Street."

"It doesn't matter," said Aggie. "It's brought us together at last."

"An' nothin'll never part us no more," said the dustman solemnly.

Jimmy looked at Bobby, and the two silently withdrew. Aggie's voice followed them on a note of dreamy happiness.

"An' to think it's all along of me dreamin' of that 'edge 'og."

## Chapter 17

# *The Hidden Treasure*

The Three Musketeers set off down the road, wearing the determined expressions that they always wore when they were out in quest of adventure. They were going to seek for hidden treasure. It was Charles's idea.

"All those smugglers an' highwaymen mus' have hid their treasure all over the place," he said, "an' prob'ly they got hung or exported – same as they used to be in those days – before they'd had time to dig it up or tell their mothers where it was. I bet the whole place is full of treasure hid by smugglers and highwaymen in ole times if only we knew where to look for it."

Put thus, the idea had seemed logical and convincing, and the Three Musketeers had set to work at once. On Charles's advice they went heavily armed with pistol, bow and arrows and a catapult that Bill had made out of a twig and a piece of elastic.

"Someone else might have got the idea," said Charles. "We might find another gang at work an' they'd probably be desp'rate."

"Why?" said Bill.

"Well, gangs are," said Charles a little irritably. "Come on. I bet the old quarry's the best place to look. There's lots of hiding-places in the old quarry."

So they had spent yesterday in a vain search of the old

quarry and today they were going to search the woods. That, too, had been Charles's idea.

"I bet if I'd been a highwayman I'd have hid my treasure in the woods," he said.

"Why?" said Bill.

"Well, stands to reason," said Charles. "People couldn't see you doin' it with all those trees about. An' I bet no one's every bothered to look under all those leaves and bushes. It's probably *full* of hidden treasure."

It was just as they were approaching the stile leading to the woods that they turned and saw Jimmy and Bobby following them.

"Go away," said Roger, sternly. "We don't want kids. I get sick of telling you we don't want kids."

"I'm nearly eight," pleaded Jimmy.

Roger put his hands on his hips and planted his legs firmly apart in an attitude of authority and resolution.

"You're seven and three-quarters," he said. "Seven and three-quarters is a kid, an' we don't – want – kids."

Jimmy made a faint movement as if to turn back, but Roger was too familiar with that movement to be deceived by it.

"An' it's no good pretendin' to go away an' then tryin' to come back when we aren't lookin'," he said. "If you go on following us, I – I won't let you share Sandy's lead any more."

Jimmy knew when he was beaten. Roger had saved up his money and bought a lead for Sandy, decreeing that Sandy – whose trusting disposition made him greet every form of transport as a long-lost friend – must not be taken on the main road without it.

"All right," he muttered, falling back dispiritedly.

"Well, don't forget," said Roger.

The two watched the Musketeers climb the stile and vanish into the wood, and then slowly and reluctantly turned homeward. Suddenly Jimmy brightened.

"I say!" he said. "Let's go treasure huntin' on our own."

"There's nowhere left to hunt," said Bobby. "They've done the quarry an' they're doin' the woods."

"I bet they didn't do the quarry prop'ly," said Jimmy. "I bet they didn't look under every single stone. I bet you anythin' there *is* hidden treasure there, an' I b-bet we find it."

Jimmy's optimism, as usual, communicated itself to his friend.

"All right," said Bobby. "When shall we start?"

"Now," said Jimmy. "At least – we'd better go armed, same as them, so we'll go home first an' get weapons an' then go to the quarry."

They parted and met at the crossroads about ten minutes later, with their weapons. Jimmy had brought a tin opener, and Bobby an old cricket stump.

"It's jolly heavy," he said. "It could stun anybody easy an' leave them conscienceless."

"Yes," agreed Jimmy, "an' this point's as sharp as a dagger any day. Well, if it can pierce tin, stands to reason it can p-pierce a person. Come on. Let's start."

They set off down the road, piercing and stunning imaginary foes to an accompaniment of threatening growls and savage gesticulations. Suddenly Bobby turned round . . . and his desperado air dropped from him.

"Gosh!" he said in dismay. "Araminta Palmer's following us."

Jimmy, too, turned round.

"What d'you want?" he said sternly.

"I wad to cub with you," said Araminta.

Araminta had had her adenoids removed three months ago, but, having talked through her nose for several years, she resolutely and despite all her parents' entreaties refused to abandon the process.

"We don't want kids," said Jimmy.

"I'b dot a kid. I'b dearly six."

Jimmy put his hands on his hips and planted his legs firmly apart in faithful imitation of Roger's attitude.

"You're five an' three-quarters," he said, "Five an' three-quarters is a kid an' we don't want kids . . . If you come with us, I won't let you join in . . . well," he ended lamely, "I won't let you join in anything of mine."

"I dode wad to joid id adythig of yours," said Araminta.

JIMMY PUT HIS HANDS ON HIS HIPS AND
PLANTED HIS LEGS FIRMLY APART.

Jimmy was silent, a little nonplussed by the impasse the conversation had reached.

"You card stop be cubbing with you if I wad to," said Araminta, pursuing her advantage.

Again Jimmy was silent, realising the truth of this.

"Well, we won't take any notice of you," he said at last.

"I dode care," said Araminta.

She joined them and walked along the road with them. They saw that her small mouth moved rhythmically as she walked. Jimmy wanted to ignore her, but his curiosity got the better of his dignity.

"What are you chewing?" he said.

"Gub," replied Araminta. "Ad Abericad gave it to be. I've had it for bunths and bunths. Have a chew?"

Jimmy hesitated. Again the temptation was too strong for him.

"Thanks," he said distantly.

He had never chewed gum and had always wanted to try. Araminta took the nauseous-looking lump out of her mouth and handed it to him. He chewed hard and in silence.

"Where are you goig?" said Araminta.

"Shan't tell you," said Jimmy. "It's somewhere where you can't come, anyway."

"Why card I cub?" said Araminta.

" 'Cause you can't," said Jimmy.

"What are you goig to play at?" said Araminta.

"We're not going to play at anything," said Jimmy. "It's deadly earnest, what we're goin' to do, an', if you don't go away an' leave us alone, we'll wait to do it till this afternoon, when you're at the dancing class an' can't bother us."

"I dode care," said Araminta.

"Let's not speak to her, Jimmy," said Bobby.

"Cad I have by gub back?" said Araminta.

A blank look came over Jimmy's face.

"Gosh! I m-mus' have s-swallowed it," he said.

Araminta's face darkened with anger.

"You've god ad swallowed by gub that I've had for bunths and bunths!" Then her face cleared, and a smile spread slowly over it. "You'll have to led be cub with you dow you've swallowed by gub. You'll *have* to."

"Yes, I s'pose we will," said Jimmy ruefully.

They spent the rest of the morning in the quarry. It would have been an enjoyable morning without Araminta. Araminta needed constant attention. She got into difficulties and had to be rescued. She got into tempers and had to be calmed. She tired of looking for hidden treasure and wanted to play at fairies, with herself a fairy queen and Jimmy and Bobby as her attendant gnomes. It was almost impossible to hunt for hidden treasure and cope with Araminta as well. They were relieved when it was time to go home to lunch.

"Tell you what!" said Jimmy to Bobby. "We'll come back this afternoon when she's at her dancing class, an' search that cave by the pond prop'ly. We were jus' goin' to do it when she started makin' all that fuss about bein' a fairy queen." He threw Araminta a stern glance and added: "You've been a beastly n-nuisance, Araminta."

"I dode care," said Araminta.

The two set to work again immediately after lunch, searching the cave without success till suddenly Bobby said: "Let's jus' look behind that big stone right at the end. We've not looked there yet."

"All right," agreed Jimmy.

He scrambled up the boulder and looked behind it.

"Gosh!" he said, mouth and eyes opening wide. "There's a s-sack here an' there's somethin' in it. I b'lieve it's hidden treasure. G-give me a hand with it. Quick!"

Together they pulled the sack from behind the boulder, and carried it outside the cave.

"C-come on," said Jimmy excitedly. "L-let's empty it out."

They held the sack by its ends, and out fell a stream of silver objects – spoons, salt cellars, candlesticks, cream jug, a teapot, a hot-water jug. Bobby and Jimmy gasped with amazement.

"It is hidden treasure!" said Jimmy. "What shall we d-do with it?"

"Let's divide it," said Bobby. "I'll give my half to my mother. It'll do for her birthday present. She's ninety-two on Saturday."

"She isn't. She's twenty-nine," said Jimmy. "I heard my mother sayin' so."

"Oh, yes," said Bobby vaguely. "I always forget which way round it is."

"I'll give my half to my mother, too," said Jimmy. "L-let's sort of jus' p-put them out for them to find for a s-sort of surprise, shall we?"

Jimmy's mother was just taking some scones out of the oven when a loud knocking resounded through the house. She went to the front door and opened it. Mrs Palmer stood there looking pale and distraught.

"Do come in," said Mrs Manning. "Is anything the matter?"

"I can't come in," panted Mrs Palmer. "I'm on my way to collect Araminta from the dancing class, and I'm late already, but – oh, my dear, I must tell you. I *must* tell somebody. I was out to lunch, and when I came back I found that burglars had been and stolen all my silver. I rang up the police, of course, but I've just passed Mrs Peaslake's house, and I happened to look through her window, and . . . Oh, I simply don't know how to tell you," her voice tailed off hysterically.

"Tell me what?" said Mrs Manning.

"You won't believe it," said Mrs Palmer. "I wouldn't have believed it myself if I hadn't seen it with my own eyes."

"Seen what?" said Mrs Manning patiently.

"Half my stolen silver on her sideboard. *Quite* half. I *know* it's my silver. It used to belong to my grandmother and I've known it since I was a child. One does hear of the most respectable people living secret lives of crime, but to think that a prominent member of the Women's Institute . . ." Again Mrs Palmer's emotion became too much for her.

"But surely," said Mrs Manning, "if she'd stolen your silver, she wouldn't have put it in full view on her side-board."

"That's the cunning of it," said Mrs Palmer. "She thought it would look so natural there that people wouldn't notice it. I once read a detective story where they did something like that. Then she'd have sold it quietly piece by piece . . . Oh dear! It's all been such a shock to me that—"

"Come in and sit down," said Mrs Manning soothingly.

Mrs Palmer followed her into the sitting room and sat down in an armchair. Then her eyes roved round the room, becoming fixed and wild as they settled on the side-table against the wall. She uttered a sound that was half-scream, half-moan.

"Good Heavens!" she said. "You're in it too."

"Whatever do you mean?" said Mrs Manning. "In what?"

"My silver sauce boat!" moaned Mrs Palmer. "My spoons!"

For the first time Mrs Manning noticed the strange collection of silver that had appeared in the room since she had last entered it.

"But I don't understand," she said faintly. "I—"

Then Jimmy burst into the room. He had arranged the silver on the table and had gone away in order that his mother might discover it by herself, making the "surprise" more perfect. He had now come to offer explanation and receive her thanks.

"Jimmy, do you know anything about this silver?" said Mrs Manning.

"Yes," said Jimmy. "It's hidden treasure. Bobby an' me found it in a cave, an' I'm givin' it to you for a p-present."

"What a wicked untruth!" said Mrs Palmer. "It was a legacy to me from my grandmother."

And then Araminta came in.

She looked reproachfully at her mother. "You dever cabe to fetch be," she said. "So I had to fetch byself. Adyway, I wanted to fetch byself, 'cause I wanted to call and see Jibby." She smiled radiantly at Jimmy. "Did you fide the hidden treasure, Jibby?"

Jimmy stared at her blankly.

"Oh, what does this all mean?" wailed Mrs Palmer.

Araminta proceeded to explain what it meant.

"He swallowed by gub, so they had to let be cub with theb, so I wanted theb to fide sub hidden treasure 'cause they'd let be cub with theb, an' you were out to lunch an' couldn't stop be, so I put sub id a sack ad hid it id a cave for theb to fide. I didn't think you wanted it, 'cause you dever use it."

"I wish you'd try and speak nicely, darling," wailed Mrs Palmer, forgetting everything but her daughter's deplorable enunciation. "You know you've had them out."

"I dow I have," said Araminta, "but I didn't want to have theb out. I liked havig theb id."

"About this silver . . ." said Mrs Manning.

The situation was explained to the satisfaction of everyone but Jimmy. The two mothers went over the road to Mrs Peaslake's to explain the situation to her. Jimmy stood glaring at Araminta across the sitting room.

"You're a m-mean, m-meddlesome, interfering girl," he said furiously. "I'm g-glad I swallowed your chewing gum, and I d-d-despise you."

"I dode care," said Araminta.

## Chapter 18

# The Black Market

"Time these Black Market crooks were brought to justice," said Jimmy's father, folding up his newspaper and rising from the breakfast-table. "Dunno what Scotland Yard's about . . ."

Jimmy followed him into the hall and watched him put on his hat and overcoat.

"Where is the Black Market?" he asked.

"No one quite knows," said Mr Manning. "If they did, it would be simpler, of course."

With that he snatched up his attaché case and ran for his bus.

Jimmy was very thoughtful during school that morning. After school he waited for Bobby, as usual, and the two of them discussed the affair on their way home.

"It's a place where crim'nals buy things," said Jimmy, "an' no one knows where it is . . . I say!" A note of excitement crept into his voice. "S'pose we found it!"

"It couldn't be anywhere round here," said Bobby. "Big crim'nals live in a place in London called the Underground. I bet that's where they have the Black Market."

"They m-might have it here," said Jimmy, "jus' 'cause they'd know that no one would think of it bein' here. Anyway, I'm goin' to keep a l-look out."

"All right," said Bobby, infected by Jimmy's

enthusiasm, "I will too."

Jimmy went home to find one of his aunts having lunch with his mother. He listened to their conversation idly at first, then with increasing interest.

"I called in to see Mrs Tallow yesterday evening," his aunt was saying, "and they were just having dinner. My dear, such a spread! Where does she get the stuff? She's in the Black Market, of course."

Jimmy finished his lunch quickly and ran across the road to Bobby.

"I say," he said excitedly, when the owl call that was their signal had summoned Bobby to the gate. "Mrs T-Tallow goes to it, so it mus' be somewhere near here. The Black Market, I mean."

"Gosh!" said Bobby.

"So we can f-find it now," said Jimmy. "We can jus' f-follow her an' see where she goes."

"When?" said Bobby.

"N-now. It's a half-holiday, so we've g-got all afternoon. Come on. Let's go to her house now."

They made their way to Mrs Tallow's house and stood uncertainly at the gate, looking at the house.

"I can see her through the window," said Bobby. "She's not gone yet. What'll we do?"

"Let's hide in the garden an' wait till she goes," said Jimmy. "Come on. We'll crawl through the hedge an' get behind those bushes."

They had been in position for about ten minutes when the front door opened and Mrs Tallow, golden-haired and immaculate as her son, emerged. She carried a large shopping basket on her arm.

"Her basket's empty," whispered Jimmy. "She mus' be goin' to it now."

"I hope it won't lead us into danger," said Bobby a little apprehensively. "She'll prob'ly get desp'rate when she's cornered. Crim'nals do."

"We can't help that," said Jimmy. "She's a Black Market c-crook, an' we've got to bring her to justice, same as Daddy said. Come on. We've got to f-follow her now."

They followed her down the lane, keeping well in the shelter of the hedge, and watched her enter the gate of Miss Pettigrew's house. She knocked at the door, was admitted by a maid and vanished from their sight.

"Come on," said Jimmy. "Let's l-look in at the window an' see what she's doin'."

They crept round the side of the house and looked in at the window . . . and there a sight met their eyes that turned them pale with horror.

In Miss Pettigrew's drawing room were ranged three stalls covered with goods – one with cakes, vegetables, and several tins and packages of food, another with fancy goods, the third with a miscellaneous assortment of odd-ments. And moving about among these stalls were various local personages all well know to Jimmy.

"Gosh!" he gasped. "It's the Black Market, an' – an' l-look at 'em all. They're all in it – even the Vicar. Gosh! I thought clergymen had to be good men. I thought they were *ob-bliged* to be good men by lor."

Miss Pettigrew, resplendent in a new purple dress, was welcoming Mrs Tallow, and leading her to the stalls.

"L-look!" went on Jimmy. "Miss Pettigrew's the head of it. Gosh! Miss Pettigrew! You wouldn't think she was a c-crook, would you? Why, she d-does the church flowers the m-month after my mother. You'd think that meant she was good, wouldn't you?"

"Let's go back to the road," said Bobby, twisting his watch round his wrist nervously. "We don't want them to catch us watchin' them."

"All right," agreed Jimmy, and the two crept down through the garden to the gate.

"Well, what are we goin' to do about it?" said Bobby.

"We've got to think hard," said Jimmy solemnly. "It's somethin' jolly important, this is – f-findin' the Black Market. We'll prob'ly be f-famous in hist'ry for it."

"I think we ought to tell the policeman," said Bobby.

"No, that wouldn't be any g-good," said Jimmy. "He's got a c-cold in his neck. He told my father so yesterday. They'd overpower him in no time. The Vicar's jolly strong. He does boxing."

"What about writin' to Scotland Yard?"

"No, that's no g-good, either," said Jimmy. "We wouldn't get an answer till the d-day after tomorrow, an' it might be too late. I think we ought to fetch the army for a b-big thing like this."

"But we don't know where it is," objected Bobby.

"Our gardener's in the Salvation Army," said Jimmy a little doubtfully.

"Yes, but he only plays the drum," said Bobby, "an' that wouldn't be any use against the Black Market."

"A J.P.!" said Jimmy with a burst of inspiration. "That's what we ought to get. A J.P."

"What's a J.P.?" said Bobby.

"I dunno exactly," admitted Jimmy, "but I think they're sort of nex' to judges. They've got somethin' to do with justice an' puttin' down crim'nals, anyway, 'cause I've heard my father talkin' about them."

"Well, how do we find one?" said Bobby.

"Dunno," said Jimmy.

And then the most amazing thing happened. Round the bend of the road came a car, and on the back of the car was a large trunk, bearing the initials J.P.

"Gosh!" said Jimmy. "There's one! An' – Gosh! He's stoppin' at the garage. Quick. Let's get him."

James Pultney, drawing up at the garage to exchange one of his "E" coupons for the wholly inadequate supply of petrol allotted to him by a stony-hearted government, and getting out of the car to ensure that every drop of it went into his tank, was amazed to find himself suddenly seized by two excited small boys.

"Come on, quick!" they said. "Down here . . . This way . . . You've got to be quick or they'll have gone."

Before he could find breath to protest, he was dragged and pushed down the road . . . in at the gate of a small house . . . into a brightly lit room with three stalls and a lot of people. They looked at him with interest and faint

"COME ON, QUICK! DOWN HERE . . . THIS WAY . . ."

surprise. He was a large florid man, whose face was vaguely suggestive of a Roman Emperor.

A parrot in a cage by the window said "miaow", and a tall woman in a purple dress bore down on him.

"I don't think I have the pleasure of your acquaintance," she said, "but I am delighted to welcome you."

"James Pultney," he said.

"The actor?" they said excitedly.

"An actor," said James Pultney modestly.

"I recognised you at once," said Mrs Tallow proudly.

But the actor's eyes had fallen on the White Elephant stall and were gleaming exultantly.

"I've been combing junk shops for that for months," he said. "I want it for my next part."

Miss Pettigrew took up the Victorian smoking cap, gaily beaded in red and purple, to which he was pointing.

"It belonged to my grandfather," she said. "I turned it out with some other old rubbish. It's in the sixpenny box."

"I want these too," said James Pultney, grabbing a pair of carpet slippers.

"Certainly," said Miss Pettigrew graciously. "They're fourpence halfpenny."

James Pultney looked around him.

"What is all this, by the way?" he said.

"It's a small sale of work to help pay for the repairs to our church clock," said Miss Pettigrew. "We are hoping to reach our target of five pounds."

"I'll give you that for the cap and slippers," said James Pultney. He turned to Jimmy. "And here's half a crown for bringing me."

"Th-thank you," said Jimmy, blinking bewilderedly as he pocketed the half-crown.

James Pultney tried on the cap. It fitted perfectly. He beamed with delight. Then his delight faded to perplexity.

"But how did the kids know I wanted the things?" he said.

He turned to the spot where Jimmy had been standing. But Jimmy was there no longer. He was walking down the lane with Bobby.

"Half a crown!" said Bobby. "It isn't bad."

"N-no," said Jimmy a little sadly, "but I'd rather have f-found the Black Market."

# Chapter 19

## Sandy Saves the Situation

"Time you started for school, Jimmy," called Mrs Manning. "It's nearly two o'clock."

Jimmy had wandered down to the bottom of the garden with Sandy after lunch and was watching him at his never-ending task of trying to come to an understanding with Henry. Sandy was a simple friendly soul who liked to know where he was with people, and he still didn't know where he was with Henry, though he spent a good part of each day trying to find out. He was standing now looking down at him, head on one side, tail waving in tentative friendliness, a puzzled expression on his brown foolish face.

Slowly Jimmy went back to the house. Sandy, temporarily abandoning the problem of Henry, followed him, pausing to examine each stick, stone and plant as he passed it, in a business-like, rather fussy manner, as if intent on some routine job of "checking-up". For Sandy always liked to make sure that things were in their right places. In the house he would even try to change the cushions if he thought they had been put in the wrong chairs. He stopped for some moments, obviously a little worried by a plant that hadn't been there yesterday.

"It's all right, Sandy," Jimmy reassured him. "Daddy

put it in last night. You needn't start tearing it to pieces. It's not a bedroom slipper."

In the hall, he caught up his school satchel, put on his cap, called "Goodbye, Mother," said "*No*" very firmly to Sandy, who as usual wanted to come to school with him, shut the front door and went down to the gate, where Bobby Peaslake was waiting for him.

"Hello," said Jimmy.

"Hello," said Bobby. "We'd better be quick or," glancing at his wrist-watch, "we'll be late."

"All right," said Jimmy.

The two set off down the road, taking up a discussion on the possibility of discovering an unknown continent at the point where they had left it the day before.

"I bet there mus' be some left," said Jimmy earnestly. "That man, Monte Cristo, can't have found them all."

"You've got it wrong," said Bobby. "Monte Cristo's a man in his'try. You're thinkin' of the man in g'ography that was called Marco Polo 'cause of him discoverin' the North Pole."

"Well, whoever it was," said Jimmy vaguely, "I'm goin' to find one when I grow up. It's a lot more excitin' than goin' to an office an' havin' meetings on planks same as my father does."

"Planks?" said Bobby with interest. "Why, is he a pirate?"

"No, I mean boards," said Jimmy, "an' I think—" He turned round.

Sandy was trotting along behind them, looking guilty but determined.

"Corks!" said Jimmy. "The side door must have been open."

"You'd better send him home," said Bobby.

"Yes, I will," agreed Jimmy, and, adopting a tone of authority called, "Home, Sandy!"

Sandy stopped in his tracks and stood there, head on one side, tail waving apologetically.

"I 'spect he'll go back now," said Jimmy. "Let's take no notice of him."

They went on for a few yards, then turned round again. Sandy was standing in the same attitude – self-conscious, apologetic, pleading – but he had advanced several yards since they last looked back, and it was clear that he had only just stopped as they turned round.

"Go *home*, Sandy," ordered Jimmy.

Sandy wagged his tail in a conciliatory manner, as if ready to comply with any suggestion that Jimmy made.

"Go home at *once*," said Bobby, and Sandy made the faint backward movement of a dog reluctantly about to go home.

"I 'spect he'll go now," said Jimmy confidently.

They walked on for some minutes, then Bobby half-turned round and looked back out of the corner of his eye.

"He's still comin' along," he said.

Jimmy turned round again. Again Sandy stopped short in his track, trying to look as if he hadn't moved since last they saw him.

"Oh, gosh!" groaned Jimmy. "An' we've not got time to take him back. Let's run fast an' . . . an' sort of dodge him round the next corner. P'raps he'll think he's lost us an' go home."

But it wasn't any use. Sandy took this manoeuvre as an invitation to join in a game, and leapt along with them in wild delight. Their short difference of opinion was, he considered, over. The hatchet was buried and they were friends and playmates once more. When the school came into sight, Jimmy and Bobby slackened their pace.

"Well, now what are we goin' to do?" said Bobby.

Jimmy looked round. They were passing Jasmine Cottage, where Miss Tressider, their form mistress, lived.

"*Tell* you what!" said Jimmy. "We'll jus' put him in that little shed outside Miss Tressider's cottage. We're always out of school first, an' we'll fetch him as soon as we're out. She won't know he's been there, an' he can't do any harm in a shed."

Bobby considered the suggestion with a judicial frown.

"Yes, that's a jolly good idea," he said. He consulted his watch again. "An' we'd better be quick 'cause there's not much time."

It proved an easy matter to lure Sandy into the shed and shut the door on him. They were just in time for school, and the afternoon passed without incident. But unfortunately Jimmy, in his efforts to avoid any trouble that might lead to his being kept in, displayed just too much interest in the lesson. It was not difficult, of course, to take an interest in Miss Tressider's lessons, for she was young, pretty and enthusiastic, but on this occasion Jimmy overdid it. The interest he displayed in fossils was so great that Miss Tressider felt it deserved some reward.

"If you'll stay behind after school, Jimmy," she said, "I'll show you some little fossilised shells that I found in a piece of stone I got for my rockery. They're at my cottage – only a few yards away, you know."

Jimmy's heart sank.

"Th-thanks," he said.

Bobby, after a moment's hesitation, decided to stand by his friend in his hour of need.

"Can I come too, please, Miss Tressider? I'm int'rested as well."

"Certainly," said Miss Tressider, thinking that Bobby Peaslake must be more intelligent than he looked.

School over, they waited for her to put her things on and, with blank set faces, accompanied her down the road to the cottage, replying so inconsequently to her remarks on coal-bearing rocks that she thought she couldn't have made the subject very clear, after all.

"Come in," she said. "I haven't locked the door. I'm afraid I never bother to lock up."

She led them into the shed, and there they received their first shock. It wasn't a shed at all. It was a kitchen built on to the cottage, and from it an open door led into the little sitting room. Sandy was nowhere to be seen, but on the hearthrug lay the remains of Miss Tressider's bed-room slippers, chewed into small fragments.

"Good Heavens!" exclaimed Miss Tressider. "Who on *earth* has done this?"

Jimmy's face was drained of expression.

"S-S-Sandy," he said.

Bobby, not knowing what else to do, consulted his wrist-watch and coughed apologetically.

"Who's Sandy?" said Miss Tressider.

"A d-dog," explained Jimmy. "We p-put him in, but we d-didn't mean him to ch-chew up your slippers. It's only s-slippers he does it to. It's not his f-fault. He c-can't help it. I'm sorry."

Miss Tressider looked at him in bewilderment.

"You see, we thought it was a shed," said Bobby, trying to make the situation clearer. "An' if it hadn't been for all those trees in rocks an' things we'd have got him out before you came."

"I don't know what you're talking about," said Miss Tressider, helplessly.

Then she looked round the room and gave a little scream.

"Goodness!" she screamed. "Someone *has* been here! That cigarette box has been moved from the chimney piece to the table. One minute . . ."

She went hastily from the room. Jimmy and Bobby looked at each other in silent dismay.

"S-Sandy couldn't move a c-cigarette box," said Jimmy.

"I dunno," said Bobby. "It's all a bit queer. P'raps," nervously, "if we went home now quick she'd forget we'd been here."

"No, she wouldn't," said Jimmy, "an' anyway—"

At that moment Miss Tressider returned to the room. She was very pale.

"A burglar *has* been," she said. "He's taken my silver teapot and all my bits of jewellery. I don't mind about that. What I do mind is that he's taken the jewellery that belonged to my mother. It was in a little box in the shape of a tortoise with a real tortoise shell for a lid. It was on my dressing table and it's gone with everything else."

Suddenly Jimmy looked out of the window. There at the bottom of the garden was Sandy, standing in a familiar attitude – head on one side, ears cocked, tail waving in tentative friendliness, looking down at something on the grass just in front of him.

"*Look!*" he said excitedly.

He plunged out of the open french window, and the others followed. On the grass in front of Sandy was a small tortoise made of silver except for the tortoiseshell back. Miss Tressider snatched it up and opened it.

THERE ON THE GRASS IN FRONT OF SANDY WAS A SMALL TORTOISE MADE OF SILVER.

"It's all here," she said. "Oh, what a relief! But what happened?"

It was clear to Jimmy what had happened. Sandy had explored the cottage in his usual inquisitive fashion and, after demolishing Miss Tressider's bedroom slippers, had gone upstairs and found a Henry – but a Henry not in its right place. Sandy knew that the right place for Henrys was at the bottom of the garden, so – jumping probably, on to the dressing stool – he had taken Henry from the dressing table in his mouth and carried him down to where he ought to be. The burglar must have come after Henry had been removed.

Jimmy explained this as best he could to Miss Tressider.

"You see, he's very meddlesome," he ended.

"Well, I'm very grateful to him," said Miss Tressider. "I don't mind about any of the other things they've taken, but it would have broken my heart to have lost my mother's jewellery. Now I'll ring up the police and then we'll have a cup of tea, and Sandy shall have a chocolate biscuit all to himself." She bent down to pat Sandy's head. "You *are* a clever dog, Sandy."

Sandy looked up at her, head on one side, smiling his foolish smile and waving his plume-like tail in agreement . . .

# Chapter 20

# A Problem Solved

"Let's do a play," said Roger. "It's a long time since we did a play."

The Three Musketeers were holding a meeting in the kitchen of the blitzed house. They had reached that recurrent phase in their affairs when their ordinary pursuits began to pall and they wanted to try something fresh.

"I'll write it," said Charles.

"You wrote the last one," said Bill, "an' it wasn't much good."

"The *play* was all right," said Charles. "You messed it up startin' fightin'."

"Well, it was about a war, wasn't it?" said Bill.

"Yes, but I didn't mean you to go on fightin' all through it, same as you did. Sally was s'posed to be a beautiful female spy, an' you never gave her a chance to come on an' do her part."

"Well, she couldn't read what you'd wrote for her to say, so it didn't matter, an', anyway, it was a jolly good fight."

"Now, about this new play—" said Roger, bringing them back to the matter in hand.

"The two best sorts of play," said Charles with a rather self-conscious air of knowledge, "are hist'ry an' detective."

"I bet a hist'ry play's difficult to write," said Bill.

"Not for me," said Charles modestly. "I bet I could do it, all right. You jus' bring in a lot of people out of hist'ry, like Julius Caesar an' Queen Elizabeth an' William the Conqueror an' Thomas à Becket an' the Little Princes in the Tower, an' – an' – an' make 'em say 'Gadzooks'. 'S quite easy."

"Why did they have to say 'Gadzooks'?" asked Bill.

"It's a swear word. They said it instead of 'damn'."

"Why did they? Why didn't they say 'damn'?"

"'Cause 'damn' wasn't invented then. They invented 'damn' later when hist'ry went out an' modern times came in, an' then they made people stop sayin' 'Gadzooks' an' start sayin' 'Damn'."

"You oughtn't to keep sayin' it like that," said Roger virtuously.

"I didn't say it loud," Charles excused himself. "It only counts as swearin' if you say it loud. Like this. *Damn!*"

"You'll get in a row if anyone hears you," Roger warned him. "They won't know you're talkin' hist'ry. Now about this other sort of play. Detective."

"That's easy too," said Charles. "You jus' have someone murderin' someone an' someone else findin' out who it was. I could write that sort quite easy."

"They'd both be jolly excitin'," said Roger. "It's goin' to be jolly difficult to choose which to have . . . *Tell* you what!"

"Yes?" said the other two eagerly.

"Why not have 'em mixed? Queen Elizabeth murderin' Napoleon or somebody an' Thomas à Becket findin' out she did it or somethin' like that."

"That's a jolly good idea," said Charles. "I don't think anyone's thought of it before."

"It'd have to be Thomas à Becket bein' murdered," said Bill, " 'cause he axshully *was* murdered. He was murdered 'cause he wouldn't let Henry the Eighth have seven wives. It comes in a play in Shakespeare. I've jus' forgot who murdered him."

"Macbeth?" suggested Roger tentatively.

"Prob'ly," said Bill. "I jus' don't remember."

"I could bring Macbeth into it easy," said Charles, "an' this Thomas à Becket could say, 'Gadzooks' when he was murdered."

"No, he wouldn't," said Bill. "He was a sort of clergy-man. He wouldn't swear. He'd just say 'Oh dear!' or somethin' like that."

"Well, how'll we start it?" said Charles.

"Toothy once told me a detective tale," said Roger, "that began with someone jus' sittin' in a chair under a tree an' a note fell down on him from the tree with 'Beware. I am on your tracks' written on it, an' it was one of the gang that was after him that had climbed the tree an' dropped it."

"All right," said Charles. "We'll have Thomas à Becket sittin' in the chair an' we'd better have one of the Princes in the Tower climbin' the tree. I bet they could climb better than Queen Elizabeth. Well, what happened then?"

"I dunno," said Roger. "Toothy didn't get any further. We saw a rat in the ditch an' started tryin' to catch it."

"Well, we've got to think out what happens next, then," said Charles.

"My father knows a man who writes plays," said Bill, "an' he says that you've got to make things happen in plays same as they'd happen in real life."

"Oh," said Charles, taken aback by this new and

startling idea. "That's goin' to be difficult."

And then Roger saw Jimmy lurking in the doorway. There was an uneasy and well-founded suspicion in Roger's mind that he had been there all the time.

"What do you want?" he said sternly.

"C-can I be a P-prince in the Tower?" said Jimmy.

"No, you can't," said Roger. "Go away."

Jimmy went away – but not slowly, disconsolately, as he usually went when dismissed by Roger. He went briskly, eagerly. An Idea had come to him. He could help Roger, Charles and Bill with the play. He could find out what would happen in real life. Thomas à Becket . . . a "sort of clergyman" . . . The Vicar was a clergyman. All he wanted was the Vicar, a tree and a note. The note was easy enough. A short visit to his home sent him on his way with a piece of paper on which was written "Bewair i am on your trax," safely hidden in his pocket. He ran quickly along the road to the Vicarage and peered through the hedge. Then he gave a gasp of amazement. At the end of the lawn the Vicar was sitting under a tree in front of a tea table in company with an elderly lady. It only remained for Jimmy to climb the tree and drop the note. He scrambled through the hedge and silently hoisted himself up into the tree.

Fortunately the Vicar and his visitor were engrossed in their conversation and the lady was talking in a deep resonant voice that drowned the few sounds Jimmy made in his ascent. The lady seemed, indeed, to be doing most of the talking. Occasionally, the Vicar said "Yes, Aunt," or "No, Aunt," in a somewhat depressed tone of voice, but was evidently all that was required of him. Half way up the tree Jimmy stopped to consider the situation. In order to drop the note where the Vicar should see it, he must climb along to the end of the branch that hung over the tea table. It didn't look too safe, but – he began to climb . . . The loud rending of the branch cut sharply through the summer air and, before the Vicar and his aunt knew what was happening, a small boy landed suddenly into the middle of the tea table, precipitating it and himself and the aunt on to the grass.

Jimmy sat up. He had watercress in his hair and a cream bun on the end of his nose. The Vicar, who was a very young man, threw back his head and laughed. The Vicar's aunt rose slowly to her feet. The upturned jam dish had fitted itself on to the top of her head as neatly as if it had been made for it, and the contents were trickling slowly down her face.

"I am going straight home, Adrian," she said in her deep resonant voice. "I shall never forget or forgive this outrage."

JIMMY LANDED
SUDDENLY INTO
THE MIDDLE OF THE
TEA TABLE.

"It wasn't my fault, Aunt," said the Vicar.

"You laughed," said the aunt in a deeper and yet more resonant voice. "You *laughed*."

"I'm terribly sorry," said the Vicar. "I simply couldn't help it. Are you hurt?"

"Physically, no," said the aunt, removing the jam dish from her head and putting it on to a chair. "In my feelings, deeply and irremediably. I can only repeat that I am going straight home."

With that she walked with slow dignity towards the house – a dignity only slightly impaired by the fact that she wore a piece of bread and butter in the small of her back. The Vicar looked after her with a brightening of the whole face. She had come to him for a week and had already stayed three months. She objected to his pipe, his dog and his habit of leaving his things about. She tried to write his sermons and run his Sunday School. She had once even tried to take a Christening for him . . .

Then he looked at Jimmy.

"You've got a nasty graze on your knee," he said. "Come into the study, and I'll put some iodine on it."

Jimmy followed him into the house.

At the foot of the stairs he paused. From above came the deep resonant voice of his aunt telephoning for a taxi. "The Vicarage . . . at *once*."

"She really *is* going," he said. "I'm frightfully grateful to you, old chap."

In the study Jimmy took out his note.

"I'm sorry I fell on you," he said. "I meant jus' to d-drop this on you an' s-see what you'd do."

The Vicar read the note. He did not seem surprised by it. Though young, he had learnt not to be surprised by anything.

"I don't think I'd have done anything different from what I am doing," he said. He opened a cupboard, "Would you like one of these? I have a friend who's just come back from Jamaica."

The Three Musketeers were discussing whether Queen Elizabeth or Napoleon should be the detective when Jimmy burst in on them. He still wore odds and ends of watercress in his hair, his face was filthy and his trousers torn, but his eyes shone with triumph.

"I say!" he panted. "I've found out what Thomas à Becket d-did when the Prince in the Tower dropped the n-note on him. He g-gave him a banana."

# Chapter 21

# *The Rehearsal*

The Three Musketeers had assembled in the kitchen of the blitzed house for the rehearsal of their play. Charles strode to and fro, waving his manuscript and issuing orders to his cast, for Charles's father was the leading light of the local amateur Dramatic Society and, on these grounds, Charles had allotted to himself the parts of author, producer, stage manager as well as half a dozen characters in the play. The original idea of combining a historical with a detective play had been abandoned – chiefly because everyone wanted to be Napoleon – and Charles had concentrated all his energies on writing a detective play that, he considered, put all other plays ever written into the shade.

"It's a jolly sight better than anythin' that old Shakespeare wrote," he said modestly. "Well, I've seen two of his plays, so I ought to know. He can't say things straight out same as I do. He gets you all muddled up listenin' to him."

The cast was at present scuffling about the kitchen, engaged in unofficial fights and arguments.

Sandy, who was cast for the part of the bloodhound, was leaping up excitedly, trying to lick the face of the murderer, whom he was supposed to bring to justice in the last act.

"I wish you'd shut up an' listen," said Charles.

"We've only got time for one rehearsal with the play bein' tomorrow, so you've got to work hard." This appeal produced no noticeable effect, so he added: "If you don't shut up an' listen, I won't let any of you see my mouse's skeleton ever again."

This threat produced comparative quiet. Charles's mouse's skeleton held a fearful fascination for his contemporaries, and had once made as much as fourpence halfpenny as an exhibit in an "animal show". Then Charles, clearing his throat, continued:

"I'll jus' go over the play, case you've forgotten what it's about. It starts with Toothy bein' an ole miser, countin' his money an' putting it in piles. Have you got your money, Toothy?"

"Yes," said Toothy, taking out five halfpennies and inspecting them anxiously. "Gosh! I thought for a minute I'd lost one. I say! If I make piles of one, I could have five piles of 'em, couldn't I?"

"Yes," said Charles. "Five piles'd be fine. Can you carry on like an ole man?"

"What do they do?" said Toothy.

"I'm not quite sure," said Charles uncertainly.

"I met an ole man once that was over ninety," said Bill.

"Well, what did he do?" said Charles.

"He couldn't hear what anyone said to him," said Bill.

"All right," said Toothy. "I'll be that sort."

"Well, while Toothy's countin' his money," said Charles, "Roger comes in. He's called Rupert an' he murders Toothy for his money an' Toothy's got a ward called Eglantine – that's Sally – an' this Rupert's in love with her but she's in love with Vivian – that's Jimmy (we didn't want to have Jimmy in 'cause he's only a kid, but Freddy

Pelham that was goin' to do it's come out in spots) – so Rupert tries to make out that Vivian did the murder an'—" he consulted his chaotic manuscript. "I got in a bit of a muddle after that, but it all comes right in the end. There's a trial an' I'm the detective an' judge an' then Eglantine marries Vivian an' I'm the clergyman that marries them an' then Rupert takes poison an' dies in ag'ny an' everyone claps. I gave you what I could remember of what I made up wrote down yesterday an' I hope you've learnt it same as they do in axshul plays. It's time we started rehearsin'."

Jimmy stood in the background, next to Bobby (who had no part and was there on sufferance), agog with eagerness and excitement. He had only been told yesterday that there was a chance of his being in the play, and

JIMMY STOOD IN THE BACKGROUND, HIS
WHOLE BEING FILLED WITH PRIDE.

he had spent most of the night either learning his part (written in Charles's execrable handwriting on a paper bag that had only too obviously once contained sausage meat) or lying awake and thinking of the glorious moment when Sally should throw herself into his arms and murmur: "Oh, Vivian, I have loved you all the time." He had dreamed of marrying Sally ever since he could remember, and now miraculously the dream seemed to be coming true. Occasionally he glanced at his paper bag to make sure that he was word perfect. "Your bileaf in me has kept up my curridge through this great ordeel. I could not ask thy hand in marridge wile my gud name was bismestched."

"Sally's not here," said Bill.

"Well, we can't wait for her," said Charles. "Let's start now. Go on, Toothy. Start countin' your money."

Toothy took his seat upon the small packing case that did duty for a chair and, spreading his five halfpennies on the larger packing case that did duty for a table, began to count them.

"Well, come on," he said irritably. "I've counted them. They're twopence halfpenny. I can't make 'em any dif-f'rent however long I count 'em."

"All right," said Charles pacifically. "Roger's the murderer. He ought to be comin' on. Where is he?"

He looked round for Roger and saw him struggling to affix a straggly all-enveloping white beard over his ears.

"You can't wear that," said Charles with asperity. "You're suppose to be a *young* man."

"I'm jolly well goin' to wear it," said Roger in a muffled voice. "Our charwoman lent it to me. Her father used to wear it to be Father Christmas in. It's a jolly good beard."

"But, listen," said Charles. "It comes out in this play

that you're this murdered man's grandson, an' you can't be anyone's grandson in a beard that comes nearly down to your feet."

"I can't help that," said Roger, speaking almost inaudibly and removing several long grey hairs that had found their way into his mouth. "I didn't make it, did I? An' our charwoman *wanted* me to wear it. She said it'd got the moth in an' it'd do it *good* for someone to wear it. Anyway a beard doesn't mean old or young in a play. It just means you're actin'."

"Look here," said Toothy, "I'm gettin' sick of countin' this twopence halfpenny."

"Oh, all right," said Charles. "Go on in, Roger."

Replacing the hook of his beard over his left ear, which at once brought the other hook off his right ear, and taking from his pocket the crumbled piece of paper containing his part, Roger strode on to the "stage".

"Ha! A miser!" he said. "I will catch his cold."

"It's 'snatch his gold'," said Charles indignantly.

"Well, why don't you write so's people can read it?" said Roger. "All right. I will snatch his gold. Old man, wilt thou hand over thy gold to me?"

There was a silence as once more Toothy counted his twopence halfpenny.

"Go on, Toothy," said Charles. "You've got to answer him."

"I thought you said I couldn't hear what people said," said Toothy testily. "Well, if I can't hear what people say, I can't answer them, can I?"

And then Araminta Palmer appeared in the doorway and beamed round the assembly, in no way disheartened, apparently, by the scowls that greeted her arrival.

"What do you want?" said Roger sternly.

"I wad to be id it," said Araminta, advancing into the room. "I wad to be the Fairy Queed."

"Well, it's not that sort of play," said Roger, "and we wouldn't have you in it, anyway, so there!"

"But I've got a Fairy Queed's costube," persisted Araminta. "Ad I cad act, I cad."

"Well, you won't act here, because we don't want you."

"I dode care," said Araminta.

"So go away."

"A'right, I'b going," said Araminta. She put out her tongue at each member of the company in turn and went towards the door. At the door she turned and added: "But I'b cubbig back," before she finally disappeared.

"Now let's get on with it," said Charles. "Go on, Roger. Murder him."

Roger seized Toothy by the collar. Toothy, obeying his natural instincts, hit him, and a somewhat protracted struggle ended with Toothy sitting astride Roger, who had been considerably hampered during the struggle by a determination not to be parted from his beard, and gasping: "Say you're beat."

"You can't go on like that," said Charles despairingly. "It's silly having the murderer beat by the man he's murderin'. Lie down an' be murdered, Toothy. I'm the detective, an' I'm comin' in now to inspect the body."

Holding in place a pair of horn-rimmed spectacles that would otherwise have slid off his nose, he entered the stage. Toothy was crawling about the floor, an agonised expression on his face.

"I've lost my twopence halfpenny," he said.

"Never mind that," said Charles in exasperation, "You're the *body*. Lie down."

"'S all very well for you," said the body bitterly, continuing his investigations. "'S not your twopence halfpenny. I was savin' it up for an ice cream."

"Hello," said Sally, entering with a flourish. "You shouldn't have started without me."

It was clear that Sally was prepared to display all the airs and graces of a leading lady.

"Well, you shouldn't have been late," said Charles with spirit. "Have you got your part with you?"

"No," said Sally. "I used it to wrap a toffee apple in and it melted. Anyway, I couldn't read it."

"Well, listen," said Charles. "You're Eglantine, an' you've got to marry Jimmy!"

Sally's face darkened with anger.

"I won't marry a silly little boy like Jimmy Manning," she said. "He's only seven."

"I'm s-seven and three quarters," pleaded Jimmy.

"Well, Freddy's spots may have gone by tomorrow," said Charles. "Then you can marry him."

"I won't marry Freddy either," said Sally. "He wears spectacles and he's frightened of cows. I want to marry Roger."

"You can't marry Roger," said Charles. "He's a murderer an' a thief an' a liar."

"He's *not*," said Sally stormily. "You're a beast to say those things about Roger. He's the nicest boy I've ever met in my life and I'm *going* to marry him."

"Oh, shut up," said Roger, with a disgust that was not untinged by gratification.

And then Araminta pirouetted into the room. She had changed into her Fairy Queen costume, and, before anyone could stop her, had leapt upon the packing case and was waving her wand over the assembly.

"I ab the fairy queed," she said. "I wave by wand, ad coudless fairies cub at by cobband."

The wand caught in Sally's hair, and Sally, losing the last vestige of her self control, pulled the intruder down and shook her. Furiously Araminta hurled herself upon Sally – kicking, biting, scratching. Sobbing with rage, Sally fought back, tugging at the tight tawny curls. Suddenly the over-wrought nerves of the whole company seemed to give way. Roger, smarting under his defeat by Toothy, flung away his beard and punched him. Jimmy, hearing Bobby mutter, "Soppy kid, Sally," hit out wildly and received in return a punch that made a struggle to the death, as it seemed, inevitable. Sandy, barking joyously, joined in all the fights without discrimination. Charles stood watching the pandemonium. It was a discouraging spectacle. But not for nothing was Charles the son of an eminent local amateur actor.

"Oh, well," he said, thrusting his manuscript into his pocket, "I 'spect it'll be all right on the day."

## Chapter 22

# *The Rescue that Failed*

The play was taking place in the spinney at the bottom of Bill's garden, on a "stage" consisting of an open space beneath a somewhat decrepit "monkey puzzle" tree. It was not the detective play originally written by Charles. That had never been performed, for Freddy Pelham's spots turned out to be chickenpox and Roger, Charles and Bill had gone down with it in quick succession. Charles had whiled away his hours of enforced inactivity by reading a collection of Wild West stories sent him by the charwoman's husband and, on recovery, had at once set to work to write a Wild West play.

"They're much more excitin' than detective plays," he said, "cause Red Indians are savager than crim'nals an' there's more of them."

His choice had been influenced by a recent craze among the junior inhabitants of the village for making Red Indian headdresses out of hens' feathers. All the neighbouring hen-runs had been ransacked and many of their occupants reduced to semi-nudity, while small boys went about in the plumage of the Rhode Island Reds and Buff Orpingtons.

The plot of the play was simple and not unduly original. Sally and Roger were to be white pioneers in a Red Indian territory, and Roger was to leave Sally in charge of the "clearing" while he rode off to borrow a tin-opener from his nearest neighbour, three hundred miles away. During his absence Sally was to be captured by Red Indians and rescued by Roger, who, assisted by Charles and Bill, was to attack and overcome the whole band and finally to be appointed their chief. To Jimmy, because of his youth, had been assigned the relatively unimportant part of tom-tom player. The tom-tom was Charles's idea. He was somewhat vague on the subject, being under the impression that a tom-tom was a bird that made a sound like a saucepan being hit by a stick, but he was quite sure that in any Red Indian play a tom-tom was necessary. Jimmy, therefore, had been told to sit behind a bush and bang a frying pan with a wooden spoon. And Jimmy, with his unbounded optimism, was beginning to consider this the most important part of the play.

The audience was a sparse one, consisting chiefly of the younger brothers and sisters of the cast, and over the whole hung a faint air of apprehension. For there was a rumour abroad that the Mouldies had planned to force their way into the audience and boo Charles's master-piece. The Three Musketeers had tried to conceal their preparations from the ever-watchful eyes of their foes, but there had been a curious smile on Archie's face the last time they met him, and the Mouldies had been seen gathering together in Archie's back garden this morning, whispering and sniggering.

"I bet they don't know we're havin' it here," said Charles optimistically. "They'll expect us to be havin' it in the quarry or the blitzed house."

" 'Course they will," agreed Roger, adding: "Anyway, Bill's garden ought to be safe from them. It's private prop'ty an' there's lors against trespassin'."

Not altogether reassured by this reflection (for all of them broke such laws with impunity every day), the audience sat on uneasy seats of pine needles and brambles and cheered the tom-tom overture that Jimmy was performing behind his bush. A fresh burst of applause greeted the appearance of Sally and Roger. After a heated argument as to whether Sally should wear her mother's Ascot hat and silver fox cape, which Roger considered unsuitable but which Sally refused to relinquish (Sally's mother was away for the day), Roger, reminded of his opening lines by the prompter, muttered something about a tin-opener and strode off the two or three yards that represented the three hundred miles. Then occurred one of those hiatuses that are the chief characteristics of amateur theatricals and that are generally accepted by the audience as part of the entertainment.

"Where are those Indians?" shouted Roger testily.

"They're not quite ready," said Toothy, who had arrived breathless from the "green room", which was Bill's family's garage. "They're paintin' their faces an' Charles is alterin' the plot. He's thought of a different ending."

Roger and Toothy hurried off together to the garage, and Jimmy, feeling that the whole entertainment now devolved upon him, redoubled his tom-tom efforts. After a few moments a crowd of boys with painted faces and feathered headdresses burst in from the bushes, uttering ferocious war-whoops, seized Sally and dragged her off. The audience cheered loudly. Jimmy's tom-tom touched heights of frenzy unreached before. Then the applause died away to an animated chatter, and another hiatus followed. And then, to everyone's surprise, a second band of feathered Indians burst upon the stage and to even wilder accompaniment of war-whoops. They stood, looking about them uncertainly.

"Where's Sally?" said Bill's voice from a mask of burnt cork.

A sudden silence fell, and gradually the truth dawned upon everyone . . . The first band of Indians had been Mouldies. Archie had managed to discover the time, place and plot of the play and had cunningly taken advantage of the gap in the proceedings to carry off Sally. For a few moments they were all too horror-stricken to be able to form any plan of action. Only Charles, with the egotism of the artist, had thought for his own affairs.

"Well, the play's ru'ned now," he said bitterly, "an' I'd thought out a jolly good ending for it. They were all goin' to eat a bear that had eaten some special native berries that turned people mad an' they'd all go mad an' die in ag'ny. It was a jolly good ending."

Roger had by now taken command of the situation.

"We've got to start off straight away an' rescue her," he said. "Half of you go to the woods with Bill an' the rest to the ole quarry with me. Come on, Charles."

Charles gave a hollow laugh.

"This *would* happen to the only play I've ever wrote right through," he said.

"Can I come with your lot, Roger?" said Jimmy.

"No," said Roger. "You've got to stay here. You're too young to rescue people. You'd only get in the way."

"I w-w-wouldn't. Honest, I w-w-wouldn't," pleaded Jimmy, almost in tears.

"Well, we don't want you," said Roger in a tone of finality. He turned to the others. "Come on quick. There's no time to lose. They may've scalped her by now. She'd be jolly easy to scalp with all that hair."

Uttering ferocious war-whoops, the motley band moved off, leaving Jimmy alone with the shame of his seven years. But Jimmy was not the boy to give way to despondency for long. Already a plan was forming in his mind. He would rescue Sally on his own . . . He didn't think that Archie would have taken her to the woods or the old quarry. He would have taken her to his home. And the Mouldies were too strong and cunning to be beaten on their own ground. It would be necessary to treat with them. In a history lesson on medieval warfare Miss Tressider had told him how the warriors of those days ransomed any of their friends who were taken prisoner. Jimmy decided to ransom Sally . . . He would ransom Sally and bring her back, while the others were still searching woods and quarry.

He set off at a run to collect his treasures. He had four ship halfpennies, one and sixpence that he was saving up for his mother's birthday present, an Egyptian stamp, a bag of bull's-eyes (his sweet ration for the week), his seagull's skull, a return railway ticket from London, some dried seaweed, a furry caterpillar in a matchbox and, in another matchbox, an insect that he described euphemistically as his "performing ant." All these he bundled into his school satchel, then ran off down the road to Archie's house. Archie was standing at the gate with Georgie Tallow. They still had painted faces and wore Red Indian headdresses.

"I've come to r-ransom Sally," stammered Jimmy.

Archie smiled his most unpleasant smile.

"Come in," he said.

Jimmy followed him into the tool shed that was used as the Mouldies' headquarters. Georgie followed Jimmy and closed the door. Shut in with his enemies and looking up into Archie's fox-like face, Jimmy knew a moment of cold terror, but he quietly conquered it. Archie was still smiling.

"Well?" he said.

"I k-knew you'd g-got her here," said Jimmy.

"Clever, aren't you?" said Archie, exchanging a wink with Georgie. "Of course we've got her here."

"I'll g-give you all these for a r-ransom," said Jimmy, pouring his treasures out into the wheelbarrow, "if you'll let her go."

Archie inspected the treasures.

"Yes," he said at last, "we'll let her go for these."

Jimmy's heart leapt.

"C-can I take her now?"

Archie and Georgie exchanged another wink.

JIMMY POURED HIS TREASURES OUT INTO THE WHEELBARROW.

"I couldn't hand her over to you," said Archie, putting a bull's-eye into his mouth. "We can only hand her over to Roger. He's the head of your gang."

"Will you *p-promise* to hand her over to Roger?" said Jimmy.

"Oh, yes," said Archie, slipping the one and sixpence into his pocket.

"Will you *write* it an' p-put it 'on your honour'?" persisted Jimmy, aghast at his own daring.

But Archie remained pleasant and obliging.

"Certainly," he said, slipping the Egyptian stamp into his wallet.

Georgie produced a notebook with pencil attached, and Archie wrote, "I promise on my honour to hand over Sally to Roger Manning," signed it and, tearing out the page, gave it to Jimmy, putting another bull's-eye into his mouth as he did so.

"Th-thanks," said Jimmy. "Well, I'll g-go now."

They opened the door and he went off down the road. He felt light-headed with relief. He'd rescued Sally . . . Not even Archie would dare to disown an "on my honour" promise. He pictured himself announcing the news to the others when they returned from their fruitless search of woods and quarry. He imagined Roger's delight and gratitude. Never again would they scorn his youth and refuse to take him with them on their expeditions. He saw them all crowding round him, congratulating him, demanding details of his exploit. "Oh, I jus' went along to Archie," he would say carelessly, "an' – I *made* him sign it." And Roger would take the note to Archie and return in triumph with Sally.

He scrambled through the hedge into Bill's garden and ran breathlessly to the spinney. And then he stopped, open-mouthed with amazement. For Sally was there with Roger, and they were evidently just starting the play again. Sally had added a parasol and handbag to her outfit.

"You are the limit, Jim," said Roger sternly, "going off like this. We give you a little job like the tom-tom, and you can't even do it properly."

"D-did you rescue Sally?" gasped Jimmy.

"She didn't need rescuing," said Roger. "They met Miss Pettigrew at the end of the road, and she made them let her go. We met her coming back. She's been here for ages."

Jimmy was silent. So even when Archie took the ransom he had known that Sally was safe with Roger and the gang.

"Oh, do get *on*," pleaded Charles distractedly. "I didn't write this play for you to go chattering an' *chattering*."

"Go an' do your tom-tom, Jim," said Roger, "you've wasted enough time."

Slowly, dispiritedly, Jimmy returned to his bush and took up his frying-pan and spoon.

He was a sadder, but perhaps a not much wiser boy.

## Chapter 23

# Archie Gets the Worst of It

The Three Musketeers with Toothy and Jimmy sat – on uneasy seats of lawnmower, wheelbarrow, seed boxes and roller – in the Mannings' tool shed, discussing the situation. Jimmy was, for the first time in his seven years, accepted as a member of the council, and he was so much overwhelmed by the honour that he could do little but blink and stammer, torn between a desire to acquit himself creditably and a fear of saying something foolish that would lower him for ever in their esteem.

Roger was presiding over the meeting.

"We've got to get Jimmy's treasures back from Archie Mould," he said.

"How?" said Bill.

"Well, that's what we've come here to talk about," said Roger a little irritably.

"Let's send him a challenge signed in our blood," said Charles.

"I'm not going to do any signin' today," said Bill. "I've got a cold comin' on an' I need all my blood for my strength."

"All right," said Roger. "It takes too long, anyway, when every moment's precious. We'll just send him a challenge."

"An ultimatum's better," said Toothy a little uncertainly.

"They're the same thing," said Roger, "only one's French."

"Which?" said Bill.

"Oh, shut up and let's get on with it," said Roger.

"I've got some paper," said Charles. He took a crumpled piece of paper from his pocket, spread it on the roller, took a stubby pencil from another pocket, inspected it frowningly, chewed a point on to it and began the composition.

"If you don't return Jimmy's treasures by the end of the afternoon," he wrote, " we declair war on you."

"War without a quarter," said Bill.

"What's that mean?" demanded Roger.

"Well, I saw it in a book," said Bill vaguely.

"War without a quarter mus' mean three-quarters of a war," said Roger; "an' we're jolly well not goin' to declare

THE THREE MUSKETEERS DRAFTED
AN ULTIMATUM TO THE MOULDIES.

three-quarters of a war. We're goin' to declare a *whole* war."

"To the d-d-death," stammered Jimmy.

"Yes, that's jolly good," said Toothy. Roger nodded approval, and Charles added "to the deth" to his challenge.

"Well, now," began Roger, and suddenly they saw Araminta Palmer standing in the doorway. "What do you want?" said Roger shortly.

"I wad to be id it," she said in her deepest and most adenoidal voice.

Roger's scornful glance went from her mop of red-gold curls to her small strap-over shoes.

"When we want kids of five," he said crushingly, "we . . . we'll ask you to come."

"I cub without askig," said Araminta, uncrushed.

"Well, we don't want you."

"I dode care," said Araminta.

"Let's take no notice of her," said Bill. "Go on, Roger."

"Well—" began Roger again.

"I'm Archie Bould's edeby, as buch as you are," said Araminta, who had evidently been listening to the conversation from the beginning.

Roger moved his position so as to exclude her from the group.

"We've got to decide when to attack him if he doesn't hand over the treasure."

"He threw Baridgold's wardrobe idto the ditch," said Araminta.

They all knew Marigold, the Palmers' family cat – a large sleek ginger creature who allowed itself to be arrayed by Araminta in the most outrageous dolls' clothes and taken out in Araminta's dolls' pram.

They continued to ignore her.

"After school would be the best," said Bill.

"It was a dice wardrobe," said Araminta. "It was ad old 'taché case of Daddy's ad I kept Barigold's clothes id it."

"We'll call out the gang," said Charles, "an' we'd better be well armed. The Mouldies are sure to have weapons."

"It's all dasty ad buddy dow," said Araminta. "I card use it."

Roger turned to her in exasperation.

"We aren't interested in your rotten old cat's wardrobe," he said.

"I dode care," said Araminta.

"And you can jolly well go away."

"I'b goig away," said Araminta with dignity. "Ib tired of listenig to you talkig dodsence. But," she added as she went, "I'b *goig* to be id it."

"Thank goodness she's gone," said Roger. "Shut the door, Jimmy."

Jimmy shut the door.

"We'll send the challenge," said Roger, "an' if we don't get a surrender, we'll attack them after school this afternoon. Now what about weapons? I'll bring that new water pistol of mine."

"I'll bring my catapult," said Bill. "It doesn't shoot very straight but it might hit someone I'm not aiming at, and that's better than nothin'."

"I'll bring a dart," said Toothy. "It really belongs to our dartboard, but," hopefully, "I don't 'spect they'll notice it's gone. I'll dip it in my father's eye lotion. It's got 'poison' on the bottle. That's what natives do, put poison on darts."

"We don't want acshully to *kill* them," said Roger doubtfully.

"You've got to be ruthless with crim'nals," said Toothy.

"I'll bring my popgun," said Charles. "My father's jus' given it me back after the kitchen window. It's only got a cork, but a cork can be pretty deadly if it hits the right spot. What about Jimmy? He'd better be armed, too."

"I'll bring the t-tin-opener," said Jimmy.

"No, you'd better stay out of the fight, Jimmy. You're too young for it," said Roger, reducing Jimmy to his proper status as a seven-year-old, only admitted to their eleven-year-old council as a special favour.

"All right," said Jimmy, determining to take the tin-opener none the less.

Roger himself put the challenge into Archie's school satchel and saw Archie's face distort itself into its most offensive sneer as he read it. He found the answer, written by Georgie Tallow at Archie's dictation, slipped into his own satchel at the end of school. "Don't you wish yude get them? Huse been cort owt?"

So after school the Musketeers collected such of their gang as could be collected at short notice, and, armed for the battle, waited to fall on their foes. It was an unequal and inglorious fight. The Mouldies had filled their satchels from a heap of stones by the roadside (left temporarily unguarded by the road mender), choosing the largest and jaggedest they could find. Pursued by the Musketeers, they fled swiftly, then turned to fling a volley of stones at their pursuers before turning again to flight, continuing these Parthian tactics all down the road. The weapons of the Musketeers proved sadly inadequate in this type of warfare. Roger discharged his water pistol ineffectively and could find no more water to fill it with. Only one of the pebbles discharged from Bill's catapult found a target and it hit a cow, who merely flicked its tail contemptuously. Toothy's "poisoned dart" lost itself in the hedge and resisted Toothy's frantic efforts to find it (for, despite his assumption of nonchalance, he had a well-founded suspicion that the dart would be missed and that its disappearance would be laid at his door). Charles's airgun refused to discharge its cork at all, and Jimmy did not even have a chance to get his tin-opener out of his pocket. The Mouldies' weapons, on the other hand, found targets in plenty, raising a lump the size of a golf ball on Roger's forehead, grazing Charles's cheek, cutting Bill's nose, entering Toothy's mouth and denting the gold brace that enclosed his teeth (already dented enough by an attempt earlier in the day to open a new tin of shoe polish with it), and bruising a particular tender point of Jimmy's shin. After half an hour the Mouldies had thrown them off, regained the sanctuary of Archie's house and had gathered at Archie's bedroom window to jeer at the Musketeers, as, battered, weary, bruised, they made their way homewards.

"Let's go to the tool shed and plan the next battle," said Roger, who had never yet been known to own that he was beaten.

Slowly, dispiritedly, they made their way back to the tool shed. And there they found Araminta arranging in a shining new attaché case the dolls' clothes in which she dressed her long-suffering ginger cat.

"I wadded to show you Barigold's dew wardrobe," she said.

"Well, clear out," said Roger shortly.

But Araminta was not a child to be thus summarily disposed of.

"I went into Archie Bould's house while you were

havig the fight ad I took *his* 'taché case," she said. "Dobody saw be."

"We'll get more of the gang together tomorrow," said Roger, "an' we'll ambush him."

"That stone went right down inside me," said Toothy. "I was jus' doin' the war cry an' I swallowed it without meaning to."

"He bade bide all dasty ad buddy," said Araminta, folding a tiny nightdress of virulent purple satin trimmed with tangled curtain fringe, and putting it into the attaché case, "so he deserved to have his taken."

"Jus' outside the wood's a good place for an ambush," said Bill. "We can hide in the bushes by the road."

"I'll probably have to have an operation," said Toothy gloomily. "People with stones inside them do."

"There was a lot of dasty old rubbish id it," said Araminta, "so I threw it odto the rubbish heap id your garden."

Suddenly Jimmy noticed the initials A.M. on the attaché case and slipped quietly out to inspect the rubbish heap. And there he stood gaping. For, flung upon the weeds, dead blooms and cut grass that formed the rubbish heap, was a pile of Archie's war saving certificates, Archie's sweet coupons, Archie's precious collection of stamps, Archie's wallet, Archie's bulging purse . . . Araminta had taken for Marigold's wardrobe the attaché case that contained Archie's dearest treasures.

"Come and l-look here," he shouted excitedly.

And they came.

It was a pale and distraught Archie who arrived ten minutes later, summoned by a curt note from Roger, an Archie armed no longer with stones and mockery, but with grovelling apologies and supplications, an Archie who brought with him all Jimmy's "treasures", packed neatly in a cardboard box, who pleaded almost tearfully for the return of his own.

"Say you're beat," said Roger sternly.

"I – I'm beat," stammered Archie.

"Then take your beastly stuff," said Roger, kicking the rubbish heap, "but 'Minta's got to keep your case. You messed hers up."

"All right," said Archie humbly.

They returned to the tool shed, Jimmy hugging his box of "treasures" lovingly to his chest. Araminta, who had been only mildly interested in the proceedings round the rubbish heap, was just packing into the attaché case a green bonnet with yellow ribbons that tied under Marigold's chin.

"Thanks awfully, 'Minta," said Roger gruffly.

Araminta gave the bonnet a final pat.

"I said I'd be id it ad I *was*," she said.

## Chapter 24

# *Speeding the Parting Guest*

"We're all jolly well sick of the beast," said Roger. "An' we've got to do somethin'."

The 'beast' was Uncle Ernest, who had come to stay with the Mannings for a week and had already stayed for nearly three. He was boisterous and overbearing and greedy and generally insufferable. He referred to Roger and Jimmy as the "kiddy-piddies" and delighted in playing practical jokes on them that made them look foolish, resenting any practical jokes that they essayed in retaliation. He was vain of his personal appearance, especially of his thick blond curly hair, and conceited about his business acumen, telling over and over again the story of a business coup that he had recently brought off in Angora. He wasn't even a real uncle, only a distant cousin of Mr Manning's who insisted on being called uncle. At first Roger and Jimmy had taken for granted that their mother and father, with grown-up obtuseness, enjoyed Uncle Ernest's company, but yesterday Roger had heard his mother saying to his father: "If he stays here much longer, I shall go mad." And Mr Manning had replied: "I'll try to get rid of him, my dear, but it's not easy. He once did me a very good turn, you know."

Roger heard no more, but he had heard enough. His father was prevented by gratitude and honour from turning out the obnoxious guest. Therefore it devolved upon him, Roger, to do it . . .

He had summoned a meeting of the Three Musketeers, and he and Charles and Bill were perched upon various garden implements in the tool shed, discussing the matter.

"What can you do?" said Bill. "He won't go jus' 'cause you tell him to . . . Could you put salt in his tea or a wet sponge in his bed or something?"

"No," said Roger. "He does that sort of thing to Jimmy and me, but, when we do it back to him, he gets angry and tells Daddy."

"I once had an aunt who went home 'cause her pipes burst. Could you write to him an' tell him his pipes have burst?"

"Pipes don't burst in summer," said Roger.

"Why?' demanded Bill.

"Well, never mind that now," said Roger. "What matters now is how we're goin' to get rid of him."

"I've got an idea," said Charles slowly.

There had been a thoughtful look on his face ever since the beginning of the conference.

"What is it?" said Roger.

"We could blackmail him."

They looked at him blankly.

"What's that?" said Bill.

"Well, I read a story where someone did it," said Charles. "You find out somethin' wicked they did in their past life an' you send them a note tellin' them that you know about it, an' – an' they jus' go."

"S'pose they haven't done anythin' wicked," said Bill.

"I bet *he* has," said Roger bitterly. "He put a drawing pin on my chair for me to sit down on yesterday an' he swung Jimmy round by his arms till he nearly made him sick an' he ate *half* the jelly that Mother made for us for tea."

"I 'spect he's a murderer," said Charles. "Lots of people are that you don't know are. Nacherally they don't do murders when people are watchin' them."

"Yes," said Bill, "but – he's jus' been out to that place" – he wrinkled his brows – "that place that's got a name like a rabbit."

"Angora," said Roger.

"Yes, that's it. He's jus' been out there on business, so he *can't* be a murderer."

"How do we know it was business?" said Charles darkly. "I bet he was out there murderin'. He's got a murderer's face."

"He might only be a thief," said Bill with a judicial air.

"How do we find out?" asked Roger.

"In this story I read," said Charles, "they went into his room an' looked through his papers."

They turned their eyes speculatively to the spare room window, which could be seen through the open door of the tool shed.

"We could do that," said Roger. "He's gone down to the village an' Mother's gone to London an' Daddy's at the office."

"All right," said Charles, "let's go an' do it now."

Without wasting any further time they went indoors and up to Uncle Ernest's bedroom.

There they stood and gazed round uncertainly. Everything looked trim and neat and innocent. Certainly there was no suggestion that a murderer inhabited the room.

"Wonder where he keeps his papers," said Roger.

"I bet they're in here," said Charles, taking an attaché case from the writing table.

"It's illegible to read other people's letters," said Bill.

"You mean illegal," said Roger.

"Well, that's what I said, isn't it?" said Bill pugnaciously.

"No, it isn't," said Roger, "but we can't waste time arguing. Go on, Charles. Open it."

Charles had already opened it and was reading the first letter had had found in it. As he read, his eyes and mouth opened to their fullest capacity.

"Gosh!" he said faintly. "He *is* a murderer."

"Read it aloud," said the others excitedly.

*"Dear Ernest,"* read Charles slowly. *"Congratulations on the Angora coup. The cut-throat competition there must have been pretty grim and I'm glad you came off best."*

"Crumbs!" gasped Roger.

"He's been in for a throat-cuttin' competition out there," said Charles. "Gosh! Jus' think of it! A competition in cuttin' people's throats. An' he *won* it. Well, that proves he's a murderer all right. Think of it! A competition in cuttin' people's throats!"

The Three Musketeers sat gaping and blinking at the mental picture summoned by these words. They had all turned rather pale.

"I should jolly well think it *was* grim," commented Roger.

"But what about this word 'coup'?" said Bill. "That might make it mean somethin' different. What does 'coup' mean?"

"I thought it was a sort of ice cream," said Roger.

Charles had seized the dictionary that formed part of Uncle Ernest's travelling library and was turning over the pages.

"Here it is," he said. "Listen. 'A stroke or blow, used to convey the idea of force or violence.'"

Again the Three Musketeers gaped and blinked. Roger found his voice first.

"Gosh! He's been knockin' people about an' cuttin' their throats in that place all the time he was pretendin' to be there on business. Well, we've got to do somethin' now."

"Let's go to your bedroom and write that note," said Charles, fastening up the attaché case.

They went to Roger's bedroom and wrote the note at Roger's homework table. It was a model of brevity.

*We gnow you are a murderer. Fle.*

"Where shall we put it?" said Bill.

"On his pillow's a good place," said Charles. "He might miss it in other places but he'll have to put his head on his pillow when he goes to sleep."

Roger slipped back to Uncle Ernest's bedroom and put the note on his pillow, then rejoined the others.

"I think we ought to tell the p'lice, too," Bill was saying as he re-entered the room. "He'll go on and on knockin' people about an' cuttin' their throats if we don't. Let's write to Scotland Yard."

That, too, seemed a good idea, and after a certain amount of discussion the letter was duly written by Roger:

*Dere Scotland Yard, Pleese send someone here quick and weel tell you about Uncle Ernest beeing a murderer.*

"Shall we sign it with our blood?" said Roger.

"No, you don't sign in blood for Scotland Yard," said Bill, who was always a little reluctant to undergo the process of blood-letting. "You only sign in blood for mortal foes or blood brothers."

"What'll we do with it?" said Roger, putting the letter into an envelope and addressing it "Scotland Yard London".

"We've got to find a stamp first," said Bill. "Anyone got twopence halfpenny?"

"Yes, I have," said Charles, "but I'm jolly well not goin' to waste it on a stamp."

"I think if you write to the government you needn't put a stamp on," said Roger. "The King pays at the other end. I know he pays at the other end when people write letters to the Income Tax, 'cause I've seen the envelopes. I bet he pays for Scotland Yard letters, too. I expect, bein' the King, he can get stamps an' things cheap."

"It would be safer to put a stamp on," said Bill.

"Well, you're not havin' my twopence halfpenny," said Charles firmly. "I'll draw a stamp if you like. I'm jolly good at drawing stamps."

He set to work on the envelope and they watched him as he laboriously executed a libellous portrait of the King's head, surmounted by a crown that looked like a turnip and an uncertain rectangle of wavy lines.

"The postman won't think that's a stamp," said Roger.

"He might," said Charles, surveying his efforts through the rosy spectacles of the creator. "It doesn't look too bad if you hold it a good way off, an' the postman's short-sighted. I heard him say in the Post Office yesterday that he needed new spectacles."

"Oh, come on," said Bill impatiently. "Let's go out an' post it."

"We'd better not post it here," said Charles. "The man in that story I read paid the postman to let him open letters, an' I bet Uncle Ernest does that. Let's go'n' post it in Eckton, then he won't know anythin' about it. Come on. An' let's be jolly careful or he'll be cuttin' our throats next."

They went downstairs in conspiratorial fashion, shoulders hunched, faces set in stern purposeful frowns, and out into the garden. At the gate they met Jimmy.

"Where are you going?" said Roger.

"I'm going indoors to fetch my fishing rod," said Jimmy. "I'm going fishing."

"Well, keep away from Uncle Ernest."

"Why?" said Jimmy.

"Never mind why," said Roger sternly. "Promise not to go near him."

"All right," said Jimmy in a puzzled voice.

He stood staring after them as they set off down the road. Then he went slowly indoors to get his fishing rod. It had been given to him last week by his godfather and had been his pride and delight till now, but now quite suddenly the interest faded from it and transferred itself to Uncle Ernest. *Why* was he not to go near Uncle Ernest? The only reason he could think of was that Uncle Ernest was sickening for scarlet fever or mumps, and Jimmy was filled with a morbid desire to watch the process . . . to see the spots appear one by one on the large rubicund countenance or the lumps swell gradually behind the prominent ears.

He got his fishing rod and went out into the garden. There he saw Uncle Ernest come in by the side gate and go up to his bedroom. He stood irresolute. He had arranged to meet Bobby at the pond in the old quarry, but he was loath now to leave the fascinating and forbidden vicinity of Uncle Ernest. Then an idea occurred to him. He would climb the copper beech at the end of the lawn and from there keep a watch on Uncle Ernest. He wouldn't be breaking his promise to Roger, because in a tree you weren't actually *near* anyone . . . He realised that to leave his fishing rod at the foot of the tree would betray his presence in it, so he wrapped the line round his waist and, manipulating the rod as best he could, climbed to his favourite position on the second branch. From there he could see Uncle Ernest in his bedroom, preening himself at his dressing table mirror. No spots yet, thought Jimmy, watching him intently.

Then Uncle Ernest disappeared, to reappear a few moments later at the side door of the house, with a deckchair in his hand. He crossed the lawn, pausing to pass a hand caressingly over his thick blond locks, and set up the chair under the copper beech.

Jimmy was torn between delight and apprehension. He could watch the spots appear on Uncle Ernest if Uncle Ernest was coming out in them. On the other hand he was practically a prisoner. He peered down through the branches. Uncle Ernest remained disappointingly spotless. The infectious disease of which Roger had seemed to be warning him had so far failed to manifest itself . . . Uncle Ernest's head drooped, and rhythmic snores came from his half-open mouth.

Jimmy became bored and restless. By Uncle Ernest's chair was a long curved twig that had been blown down in a recent gale. Jimmy remembered his fishing rod and idly decided to occupy himself by trying to hook it up into the tree. He extricated himself from line and rod and, lowering the line, began to angle for the twig . . . He'd nearly got it . . . He leant forward, almost overbalanced and clutched at the branch above his head. The rod swayed wildly . . . the hook caught in something. Instinctively, intent only on concealing his presence, Jimmy tugged it up, then, gazing down, saw at the end of the line a thick mop of blond hair and, below that, the wigless face of Uncle Ernest, distorted by rage.

It so happened that the course of Jimmy's short life had never as yet brought him into contact with the idea of a wig. He dropped the rod, scrambled down the tree and fled from the scene in blind terror, pursued by angry bellows of rage from Uncle Ernest.

He didn't return until half an hour later. Roger and Charles were just coming in at the gate. They had decided to go even further than Eckton to post the letter, and had posted it with such elaborate precautions of secrecy that

THE ROD SWAYED WILDLY . . . THE HOOK CAUGHT IN SOMETHING.

the whole process had taken them nearly an hour. Jimmy followed them into the hall. Mrs Manning had just come back from London and was standing there reading a note.

"How extraordinary!" she said. "Uncle Ernest says he's been called away suddenly. He went by the three-five train. He gives no explanation."

Roger and Charles exchanged a significant glance.

Mrs Manning looked up from the note. "Do you boys know anything about it?"

"Yes," and "Y-yes," said Roger and Jimmy simultaneously.

"What do you know, Jimmy?" said Mrs Manning.

"He's a murderer," burst out Roger.

"N-no, I'm not a m-murderer," pleaded Jimmy. "I only s-scalped him by m-mistake."

*Chapter 25*

# On the Rocks

Jimmy and Bobby stood on the top of the cliff, looking down at the steep shelving rock beneath them. They had come with their families to spend a day at the sea and had wandered away from the others, climbing the grass-covered hill till they reached the point from which the cliff dropped almost sheer down to the sea.

"I bet I could climb down it," said Jimmy.

Bobby considered.

"I bet you couldn't," he said. "It sort of slopes in."

"Well, there's stones an' b-bushes an' things to hold on to," said Jimmy.

"It'd be dangerous."

"Well, it's a long time since I did anything d-danger-ous," said Jimmy. "I bet Christopher C-Columbus an' – Dick Turpin an' those people did d-dangerouser things than this. I bet I could do it."

"You got stuck in Bill's pine tree," Bobby reminded him.

"That was over a w-week ago," Jimmy said with dignity. "I was y-younger then . . . I'm goin' to try, anyway. You n-needn't come if you don't want to."

Bobby hesitated.

"I will if you're goin' to," he said at last, "but I still think it's dangerous."

"Well, come on," said Jimmy impatiently.

The two clambered down the first part of the cliff successfully, clinging to precarious footholds of rock and still more precarious handholds of bushes, but it shelved inward more than they had realised and they found themselves at last crouching on a narrow ledge, with the rock above them shelving sharply outward and the rock below them shelving sharply inward and no available foothold either above or below.

"Well, we're stuck now," said Bobby.

"Yes," agreed Jimmy. They were both rather pale. "I'm s-sorry I've led you into d-danger."

"It's all right," said Bobby. "I didn't really want to be out of it if you were goin' to be in it."

"Someone m-might see us an' rescue us," said Jimmy.

"I don't suppose they will," said Bobby, who was always inclined to take a pessimistic view of any situation.

"They d-do in books."

"I've read books where they don't," said Bobby. "I've read books where they found skeletons hundreds of years afterwards."

Jimmy went still paler. He peered over the edge of the cliff.

"I w-wonder if the sea gets up as f-far as this," he said. "If it does we'll jus' d-drown. We won't even be skeletons."

"I'd sooner drown," said Bobby after consideration, "because if you're a skeleton it means you died of hunger."

"Gosh!" said Jimmy, horror-struck. "How long do people live without food? If n-no one rescues us, I mean?"

"Dunno," said Bobby, frowning thoughtfully. "I 'spect it depends on how much you've got inside you to start with. What did you have for your dinner?"

"Shepherd's pie an' t-two helpings of apple t-tart."

"I had shepherd's pie, too," said Bobby, "but I only had one helping of stewed plums. So you'll live longer. P'raps a day longer. You're lucky."

"I d-dunno," said Jimmy doubtfully. "It'll be sort of l-lonely . . . We'd better start shoutin' for help now, hadn't we?"

They shouted loudly, but the sound of the sea breaking on the cliffs below carried their voices away unavailingly. After a few minutes they stopped for breath.

"S'no good goin' on like this," said Jimmy, trying to conquer the fear that was creeping over him. "We'll jus' wear ourselves out an' t-turn dumb. You've only g-got a certain amount of shout in your th-throat, you know, an' when you've used it all up you t-turn dumb."

"Oh," said Bobby, still further dismayed by this thought.

"So we ought to save up our throats an' have a g-good shout in turns – say, every t-ten minutes."

"All right," said Bobby, glancing at his watch.

"It's no good looking at that," said Jimmy. "It doesn't go."

"I never said it did," said Bobby distantly, "but it's a good one . . . an' I left it you in my will."

"That's not much use now," said Jimmy.

Their minds went back to the sunny afternoon when, stretched under the shadow of an old haystack, on their way home from school, they had made their wills on pages torn out of their arithmetic exercise books.

"I left you everything I'd got," said Bobby, who was still feeling piqued by Jimmy's reference to his watch, "an' you didn't leave me much."

"Well, I had Roger to think of," said Jimmy. "I left you my ship halfpennies, didn't I?"

"Yes, but you spent them last week."

"Well, T-Toothy was sellin' his l-leopard claws off that rug his mother gave him 'cause it g-got the moth in an' I wouldn't have had enough m-money to buy them without my ship halfpennies. I'd have c'lected some more if I'd l-lived. Anyway, d-don't let's quarrel. If we've got to stay here till we're skeletons, it's no good quarrelling."

"No," agreed Bobby. "I wish I'd made another will an' left something to my mother. She's always been jolly good to me . . . I say, shall we have another shout now? I'll start."

His voice rang out loudly for some minutes then he stopped, breathless.

"L-let's wave our shirts to attract a p-passing ship," said Jimmy.

"There aren't any passing ships," said Bobby, scanning the empty horizon.

"N-never mind," said Jimmy. "I'm goin' to wave it. There might be a l-liner so far off that we can't see it."

"Well, if we can't see it, it can't see your shirt," said Bobby.

"Yes, it could. Sailors have speshully p-piercing eyes." He stripped off his shirt and waved it in the breeze. The breeze caught it and carried it off out of sight round the corner of the cliff.

"I'm s-s-sorry," said Jimmy.

"It's all right," said Bobby resignedly. "You couldn't help it. I'll try mine now."

"P'raps you'd better not," said Jimmy. "You'll need it for the night. It gets cold at nights an' we might be here for d-days an' d-days."

They were silent for a few moments, then:

"I bet it's about ten minutes now," said Bobby. "It's your turn to shout."

Jimmy's voice rang out, mingling with the sound of the sea and the wind. Finally he stopped.

"I'd better save it for a bit now," he said. "I can feel it gettin' wore out."

"I'm jolly hungry," said Bobby pathetically.

"Let's see what f-food we've got," said Jimmy. "I've got an acid d-drop somewhere."

He turned out his pockets. They contained two acid drops, heavily coated with fluff, a collection of small shells and pebbles, his three leopard claws, an over-ripe plum impaled on a red crayon, a pine cone and a dead beetle. He looked at the last with concern.

"Gosh!" he said. "It was all right when I put it in."

"Well, it's dead now," said Bobby.

Jimmy examined it carefully.

"I d-don't think it is," he said. "I think it's only tired. I think its eyes are open."

"Well, it's no good for food, anyway."

"It might be," said Jimmy. "They eat s-snails in France an' I d-don't see why we shouldn't eat beetles. We may be glad of it when we're s-starving."

He separated the plum from the crayon and laid it on the rock with the acid drops, beetle and pebbles.

"The pebbles'll do to suck," he said. "They stop you goin' m-mad with thirst."

"There's not much room to go mad in," said Bobby, anxiously surveying the narrow ledge of rock on which they crouched.

"What've you got?" said Jimmy.

Bobby's pockets contained half a biscuit, some

dubious-looking crumbs, a magnet, a screw, a tiddly-wink, a marble, a piece of clay and a curiously shaped twig that Bobby used as a revolver. Jimmy put the biscuit on one side, together with as many crumbs as he could detach from the lump of clay.

"We've got to make them last," he said. "We'll eat the acid drops tonight an' the biscuit tomorrow. We'll leave the beetle till the end."

"I once read a story," said Bobby slowly, "where there were two men starving on a raft, an' they drew lots which should kill an' eat the other."

Jimmy glanced apprehensively at his friend.

"It'd be jolly difficult to k-kill an' eat someone," he said.

"We may be driven to it," said Bobby darkly. "Let's have another shout. It's your turn."

Jimmy shouted loudly and unavailingly . . . then they sat in silence, gazing gloomily over the expanse of water.

Bobby sighed. "I wish I'd been kinder to our cat," he said.

"Well, it's never been kind to you," said Jimmy, trying to dispel the gloom that was gathering over the atmosphere. "It's an awful scratcher."

There was another silence.

"I'm sorry I said your watch didn't go," said Jimmy.

"It's all right," said Bobby, heaving another deeper sigh. "It doesn't."

There was another long silence. Then Bobby spoke in a small choking voice.

"My mother'll miss me an awful lot," he said.

"Let's shout again," said Jimmy. "It m-might cheer us up. It's your t-turn."

Bobby raised his voice, but it broke on a high note and he abandoned himself unrestrainedly to tears.

"I can't help it," he said between his sobs, "I keep – thinking about – my mother."

Jimmy thought of his mother, and desolation closed over his spirit. He blinked hard, and the corners of his mouth took a downward curve.

Suddenly a boy's face appeared out of the bush that grew from the rock just at the side of their ledge.

"Hello," said the boy.

"Hello," said Jimmy. "Have you c-come to r-rescue us?"

"Rescue you?" said the boy. "What from?"

"Well—" began Jimmy, but the boy went on: "No, I've just come up the staircase."

"Staircase?" gasped Jimmy.

"Yes," said the boy. "It's just round the corner of the cliff. You can't see it from here, but it's quite close. You can crawl to it along this little path behind the bush."

A BOY'S FACE APPEARED OUT OF THE BUSH. "HELLO," SAID JIMMY. "HAVE YOU COME TO RESCUE US?"

Jimmy and Bobby were silent, digesting the startling fact that, all the time they had been sitting on the ledge of rock, there had been a way of escape within a few yards. So taken up had they been with the cliff above them and below them that they had never considered anything else.

"I often crawl from the staircase along the little path behind this bush to this place," went on the boy, "and pretend that I'm on a desert island, watching for a sail."

"Yes," said Jimmy, putting up a fairly good show of nonchalance, "we were playing that."

"Well, there's no room to pass," said the boy, "so I'll crawl back and you can crawl on till we come to the staircase."

In less than a minute Jimmy and Bobby were on a solid wooden staircase that ran up from the beach to a house on the cliff. They looked at each other sheepishly and walked down in silence.

At the bottom Jimmy's shirt was waiting for them, outspread gracefully on a flat rock.

"It must be about tea-time," said Jimmy as he put it on. They walked along the sands till they came to their families, sitting round a picnic tea in the shelter of the cliff.

"Where have you been?" said Bobby's mother. "We thought you were never coming."

"We were p-playing on the cliff," said Jimmy.

"You made enough noise about it," said Jimmy's mother. "We heard you all over the bay. What were you playing at?"

Jimmy met Bobby's eyes and looked away quickly.

"Oh, j-jus' a game," he said vaguely.

## Chapter 26

# *Jimmy's Gang*

"We'll get 'em back," said Roger grimly.

"Or perish in the attempt," said Charles, who was an avid reader of sensational fiction.

"He's a robber an' a liar," said Toothy.

"He's a villain of the deepest dye," said Charles.

"P-please, c-can Bobby an' me help?" said Jimmy.

"No, you can't," said Roger. "You kids can jolly well keep out of this."

The villain was, of course, Archie Mould, and the crime was the theft of the ten surviving leopard's claws that Toothy's mother had given him when her leopardskin rug had finally succumbed to the ravages of the moth. At first Toothy, needing money to buy an aeroplane kit on which he had set his heart, had sold these to his schoolfellows. Jimmy had bought three for twopence each and had subsequently sold one to Bobby for three-halfpence.

It was Charles who read the story of the savage tribe who treasured the claws of any leopard they killed, in the belief that the courage and strength and resourcefulness of their fallen foe passed into their own natures.

"An' I bet there's somethin' in it," Charles had said as he recounted the story to the Three Musketeers.

"Those savages had jolly good brains. They didn't get

'em all worn out goin' to school an' learnin' lessons like we do."

A timely tip from an aunt enabled Toothy to buy back all the leopard's claws and present them proudly to Roger as the leader of the gang.

"What did they do with them, Charles?" said Roger, gazing awestruck at the formidable array.

"I think they wore them round their necks," said Charles vaguely.

"I bet my mother'd notice an' stop me," said Bill. "She's always lookin' at my neck to see if it's clean. Savages' mothers had a bit more sense than ours have."

In the end the leopard's claws were put into an old cocoa tin, labelled "Valluble and dangerus not to be tutched" and placed on the chimney piece of the kitchen of the blitzed house. After that, whenever the gang held meetings there, the leopard's claws were taken out and laid in a row in the centre of the group. And – so it seemed to the Three Musketeers and their followers – their affairs prospered as a result. They came off best in several skirmishes with the Mouldies. Charles said he had a distinct leopard-feeling when he knocked Archie down in the playground for tripping him up with a cricket stump, and Toothy, after an unpleasant interview with the headmaster on the subject of his persistent lateness for morning school, said that he had felt a curious and almost overpowering desire to spring on him and maul him. It was, from their point of view, eminently satisfactory. And then came the catastrophe . . . Yesterday, taking down the box before a meeting of the gang in order to lay out the claws, Roger had found it empty. He guessed at once what had happened. He had seen Archie Mould and Georgie Tallow sniggering outside the gate of the blitzed house the day before. Archie must have discovered the secret of the leopard's claws and struck this shattering blow at the pride and prowess of the gang. Taxed with the theft, he denied all knowledge of it with a blandness that confirmed their suspicions.

"Gosh!" said Charles. "Now they'll have all the strength and cunning of the leopard, and we shan't have any."

"Oh, yes, we will," said Roger grimly. "We'll get them back all right."

"I wonder where he keeps them," said Bill.

"I bet he keeps them in that attaché case with his initials on," said Toothy. "The one where he keeps his war savings certificates an' stamps. He keeps all his treasures in it. An' I know where it is, too. It's on the top of the wardrobe in his bedroom."

"An' I know somethin' else, too," said Charles. "He's goin' to the pictures this afternoon an' his mother's out an' there'll be no one in the house. So we can jus' climb in through his window an' get it."

"C-can't Bobby an' me jus' be on g-guard?" pleaded Jimmy.

"No, you can't," said Roger again. "This is men's work."

The two watched wistfully as the gang set off down the road.

"*Tell* you what," said Jimmy suddenly.

"What?" snapped Bobby, who was feeling peevish and irritable at being excluded from the adventure.

"Let's have a gang of our own."

The idea was so stupendous that for a moment or two it took Bobby's breath away.

"We c-couldn't," he gasped.

"Yes, we could," said Jimmy. "We could jus' c'lect one same as they did."

In a remarkably short time a motley crowd of small boys was assembled in Jimmy's back garden. It was not a dignified gathering. One member, who had insisted on joining the gang, though told that his extreme youth disqualified him, clasped a teddy bear in his arms. Another sucked an ice cream cornet. Another carried a balloon on a stick. Another was under the impression that he was coming to watch a Punch and Judy Show; while another, who was "minding" his baby sister, brought her along in her pram. Partial silence was enforced for Jimmy's opening speech.

"Now we're a gang same as Roger's," he said, "an' we've got to start practisin'. We can't start on big things like gettin' leopards' claws from Archie Mould same as they do. We've got to start on somethin' small an' w-work our way up to l-leopards' claws an' things. An' we've got to start on a smaller enemy than Archie Mould."

"Hip, hip, hurray," said the youth with the teddy bear, waving that animal aloft.

"Shut up," said Jimmy, sternly.

"Georgie Tallow," suggested Bobby. "He's smaller than Archie."

"Yes, he is," said Jimmy, "an' he's always takin' things from people."

"When's Judy coming on?" said the Punch and Judy enthusiast anxiously.

"S-shut up," said Jimmy again.

"He took the box of pencils my auntie gave me," called Frankie Keston, a boy with platinum blond hair and spectacles.

"Oh, he d-did, did he?" said Jimmy, a purposeful note

coming into his voice.

"Yes, but I don't care," said Frankie. "My auntie gave me another."

"That doesn't matter," said Jimmy, raising his voice to be heard above the baby, who had begun to howl. "He took it from you, so we'll get it back. That's the first thing we'll d-do now we're a gang. We'll g-get Frankie's box of pencils back for him."

"How?" demanded Bobby.

"We'll jus' f-find out where he k-keeps it an' g-get it," said Jimmy.

"I 'spect he keeps it in his playroom," said Bobby. "His playroom's that loft place over the garage."

"All right," said Jimmy, adopting a tone of leadership copied faithfully from Roger's. "We'll all g-go there now an' g-get 'em."

The motley collection straggled off down the road to Georgie Tallow's house. Fate was kind to them in that the playroom over the garage was obviously empty and the back of the garage screened by trees from both house and road, but unkind to them in that the garage door was locked and the window of the playroom, though open, so high that they could not reach it.

"Tell you what!" said Jimmy. "There's a ladder in our t-tool shed that the g-gardener uses. Some of you go an' g-get that."

Four or five members of the gang ran back to Jimmy's garden, and returned a few minutes later, staggering under the weight of the garden ladder. They dropped it and fought over it and got tied up in it, but finally they set it against the wall. Then Jimmy climbed up it and vanished into the room. Soon he reappeared at the window holding a pencil-box.

"Is th-this it, Frankie?" he said. "It was on his s-shelf."

"Yes, that's it," said Frankie.

Slowly, carefully, Jimmy climbed down the ladder. Joyfully, with carefree abandon, their voices raised exultantly, the new gang trooped back behind its leader.

"We've g-got to put back the ladder," said Jimmy, and led them in at the gate and round to the tool shed. There stood the Three Musketeers, their faces set and scowling.

SOON JIMMY REAPPEARED, HOLDING A PENCIL-BOX.

"So *you'd* taken the ladder," said Roger angrily.

"Y-y-yes," admitted Jimmy apologetically.

"Well, we'd have got back the leopard's claws if it hadn't been for you, then," said Roger. "You've gone and messed the whole thing up."

"H-h-how?" said Jimmy.

"If we'd been able to get on to the scullery roof we could have climbed up to Archie's window, and we sent Toothy back for the ladder, and it wasn't there, so we couldn't do it. And now it's too late, 'cause he's come back from the pictures. And you've stopped us gettin' back the leopard's claws an' it's jolly well your fault now if the Mouldies conquer us."

"I'm s-sorry," said Jimmy, dismayed almost to the

point of tears. "You see, we were b-being a g-gang an' we wanted to g-get Frankie's pencil box back from G-Georgie." He took the box from his pocket. Roger eyed it savagely.

"As if a few rotten ole pencils mattered," he said, "compared with our leopard's claws. A few rotten old pencils that—"

He stopped suddenly. He had taken the box and opened it. It was empty of pencils, but inside were the ten leopard's claws.

## Chapter 27

# The Paper-Chase

The paper-chase had been Roger's idea, and at first Jimmy, with his never failing optimism, had hoped to be allowed to play at least some minor part in it.

"Can't I jus' s-sort of l-look after the trail for you, Roger?" he pleaded. "I could stop cows eatin' it an' . . . an' that s-sort of thing."

"No," said Roger firmly. "It's a paper-chase for me an' Charles an' Bill an' you can jolly well mind your own business."

Jimmy would have given up all thought of the paper-chase after that. It was Bobby who suggested that the two of them should have a paper-chase on their own, and for the past week they had been busy collecting paper. Jimmy was anxious to model his chase on Roger's and had watched Roger's preparations closely. Roger packed his school satchel with torn-up paper, so Jimmy did the same . . . Roger kept a suspicious eye on these activities of Jimmy's.

"If you go messing up our paper-chase—" he said darkly.

"No, we won't," promised Jimmy earnestly. "Honest, we won't."

The news of the paper-chase leaked out among their friends and foes.

"Yah!" jeered Georgie Tallow, meeting Jimmy in the village on the morning of the chase. "Who's having a baby paper-chase on his own 'cause Roger won't let him join in the proper one?"

"Huh!" answered Jimmy stoutly. "Roger'd be jolly glad to have me in his paper-chase, but Bobby an' me had fixed this up an' we couldn't c-change our arrangements."

"Oh," sneered Georgie, "Well, when you're joining in a proper paper-chase with Roger, send me a postcard, will you."

"Yes, I will," said Jimmy and walked away with as much dignity as he could muster, pursued by jeers from Georgie.

The afternoon of the paper-chase was fine and sunny. The Three Musketeers set off down the road, Roger carrying his satchel full of torn-up paper over his shoulder. About twenty yards behind walked Jimmy and Bobby, Jimmy carrying his satchel full of torn-up paper over his shoulder. Occasionally Roger turned round to frown disapprovingly at the couple. Then suddenly both Roger and Jimmy turned round . . . and Jimmy's expression reflected all the horror and indignation of Roger's. For behind Jimmy walked Araminta Palmer, pushing a dolls' pram that contained a battered toy monkey known as Sinbad, and carrying over her shoulder a miniature satchel full of torn-up paper. They all stopped and waited for her.

"What are you doing?" said Roger sternly.

"Ib goig to play fairies id the wood," said Araminta blandly. "Would you like to cub ad play fairies with be?"

"*No!*" said Roger, then, with mounting suspicion: "what have you got in that satchel?"

"Paper," said Araminta.

"What for?" scowled Roger.

"To play fairies with," said Araminta. "I'b going to play Hadsel ad Gretel. I'b going to fide a little witches' house bade of cakes ad I'b goig to drop little bits of paper od the ground so's I cad fide my way back. It's a *dice* gabe. Why wode you play id?"

"We don't want to play your silly baby games," said Roger furiously.

"I dode care," said Araminta.

"And you can jolly well keep right away from our paper-chase."

"Ad you cad keep away frob by gabe," retorted Araminta with spirit.

"Come on," said Roger to Charles and Bill. "Take no notice of her."

Araminta turned to Jimmy.

"You'll play fairies with be, wode you, Jibby?" she said.

"No, I won't," said Jimmy, imitating Roger's tone of stern contempt.

"All right," said Araminta. "I dode care."

The three parties separated . . . Jimmy never knew quite what went wrong with the paper-chase. There were so many trails of paper through the wood that it was more like a jigsaw puzzle than a paper-chase. There was Jimmy's trail of newspaper; there was Roger's trail of exercise book paper, each fragment plentifully adorned with red ink; there was Araminta's trail of highly coloured "comics". At the end of the afternoon Jimmy and Bobby ran into each other by chance at a point where two paths met.

They were hot, tired and hungry. Jimmy had fallen into a stream, and Bobby, trying to spot the "hare", had climbed a tree and fallen painfully out of it.

"Well, you made a jolly rotten trail," said Bobby irritably, "all mixed up with other people's."

"That wasn't my fault," said Jimmy. "You're a jolly rotten trail-finder, an' I bet Roger will be mad with us. I kept tryin' to keep away from his an' gettin' mixed up in it."

"It was that beastly little Araminta that messed everything up," said Bobby. "Come on. Let's go home."

They set off down the path. And then, quite suddenly, they came upon Araminta. She was sitting in a clearing in the wood, and round her were five little piles of biscuits in a circle. In front of each pile was a daisy chain. In the middle of the circle on the ground was a large plum cake. Beside Araminta lolled the grotesque moth-eaten figure of Sinbad.

"What are *you* doing here?" said Jimmy sternly.

"I'b havig a fairy feast id a fairy rig," said Araminta. "I've fidished playig Hadsel ad Gretel ad I'b predending that I've broken up the witch's little house of cakes, ad I'b havig a fairy feast id a fairy rig."

"You've messed up all our trails with yours," said Jimmy still more sternly.

"I couldn't help that," said Araminta, unperturbed. "I couldn't bake up by mide where I wanted to

SUDDENLY THEY CAME
UPON ARAMINTA . . .

be, ad I had to leave trails to all the places I tried, id case I got lost. Will you play fairies with be dow?"

"*No!*" said Jimmy.

"If you played with be," said Araminta indifferently, "you could have sub biscuits ad cake, but you'd have to pretend to be fairies."

They hesitated. The cake looked rich and plummy. The biscuits were an exciting mixture of chocolate biscuits, wafers, shortcakes and gingerbreads.

"Well—" said Jimmy, his mouth watering.

"You'd have to wear daisy chaids ad call be Your Bajesty, 'cause I'b the Fairy Queed."

"Where did you get it all from?" said Jimmy.

"It cabe id a food parcel from abroad this mordig," said Araminta. "By bother was out for lunch, so I opened it ad took out the things I wanted for the fairy feast. I brought theb id the prab under Sidbad."

"Does your mother know you've taken them?"

"No," said Araminta, "but it's all right. I left her a tid of dried bilk."

"Gosh!" said Jimmy, aghast at the enormity of the crime. "You'll get into an awful row."

"No, I wode," said Araminta. "I'b a growig child. I deed food."

They looked at her in unwilling admiration. It was well known that Araminta could twist both her parents round her little finger.

"Cub ob if you're cubbig," she said impatiently. "We're jus' going to begid."

And suddenly there they were, sitting in the "fairy ring", crowned with daisy chains, mumbling "Your Majesty" to Araminta, wolfing plum cake, chocolate biscuits and wafers.

And then the worst – or what seemed to Jimmy the worst – happened. Roger, Charles and Bill appeared suddenly in the clearing – hot and cross and dirty.

"You jolly well messed up our paper-chase," said Roger, glowering angrily from Jimmy to Araminta, then he stopped short, gazing at the feast outspread on the ground.

"What on earth—?" he said.

"It's a fairy feast," said Araminta. "Cub od if you're cubbig, but you must pretend to be fairies ad wear daisy chains ad call be Your Bajesty 'cause I'b the Fairy Queed."

None of them knew whether it was Roger, Charles or Bill who made the first shameful movement of surrender (it was a fruitful source of argument for months to come) but, before any of them quite realised what was happening, they too were seated in the fairy ring, crowned with daisy chains, mumbling "Your Majesty", wolfing cakes and biscuits. They sat there abashed, with hangdog looks, avoiding each other's eyes, Samsons shorn of their locks, but making the most of every golden moment, every precious biscuit and slice of cake. And in the place of honour sat Araminta, that redoubtable child, daintily nibbling a wafer.

It was a strange procession that wended it s way homewards to the village. First went Araminta, walking airily and unconcernedly, wheeling Sinbad in his pram. Behind in single file walked the Three Musketeers, Jimmy and Bobby, keeping a constrained and sheepish silence.

At the door of her house Araminta turned to them: "Put Sidbad's prab id the garage," she ordered, "ad thed," generously, "you deedn't be fairies ady bore."

Inside the sitting room she found her mother gazing distractedly at the empty wrappings of the food parcel.

"Whatever's happened to all the food in it?" she said.

"I took it," said Araminta calmly. "Ib a growig child. I deed food. I left you a tid of dried milk."

"But, darling," wailed Mrs Palmer, "you can't have eaten it all."

"No," said Araminta. "The fairies ate bost of it."

"The fairies, darling?" said Mrs Palmer bewildered. "What fairies?"

"Those," said Araminta, pointing to the window.

Mrs Palmer looked out of the window, as the five fairies, cowering, shame-faced, with bits of daisy chains still adorning their tousled hair, crept past before her astonished gaze.

"I – I shouldn't tell anyone about this, Jimmy," said Roger, when the two of them were walking up to the front door of their house.

"No, I w-won't," said Jimmy, "an' I'll tell Bobby not to."

The gulf of four years that usually separated them had been bridged by the events of the afternoon. They were united by the bond of human frailty, by the memory of the shameful "fairy feast", by the mental vision of five boys, garlanded with daisy chains, addressing a despicable human atom as "Your Majesty" . . .

"It's all been a bit of a mess-up," went on Roger. "We'll have another nex' Saturday, an' you an' Bobby can be in it."

Jimmy's face shone.

"Th-thanks *awfully*, Roger," he said.

Roger went into the kitchen, where his mother was preparing the dinner.

"How did the paper-chase go off, dear?" she said.

"All right," said Roger vaguely. "When it was over we

had a game with Araminta Palmer. She wanted us to, and it seemed a shame to disappoint the kid."

"How kind of you, dear!" said Mrs Manning. "Where's Jimmy?"

"I think he's upstairs," said Roger.

Jimmy was upstairs, writing a postcard to Georgie Tallow.

*Roger and mees havving a propper papper chace toogether on satdy snukes to yu.*

## Chapter 28

# *A Present for Uncle Peter*

"The difficulty's goin' to be the paper," said Roger. "We'll want lots of paper, an' Mother says we mustn't use any more from her newspaper pile, 'cause she wants them for when we have the ceilings done, to cover floors an' things."

The day of the great paper-chase had arrived. The Three Musketeers, Jimmy, Bobby and most of their friends were to take part in it, and, as Roger said, the great difficulty was paper.

"*Tell* you what!" said Jimmy, eager to prove his fitness to be included in their council. "There's a lot of old newspapers in that t-tin trunk in the boxroom."

Investigation proved that Jimmy was right.

"Gosh, yes!" said Roger. "An' they're years before the war. No one'll want them. Let's tear them up."

They tore them up, and the paper-chase started. It was the most successful paper-chase they had ever had, lasting so long that it was Jimmy's bedtime when they reached home. Roger gave his mother a detailed account of it, but she seemed distrait and absent-minded.

"Your Uncle Peter's coming to stay tomorrow, you know, dear," she said, "and there's a lot to see to."

Later he heard his father and mother discussing the visitor.

"I suppose his chief interests are still boxing and the black North," smiled his father.

"Oh yes," said his mother. "He still means to write that book on boxing miners that he's been planning for years. Famous Boxing Colliers, he wants to call it. He left all the material with me, you know, when he went abroad. Stacks of old newspapers with accounts of every match that any miner had ever taken part in. I thought I'd put them all in that old tin trunk in the boxroom, but I've just looked and they're not there. I must have a good hunt for them tomorrow."

Roger was very thoughtful for the rest of the evening, and the next morning he called his band together.

"We've got to c'lect all those bits of newspaper we used in the paper-chase an' stick 'em together," he said. "Uncle peter wants 'em for writing a book on Boxing Colliers an' we *got* to get 'em back."

The gang scattered over woods and fields, but it had rained heavily in the night, and such pieces of paper as could be found were sodden and indecipherable.

Charles found an almost complete letter from a reader who had been cured of rheumatism by carrying a nutmeg in his pocket, and Toothy carefully pieced together what turned out to be instructions for making a tea cosy out of old gloves, while Bill found a fragment with the two words "seconds" and "hands" still decipherable, which might have applied either to a watch or a boxing match . . . but otherwise their search was in vain . . .

Again they assembled in the tool shed to discuss plans of action.

"Well, we've lost his old newspapers, so we've got to get him some more," said Roger.

"How can we?" said Bill.

"I've still got some we haven't looked through yet," said Charles, bringing a sodden pulp of paper from his pocket.

"Well, we'll look through them," said Charles, "an'" – his eye swept round the circle – "Jimmy can go down to the second-hand shop an' buy some more old newspapers. They're sure to have some. How much money have we got?"

Pockets were turned out, pennies and halfpennies separated from bits of string, lumps of putty, marbles, grimy handkerchiefs and penknives and poured out into the wheelbarrow.

"Tenpence halfpenny," said Roger. "Well, we ought to get some jolly good old newspapers for that. Bring all they've got, Jim. Old ones. Before the war, remember."

Jimmy took the tenpence halfpenny and set off to the village. He spent a few minutes gazing through the window of the junk shop at the fascinating jumble of skates, gas brackets, venetian blinds, croquet mallets and oil lamps that filled the window. Then he entered the shop. The proprietor happened to be out and the new assistant – an earnest ambitious youth of fifteen, who had recently read a book on Salesmanship and had made a resolution that no customer should go away empty-handed – was in charge of the shop.

"What can I do for you?" he said to Jimmy in his most impressive manner.

Jimmy poured out his collection of coins on the counter.

"I want tenpence halfpenny worth of old newspapers, please," he said.

The youth looked a little – just a little – startled.

"We haven't any at the moment," he said, quickly recovering himself. "What do you want them for?"

Jimmy considered, realising how extremely vague he was on the subject.

"I want them for a man that wants to write a b-b-book about them," he said at last.

"A book about old newspapers?" said the boy.

"N-not exactly," said Jimmy. He paused, wrinkling his brows as he tried to remember the elusive title of Uncle Peter's book. "Something abut collar boxes," he said at last.

"Collar boxes?" said the boy. "People don't write books about collar boxes."

"He does," said Jimmy, deciding to take a firm line.

"He must be bats, then," said the boy, also deciding to take a firm line.

"Well, he may be," admitted Jimmy, "but that's what he wants to do. He wants to write a book about—" Something of his certainty faded. "It began with coll—, anyway."

The boy brightened as wider fields opened out before him. He began to turn over a pile of books.

"*Treatment of Colitis*?" he said hopefully.

Jimmy shook his head.

"I'm sure it wasn't that."

"*Our Colonies*?" said the boy, scattering the books far and wide in his search. "*The Colorado Beetle*? *Famous Colleges*? *Collotype*?"

Jimmy shook his head at each.

"It *must* be one of them," said the young salesman, trying not to lose patience. "*Life of Coleridge*? How's that?"

Again Jimmy shook his head.

"Dogs?" said the boy. "We've got several books about dogs and they're bound to mention collies . . ."

"I'm sure it wasn't collies," said Jimmy, trying to dispel

the mists of confusion that were growing thicker and thicker around him.

"I've got a dog collar," said the youth, with a burst of inspiration, bringing one out from between a fire extinguisher without a top and a saucepan without a bottom.

"I don't think it was a dog collar," said Jimmy.

"Well, look here," said the young salesman persuasively, "Let's forget it. I've got some wonderful bargains for tenpence halfpenny. If you want a book, here's a *Life of Florence Nightingale*. Part of it's missing, but that all to the good, because it must have been far too long to start with. It's been a good book. Look! It once belonged to someone in London, W.I. Well, that speaks for itself, doesn't it? And if you don't want a book— Well, what would you like?" He waved his hand in a sweeping gesture round the shop. "Everything comes in useful sooner or later, if you keep your weather eye open."

Jimmy's confusion was approaching nightmare proportions. He clung to his first conviction as a drowning man clings to a spar.

"No," he said. "It was something about a collar box . . ."

The boy dived suddenly into a pile of junk on the floor and emerged triumphant.

"Well, here *is* one," he said. "That's a piece of luck, isn't it? The boss said I could price things how I liked, so you can have it for tenpence halfpenny. It's been a good one."

Jimmy inspected the battered discoloured leather receptacle, frowning judicially.

"It's a b-bit squashed up, isn't it?" he said.

"That's because it's empty," said the boy. "Look, I'll fill

it up with something, and you'll see the difference."

He turned to a pile of tattered engravings that lay on the floor behind the door. "The boss said this stuff was unsaleable and might as well go as salvage, so I'll use it to fill the box and you'll see the difference."

He took up a handful of engravings, rolled them round and put them into the collar box. It stood up drunkenly, looking more battered and discoloured than ever. "There!" he said. "Good as new, isn't it? Well, nearly, anyway . . . Tenpence halfpenny. *Thank* you. *Good* morning."

And Jimmy found himself on the pavement outside, holding his collar box, his heart full of bewilderment and misgiving. He was so bewildered that he hardly knew what had happened or how it had happened, but he did know that he'd been sent out to buy old newspapers and that he was coming home with a collar box. Slowly, draggingly, apprehensively, he entered the tool shed, where the Three Musketeers were awaiting him.

"Uncle Peter's come," said Roger urgently. "Have you got the newspapers?"

"N-n-no," admitted Jimmy. He held out the collar box. "I g-got this inst-instead."

They stared at him with incredulous horror.

"Do you mean to say," said Roger sternly, "that—"

Then Uncle Peter entered the tool shed. He was a large genial man with kindly grey eyes.

"There you are, kids!" he said. He looked at the collar box. "Hello, what's that?"

"It's a c-collar box," said Jimmy.

"So I see," said Uncle Peter, "but what's it for?"

"It's for y-you," said Jimmy desperately. "It's inst-instead of old n-newspapers."

"IT'S FOR Y-YOU," SAID JIMMY DESPERATELY.
"IT'S INST-INSTEAD OF OLD NEWSPAPERS."

Uncle Peter took it and opened it. He drew out the engravings and examined them. Then he dropped all but one and gave a shout of delight.

"Good Lord! It's the fight between Ramsbottom and Greenhalsh in 1892. I've been hunting for it for years for the frontispiece of my book. I'll buy it from you. How much do you want for it?"

"Tenpence halfpenny," said Jimmy with a great relief at his heart.

Uncle Peter gave a bellow of laughter.

"I'll give you more than that," he said.

Roger cleared his throat.

"Those newspapers," he said with a gulp, "that you gave to Mother to keep for you—"

"Oh, those!" said Uncle Peter. "Dunno why I asked her to keep them. I'd made notes of everything I wanted. No, this engraving's all I need. And I say! We'll celebrate the occasion. I'll take all you boys up to London to the pantomime. I'll go and get the tickets now."

He was gone. They heard him whistling his way to the house.

The four boys stared first at each other then at Jimmy.

"How did you know he wanted it, Jimmy?" said Roger at last.

"I d-d-didn't," said Jimmy. "But," airily, "everything c-comes in useful sooner or l-later, if you keep your eye open on the weather."

# Chapter 29

## Sandy Does His Turn

Roger and Jimmy stood on the lawn watching Sandy, who was engaged in his favourite pursuit of trying to persuade Henry to come out of his shell and have a romp.

"We'll have to polish up his tricks again," said Roger, frowning thoughtfully, "an' we might teach him a few more."

It was the day of the local Flower Show, and at the end of the proceedings there was to be a short sketch, called "Robin Hood," written by Miss Pettigrew and acted by the children, followed by a children's Dog Show. Roger was figuring in both events, as he was taking the part of Robin Hood in the play and had entered Sandy for the "most intelligent mongrel" competition.

"There's that trick of walkin' on his hind legs," he said, "with us walkin' with him and holdin' a paw each. He does that jolly well. And there's beggin'. He does that all right if you hold the biscuit right over his head."

"Yes," agreed Jimmy, "an' there's that one where he jumps through a hoop. We've only got to make him see there's no other way of gettin' out an' he jumps through it all right. An' there's that tightrope walkin' one we were goin' to teach him."

"Yes . . ." said Roger. "Gosh! I wish there was a rattin' competition."

For Sandy's greatest accomplishment was ratting. He would bring the mangled remains of his victims from field or ditch and lay them proudly at the feet of any members of the family he could find. If he couldn't find anyone, he left them in conspicuous places as trophies of his skill and prowess. Mrs Manning had had to accustom herself to finding them on her drawing room carpet, outside her bedroom door, on the bathroom mat. Sandy's obvious confidence that their pride and delight would equal his own, made it difficult for even Mrs Manning to be cross with him.

"Well, now, look here," went on Roger. "I've got to go and rehearse this old Robin Hood thing, an' then I've got to go straight down to the Show, so you an' Bobby mus' look after Sandy an' bring him along in time for the competition. He was washed yesterday, so mind you don't let him get dirty. You can make him practise his tricks till it's time to go down to the field."

"Yes," said Jimmy earnestly. "We'll d-do that."

Roger went off to his rehearsals, and Jimmy and Bobby set to work on the last-minute training of their candidate. The responsibility, they felt, was a heavy one, but Sandy seemed unaware of the importance of the occasion. He leapt about exuberantly; he worried a doormat and one of the verandah cushions; he scattered a pile of seed boxes; he threw Mr Manning's gardening boots high into the air and chased them round in circles; he tried to play tennis, with Henry as the ball.

"*Stop* it, Sandy," said Jimmy sternly. "We've got to *w-work* this afternoon."

Even that failed to check Sandy's exuberance. Faced with his Jumping Through a Hoop trick, he showed such ingenuity in finding other exits than the hoop from his improvised prison that Jimmy and Bobby finally gave up the attempt in despair. Instead of begging for his biscuit, he jumped up for it, and fell over backwards. He knew by some uncanny instinct when his Walking on his Hind Legs trick was coming and eluded all attempts at capture.

"Well, it isn't any good tryin' that tightrope trick," said Jimmy despairingly. "He'd only chew the rope up before we'd started . . . *Tell* you what!"

"Yes?" said Bobby.

"Let's take him for a walk. It'll sort of tire him a bit. Then we can start trainin' him when we come in. There's lots of time."

The three set out of the gate and down the road. For a few minutes Sandy trotted decorously and happily behind them while they discussed the tightrope trick.

"We'll start with the rope on the ground an' we'll put a biscuit half-way along an'—" He turned round. Sandy was nowhere to be seen.

"Sandy!" he called.

Almost immediately Sandy emerged from the ditch and leapt up at them, waving his tail as if congratulating himself on his prompt obedience. They stood and stared at him in dismay. The bottom of the ditch was full of mud and Sandy had evidently burrowed so wholeheartedly in it that he was covered – face, body, tail and legs – in black slime.

"Gosh!" said Bobby. "We can't take him to the show like that."

"No," said Jimmy. "We'll have to wash him."

He spoke doubtfully. Sandy was not an easy washing subject, and the operation had always been performed previously by Mr or Mrs Manning. This afternoon Mr

Manning was at the office, and Mrs Manning was on duty in the tea tent at the Flower Show.

"We'll j-jus' *have* to," he said. "It mus' be p-possible. I've seen them do it. You jus' p-put him in water an' s-soap him."

Sandy accompanied them home, waving his tail complacently, as if he had done all that could possibly be expected of a dog. They went into the kitchen, where Bobby half-filled the sink with water, while Jimmy secured Sandy and put him in. Then together they began to soap him. Sandy was at first unexpectedly docile, standing in the sink, panting and grinning and trying to lick Jimmy's face whenever it came within range.

"We mus' be careful not to let the soap get in his eyes," said Bobby. "We'd better not wash his face."

"We've *got* to wash it," said Jimmy. "It's all over black. I'll do it very c-carefully."

They never knew whether it was the soap or the dog's natural exuberance, but, before either of them realised what was happening, Sandy had wrenched himself from their not very secure grasp and was streaking off – sleek and shining with soap – through the open kitchen door into the garden. Mr Manning had mown the lawn the night before and a heap of grass cuttings lay on top of the rubbish heap. On to this Sandy hurled himself, rolling about in a frantic effort to rid himself of the obnoxious substance that covered him. Then – coated all over with grass cuttings – he shot like an arrow from a bow out of the gate and down the road.

"*Crumbs!*" gasped Bobby.

"We'll have to f-find him," said Jimmy, pale with horror. "We'll have to f-find him an' f-finish w-washin' him."

BEFORE EITHER OF THEM REALISED WHAT WAS HAPPENING, SANDY
HAD WRENCHED HIMSELF FROM THEIR NOT VERY SECURE GRASP.

But Sandy seemed to have vanished completely. A
search of the village and the gardens of all their friends
revealed no trace of him. With sinking hearts they made
their way to the field where the Flower Show was in
progress.

"We'll have a g-good look round," said Jimmy, "an' if
we can't find him I s-s'pose we'll have to t-tell Roger."

It was Bobby who met Roger coming out of the tent
where the children were changing for the Robin Hood
play. He wore a green tunic and his ordinary school
shorts.

"Sandy all right?" he asked anxiously.

"He was when I saw him last," said Bobby, temporis-
ing.

Roger nodded as if relieved.

"Did you put him through his tricks?"

"Yes, we – we tried to," said Bobby.

"Where is he now?"

Bobby gulped.

"I think Jimmy's bringing him."

"I hope he won't be late," said Roger.

Then someone called him in to finish changing, and Bobby went off to find Jimmy. He met him coming out of the vegetable tent.

"I c-can't find him," said Jimmy. "I've l-looked everywhere."

At that point a bell warned them of the opening of the Robin Hood play and they wandered disconsolately over to the roped-in space at the end of the field, where it was to take place.

"We'd better tell Roger when he's finished acting," said Jimmy.

The play began well enough. Roger, wearing his Robin Hood costume, came on with a motley collection of Merrie Men and there followed a desultory conversation on the delights of Outlaw life, in which the prompter took a prominent part. Then Roger, looking in the direction of the tent, said: "Here comes Maid Marion in her kirtle of green, bearing a goodly repast." And no Maid Marion appeared, for the small child who was taking the part (Sally was away) had succumbed to stage fright and was sobbing hysterically in her mother's arms, deaf to Miss Pettigrew's admonitions and the pleas of a circle of aunts and grandmothers.

Roger repeated his line and still nothing happened. Frowning impatiently, he repeated it again. And then something did happen. Through the hedge just behind him came Sandy, still covered with grass cuttings, creeping abjectly, every line of his body expressing contrition and apology. He knew that he had behaved outrageously. He had refused to do his tricks. He had escaped from his bath. He had gone off, rampaging over the countryside, on his own. But he brought a gift that, he was sure, would win him pardon. Still cringing abjectly, tail waving slowly and deprecatingly, he laid his rat at Roger's feet. There was a burst of clapping from the audience, and Sandy leapt round to face it, knowing himself forgiven, tail waving wildly, head on one side, grinning his foolish friendly grin, as if acknowledging the applause.

Roger looked round for Jimmy and Bobby, but they were not there. They were busy putting as much distance as possible between them and the scene of their disgrace.

# Chapter 30

## *The Little Jade Horse*

Jimmy and Bobby were sauntering idly through the village. It was not often that time hung heavily on their hands, but it did this afternoon. School started next week, and they were in a sort of no man's land between holidays and school . . . They had successfully carried out all the plans they had made for the holidays (they had even crawled along the bed of the stream where it went under the road, emerging triumphant but almost unrecognisable) and it didn't seem worthwhile making any further plans. Roger had gone to spend the night with a godmother and life seemed just a little flat. Passing Miss Pettigrew's cottage, they felt, might provide some diversion, and any diversion was better than none. The only diversion it provided, however, was the sight of the front door opening and Miss Tressider emerging from it. Miss Pettigrew stood in the doorway taking leave of her.

"Goodbye, dear," they heard Miss Pettigrew say. "It's been so nice to see you."

"Good-bye," said Miss Tressider. "I'll bring that recipe tomorrow."

Jimmy and Bobby hovered at the gate till Miss Tressider reached it.

"Have you had nice holidays?" said Miss Tressider.

"Yes, thanks" said Jimmy. "They g-go too quickly."

"I know," sighed Miss Tressider. "They're gone before they've started. Tell me all you've done."

They told her all they'd done, with those slight recon-stuctions of actual facts that were perhaps inevitable in the circumstances, glossing over failures and humilia-tions, omitting the setbacks and ignominious endings that marked so many of their exploits. Miss Tressider's interest and admiration were gratifying. They began to swagger a little, to add shameless embroideries to the never very plain fabric of their stories . . .

"We went to the sea an' climbed a cliff an' got cut off by the tide."

"We had to risk our lives gettin' away."

"We went to a fair an' we were nearly attacked by a lion. It was jolly savage. We were as near as we are to you an' the bars looked thin as thin."

"An' we were set on by a dog yesterday. I bet it was a bloodhound."

"We only jus' got away with our lives."

"An' las' week . . ."

In the middle of one of Jimmy's stories Miss Tressider stopped outside the second-hand shop at the end of the village.

"Well, I have to go in here," she said, "so I'll leave you now."

But Jimmy and Bobby didn't want to be left by her. They were tired of each other's company and found her an unusually satisfactory audience.

"Can we come in, too?" said Jimmy.

"If you like," said Miss Tressider, going in at the shop door.

Jimmy and Bobby followed her. They were always glad of an excuse for going into the junk shop. It was an

Aladdin's Cave of treasures, treasures whose battered and incomplete condition seemed to endow them with a fascination that the perfect article would have lacked. Leaving Miss Tressider to approach the counter, where Mr Prosser, the proprietor, peered at her short-sightedly over a pair of steel-rimmed spectacles, balanced precariously on the end of his nose, they began to burrow in a pile of junk behind the door. Bobby was just devising a new form of transport from a roller skate and a broken ski, when Jimmy, tiring suddenly of the whole situation, joined Miss Tressider at the counter. She had taken a small green horse from her bag and handed it to Mr Prosser.

"It's jade," she said. "My aunt left it to me and I don't really want it. I'd rather sell it and buy something I really want. How much would you give me for it?"

Mr Prosser took the little horse and examined it through a magnifying glass.

"It's got a little chip on its ear," said Miss Tressider. "Otherwise it's all right."

"It's very nice," said Mr Prosser. "Very nice indeed. I have a client who's interested in jade, so if I may keep it for a day or two—"

"Certainly," said Miss Tressider. "I'll call in at the end of the week."

She went out of the shop, still accompanied by Jimmy and Bobby. Walking one on each side of her, they continued their interrupted duet of self-glorification till they reached the gate of her cottage, where slowly and reluctantly they took their leave of her.

It was the next afternoon that Jimmy heard his mother say to his father, "Miss Pettigrew's had that valuable little jade figure stolen yesterday. I always told her it was foolish of her to keep it on her drawing room mantel-piece."

Pale with horror, Jimmy ran across the road to tell the news to Bobby.

"She mus' be a thief, Bobby," he said. "She mus' have s-stolen that jade thing from Miss Pettigrew when she went to t-tea there yesterday. Gosh! She was silly to take it to Mr Prosser an' pretend that an aunt had l-left it to her. The p'lice'll find it there an' he'll tell them she t-took it an' she'll get put in p-prison."

"She doesn't look like a thief," said Bobby slowly.

"They don't," said Jimmy with an air of wisdom. "They've g-got to look like good people or they'd get c-caught. Anyway, even if she is a thief, she's our f-friend an' we've got to help her. She was jolly d-decent to us yesterday."

"Yes, she was," agreed Bobby, "listening to all those things we told her an' being interested an' – an' all the time they weren't abs'lutely true."

"It *did* look a jolly savage lion," said Jimmy.

"Well, we knew the dog wasn't a bloodhound an' we weren't cut off by the tide."

"It was the same as bein' cut off by the tide. Well, nearly the same."

"It wasn't quite, anyway."

"Well, never mind," said Jimmy. "We can't waste time arguin'. It's a matter of life an' death an' we've got to do somethin' quick to help her. Anyway, if she goes to prison we m-might have ole Squashy to teach us Arithmetic, an' he can see when you c-count on your fingers." He was silent for a few moments, then said: "*Tell* you what!"

"Yes?" said Bobby.

"We'll go to Mr Prosser's shop an' take it back an' put it on Miss Pettigrew's mantelpiece, an' then it'll be all r-right an' Miss Tressider won't be a thief any longer."

Bobby considered this.

"No, but *we* will," he said.

"No, we won't," said Jimmy. "It doesn't b-belong to Mr Prosser, so it's wrong for him to k-keep it, so it's right for us to take it away."

Bobby wrestled with this problem in silence for a few moments, then abandoned it as beyond his comprehension.

"All right," he said,. "When shall we start?"

"Now," said Jimmy. "How much money have we got?"

Bobby took his money from his pocket and counted it.

"Two halfpennies an' half a Canadian stamp an' a coin someone brought me from abroad," he said. "It's about a tenth of a penny."

"Well, that doesn't count," said Jimmy, turning out his own pockets. "I've got two halfpennies too, an' half a bad half-crown that someone g-gave me an' that doesn't count either. I've got a ninepenny bus ticket, too, but it's used, so I s'pose it's no good."

"That makes tuppence between us," said Bobby. "What'll we do with it?"

"We'll go to the shop," said Jimmy, "an' you buy something for t-tuppence, an' while you're doin' it I'll get Miss Tressider's horse, an' then we'll take it back to Miss Pettigrew."

"Yes," said Bobby doubtfully. It all sounded so much simpler than he felt it was going to turn out to be.

Feeling slightly apprehensive, they entered Mr Prosser's shop. Mr Prosser, who appeared at first to be marooned in a sea of Venetian blind slats and gas brackets, came forward, peering at them over his steel-rimmed spectacles.

"And what can I do for you?" he said, pausing to lift an 1890 model phonograph from the floor and put it onto a 1900 model bamboo table.

"P-please have you got anything for tuppence?" said Jimmy.

"What sort of thing?" said Mr Prosser.

"Anything," said Bobby.

Few things surprised Mr Prosser, but he looked slightly surprised by this.

"Don't you mind what it is?" he said.

"No," said Jimmy.

Mr Prosser waved his hand to a cardboard box that bore a notice: "Everything here 2d."

"You go through them, Bobby," said Jimmy, "an' I'll have a l-look round."

Bobby burrowed in the cardboard box, while Jimmy edged his way to the shelf where he could see the little jade horse. Mr Prosser was concentrating his attention on Bobby. The phenomenon of a small boy wanting to spend tuppence and not caring what he bought with it puzzled and interested him.

"You really don't know what you want?" he said.

"No," said Bobby, taking up a photograph of a buxom woman in a tight-fitting evening dress and putting it back again. "Anything'll do."

"You really don't care what you buy?" said Mr Prosser with increasing surprise.

"No," said Bobby.

"Curious," said Mr Prosser. "Most curious . . . I have a nice cricket bat for one-and-six. The handle's missing, but with a little ingenuity—"

JIMMY EDGED HIS WAY TO THE SHELF . . .

"No, thank you," said Bobby, "we've only got tuppence."

Jimmy joined them. He looked very flushed, and, glancing round, Bobby saw that the jade horse had gone from the shelf. He dived into the box, took out an egg cosy, unevenly knitted in an execrable shade of purple, thrust twopence into Mr Prosser's hand and plunged from the shop, followed by Jimmy.

"Gosh!" he panted, "it was awful!"

"Well, we've done it," said Jimmy. "Now all we've g-got to do is make some excuse for goin' to see Miss P-Pettigrew an' put it back on her mantelpiece when she isn't lookin'."

"What excuse shall we make?" said Bobby.

"We'll think of it on the way," said Jimmy.

Like Bobby, he was beginning to realise the magnitude of the task they had so lightly undertaken.

He still hadn't thought of the excuse when he stood on

Miss Pettigrew's doorstep and rang the bell. Inspiration only came when Miss Pettigrew herself opened the door and looked at him inquiringly.

"P-please, can you t-tell us the t-time?" he said.

Miss Pettigrew looked round vaguely.

"The hall clock's wrong," she said, "but I think the drawing room clock's right."

She went into the drawing room, followed by Jimmy and Bobby. The parrot greeted them with a sardonic "miaow", but what held them spellbound with amazement was a cake of almost incredible magnificence that stood on the tea-table. It had layers of cream, thick icing and sugar decorations.

"Yes, isn't it wonderful!" smiled Miss Pettigrew, "Miss Tressider and I were discussing pre-war recipes yesterday and I asked her to come in today so that she could taste my masterpiece. I'll have to starve for months, of course, to make up for it. Well, now you're here, you must stay and share it . . . Oh, here's Miss Tressider."

While she went to the door, Jimmy slipped the jade horse on to the mantelpiece. His face was set and tense, but there was a great relief at his heart. All was well now. Miss Tressider was saved . . .

She entered, and she, too, gave a gasp as she saw the cake.

"I simply can't believe my eyes," she said. "But, first of all, have you had any news of your jade goddess?"

"Oh, yes," said Miss Pettigrew. "I've just heard that they've caught the thief. Did you sell your jade horse, by the way?"

"Mr Prosser thinks—" began Miss Tressider, then her eyes went to the mantelpiece and her mouth fell open.

"Did you buy it?" she said faintly.

Miss Pettigrew's eyes followed her friends, and her mouth, too, fell open.

"No," she gasped, "I've never set eyes on it till now since you showed it to me yesterday."

"How on earth did it get here?" said Miss Tressider.

"Well, I know it wasn't here before these boys came," said Miss Pettigrew. "I know it wasn't." She looked at Jimmy. "Can you explain it, Jimmy?"

Jimmy gulped and swallowed.

"Yes," he said, "but it'll take rather a l-long time. C-can I have a piece of cake first, please?"

## Chapter 31

# A Bid for Fame

"I'd like to be f-famous before I grow old," said Jimmy, a note of anxiety in his voice.

"Well, you're not old yet," said Bobby.

"No, but I'm getting on," said Jimmy. "I'm s-seven. I'd be m-middle-aged if I was a dog."

"Well, you're not a dog," said Bobby.

The two were walking along the path by the river, idly kicking into the water such stones as lay in their way.

"Anyway, how could you be famous?" said Bobby after a short silence. "I bet I can kick that stone right across to the other bank."

"I bet you can't. There! I knew you c-couldn't. I could s-save someone's life or invent somethin' or f-find an undiscovered country. There's l-lots of ways of gettin' famous."

"Well, everyone can't be famous," said Bobby. "There's got to be some . . . some infamous ones."

"I know, but I w-want to be one of the famous ones."

"Well, how'll you start?"

"I'd like to start by s-savin' someone's life. I've always w-wanted to save someone's life."

"Yes, but you've got to have a fire or a shipwreck to do that, an' there aren't any round here."

"You n-needn't," said Jimmy, kicking at a stone and

missing it. "I once read a story about a man that got a let-ter in a b-bottle washed up by the sea an' it was from a man that was in d-deadly peril an'—" He stopped short, staring at the ground. "Gosh! L-look!" he said.

There on the edge of the river bank, just near his feet, lay a bottle.

"It mus' have been washed up by the river," he said excitedly. "I b-bet there's a letter in it."

"I bet there isn't," said Bobby.

Jimmy took the cork out and looked inside.

"There is," he said in an awestruck voice. "There's a l-letter in it."

He drew out a piece of paper and unfolded it.

"Look!" he said with a gasp. "It begins with 'sos'. That means danger. SOS means danger."

"Then 'bank'," said Bobby. "What does that mean?"

"Let's go on to the next," said Jimmy. "P'raps it'll t-tell us."

"All right." The two heads bent over the paper. "It says '1s.' an' then on the next line 'land'."

"I say! That's 'island'," said Jimmy.

"Why did he write it in halves?"

"I 'spect he was too w-worried to think prop'ly. What's the n-nex' word?"

"It looks like p-e-r-r-i-l."

"That's 'peril'. Gosh! It *is* from someone in d-deadly danger. What's the nex' word?"

" 'Quick'."

"That's the m-message, then. 'SOS Bank. Island. Peril. Quick.' It's from someone in peril on the bank of an island an' they w-want help quick."

They stared at each other, open-mouthed.

"But there isn't an island anywhere round here."

"Yes, there is," said Jimmy. "There's one in the m-middle of the river opposite that house where Sir George Bellwater lives."

"Yes, but it belongs to him," said Bobby, "an' he's mad if anyone goes there."

"Well, we can't help that," said Jimmy. "It's a m-matter of life an' d-death. There's someone there on the b-bank in d-deadly peril that wants help quick. We're goin' to save someone's life at last. Come on."

Doubtfully, apprehensively, Bobby accompanied his friend along the river path till they reached the hedge that bounded the spacious grounds of Sir George Bellwater's house.

"We'll have to go through his g-garden," said Jimmy. "There's no other way of getting to the island."

"We'll get in an awful row if he catches us," said Bobby.

"Well, we c-can't help that," said Jimmy. "I keep t-telling you it's a matter of life an' d-death."

They scrambled through the hedge onto a lawn that swept down to the river and, keeping in the shelter of the hedge, made their way to the ornamental bridge that led from the garden to the wooded island. There they stood, looking round them uncertainly.

"I don't hear any cries for help," said Bobby.

"I hope we aren't t-too late," said Jimmy anxiously. "P'raps the w-worst has happened."

"Look!" said Bobby excitedly. "I can see someone on the bank. Over there. On the other side."

"Quick, then!" said Jimmy.

They plunged through the undergrowth and hurled themselves on the man who sat, ensconced among the bushes on the further side of the island, holding a fishing rod.

"We g-got your bottle," shouted Jimmy. "We've come to s-save you."

Sir George Bellwater rose with a bellow of rage, for the tempestuous arrival of the two had disturbed the first suspicion of a nibble that he'd had all day.

"Bottle indeed!" he roared. "I'll bottle you! . . . I'll teach you to come trespassing . . . disturbing the fish . . . playing the fool . . ."

Sir George Bellwater was a notoriously irascible man. He flung himself after them through the bushes, obviously determined to execute summary justice upon them.

"Wait till I get hold of you, you little devils!" he bellowed. "I'll make an example of you . . . I'll put an end to this trespassing once and for all."

Jimmy and Bobby fled in terror, scrambling through thick undergrowth, through bogs, over boulders. Once or

"WE G-GOT YOUR BOTTLE," SHOUTED JIMMY. "WE'VE COME TO S-SAVE YOU."

twice Sir George almost caught them, but at last they escaped across the bridge, and Sir George, muttering savagely to himself, returned to his interrupted fishing.

In the safety of the river path the two stood and faced each other – panting, dishevelled, almost speechless with terror and exertion.

"It couldn't have been him that sent it," said Bobby at last.

"No," gasped Jimmy. "We were t-too late, after all. The worst mus' have happened."

"What worst?" said Bobby.

"The m-man that sent the letter wasn't Sir George Bellwater, an' there was no one else there, so I b-bet Sir George Bellwater had killed the m-man that wrote the letter. I bet he'd started killin' him when he wrote it, an' that's why he s-said 'quick'."

"I don't think Sir George Bellwater can be a murderer," said Bobby. "He opened the Church Bazaar las' month."

"That's the s-sort of thing m-murderers do," said Jimmy earnestly, "to p-put people off the scent. He c-carried on jus' like a murderer. I b-bet he was fright-ened of us f-findin' the body."

"Well, what are we goin' to do?" said Bobby.

Jimmy considered.

"We'll have to get Scotland Yard to h-help," he said at last.

"We can't," said Bobby. "We don't know where it is."

Jimmy sighed.

"No . . . I'm afraid I'll have to ask my m-mother. I'd wanted to do it without g-grown-ups, but I think we'll have to t-tell her about it. Come on."

Bursting into Mrs Manning's drawing room a few minutes later, they found several of her friends having tea with her. A small stout woman was talking animatedly.

"I always make out a shopping list and I always lose it. I thought I'd make sure of it this morning, so I put it inside a bottle I was taking to the grocer's for vinegar, and – you'll hardly believe it." She chuckled. "I lost the bottle."

"How did you manage that?" said Mrs Manning.

"I went by the river path, and I just put my basket down to rearrange the things in it and – I must have left the bottle there."

"What was on your l-list?" said Jimmy.

She looked at him in some surprise.

"Well, fancy you being interested, Jimmy." She said kindly. "First of all there was sausages. I always put 'sos' for those. A sort of joke with myself, you know. Then I had to call at the bank. Then I had to get one sweet ration, for Johnny. I put '1s.' for that. Then I had to call for the lard. The man forgot to leave it with the other things yesterday. Then I had to get a pencil. I'd lost mine."

"Oh, was it 'pencil'?" said Jimmy blankly.

"Yes, dear, pencil. Then I had to call at the nursery-man's to order some plants, because my husband wants to grow a Quick hedge round the kitchen garden. I remembered them all but the lard. Anyway," again she chuckled, "I write so badly that often, even if I've got the list, I can't read a word of it. You see, Jimmy—"

But Jimmy was no longer there. He was in the garden, hands in pockets, gazing morosely in front of him.

"All that t-trouble for nothin'," he was saying bitterly.

"Never mind," said Bobby. "There's still inventin' something or findin' an undiscovered country."

Jimmy shook his head.

"I bet those would be w-wash outs, too," he said. "No, I think I'll jus' have to go on bein' infamous."

## Chapter 32

# The Fire Fighter

The usual morning procession of children was making its way down the road where the Mannings lived.

First went Roger, Charles and Bill, their satchels over their shoulders, discussing the weighty affairs of the world in which they lived. Occasionally they unbent so far as to scuffle, kick stones, or investigate something in the ditch, but on the whole their progress had a certain dignity, as befitted the advanced ages of eleven, eleven and a half, and twelve-next-month.

After them came Jimmy and Bobby, also with satchels over their shoulders, also stopping occasionally to scuffle, kick stones, and investigate ditches with seven-year-old abandon unhindered by any attempt at dignity.

The two groups ignored each other, or rather the first group ignored the second. Roger and Jimmy lived together at home in comparative friendliness; but, from the moment they set out for school in the morning till the moment they returned, Jimmy, in Roger's eyes, did not exist. He passed him in the school playground as if he had never seen him before. If Jimmy so far forgot himself as to speak to him, Roger answered shortly or not at all. It was, of course, a surface disregard. Actually, Roger was aware of almost everything Jimmy said or did at school throughout the day – aware with an acute and intense anxiety lest Jimmy's youth and foolishness should expose him or the school to ignominy and contempt.

Till this term things had gone fairly smoothly – Jimmy, despite his youth and foolishness, had so far brought no real discredit on his elder brother – but this term the situation had become more complicated. For next door to St Adrian's was a small kindergarten school, whose pupils were looked on by the pupils of St Adrian's as the lowest form of life, and to this school Araminta Palmer had just been admitted. Roger had given Jimmy strict injunctions to have no dealings with her of any kind.

"You know what she is, Jim," he had said. "She'll try to talk to you goin' to school an'" – his face stiffened with horror – "she might even try to talk to you through the hedge when you're in the playground at school. You've got to take no notice. We can't have St Adrian's people talking to kids in a kindergarten. You do understand, don't you?"

"Yes," said Jimmy, his heart sinking as he contemplated the narrow and slippery plank of social behaviour that he must now tread. He disliked Araminta, but he was a boy who found it difficult not to respond to friendly advances of any kind, and Araminta, though her advances were sometimes far from friendly, generally managed to attach herself to him. The first day was all right, because her mother took her. The second day was all right, because her aunt took her. But this was the third day, and Araminta was now going to school alone, clasping her battered, moth-eaten toy monkey, Sinbad, in her arms. At first she had tried to join Jimmy and Bobby.

"I'll cub with you if you like," she had said condescendingly.

"Well, we don't like," Jimmy had replied, aware that

Roger had turned round and was watching him with a frown. "We don't want you."

"I dode care," said Araminta a little disconsolately. "I dode want you."

But she had persisted in trying to walk with them till Jimmy, driven to ruthlessness by the knowledge that Roger was still watching him, had pushed her unceremoniously to their rear. And there she stayed, walking slowly down the road, forming, with Sinbad, the third group of the procession. But not in silence.

"You're a dasty udkide boy," she said, raising her voice, "ad I wouldn't walk with you dow even if you asked be to."

"Well, I told you we d-didn't want you," said Jimmy, speaking almost in a whisper, because Roger, hearing their voices, had turned round again.

"Ad I tode you I didn't wad you," said Araminta with spirit. "I'b walkig with Sidbad. I'd sooder have Sidbad thad you ady day."

"Well, don't talk to us," said Jimmy.

"You card stop be talkig," said Araminta.

Jimmy made no answer.

"Your stockigs are right dowd over your shoes," said Araminta.

Jimmy looked down.

"They're not," he said.

"I bade you say subthig," said Araminta with quiet triumph.

Roger had turned again to frown at Jimmy. Jimmy gazed self-consciously at the trees, avoiding his eye.

"You've got your cap od back to front," said Araminta.

Jimmy felt it.

"I haven't," he said.

"I bade you say subthig agaid," said Araminta.

"Shut up," said Jimmy.

The uncomfortable journey came to an end at last.

Araminta passed into the portals of Miss Truefit's Kindergarten, leaving Jimmy to walk ten yards at any rate in peace before he entered the portals of St Adrian's.

He tried to avoid Roger as he went to his classroom, but Roger was waiting for him at the door.

"Talking to that kid all the way down!" he said severely.

"I couldn't help it," pleaded Jimmy. "She t-t-talked to me."

It was while he was hunting for caterpillars in the hedge that divided the two schools during "break" that he heard Araminta's urgent "Jibby" from the other side of the hedge. His first impulse was to retreat without answering, but there was something strangely pathetic, almost tearful in the voice, and he hovered uncertainly about the spot.

"What do you want?" he said in a tense whisper.

"Jibby, do cub id ad help be. A dasty boy's beed udkide to be."

Jimmy glanced round apprehensively. The worst had happened. From the other side of the playground Roger was watching him, looking stern and horror-stricken. But still Jimmy couldn't find it in his heart to go away.

"What's he done?" he asked miserably.

"He's taken Sidbad ad put hib od the roof of the studio. I card get him down. Do help be, Jibby."

Jimmy looked through the hedge at the studio. It was a building of corrugated iron, with a flat roof, at the bottom

of the garden. He could see Sinbad perched ignomin-
iously on the top of a stove-pipe.

"Tell one of the b-big ones," he said. "They'll g-get
him down."

"I dode wad to," said Araminta. "I dode like theb. They
laugh at Sidbad. They bake fud of hib."

Jimmy looked round again. He was already so deeply
in disgrace with Roger that nothing he did now could
make any difference. He measured the distance with his
eye and on a sudden impulse squeezed through the
hedge. The coast seemed to be clear. All the other
children were playing at the further end of the lawn. A
garden ladder was placed against a tree conveniently
near the studio.

"Oh, Jibby, you are kide," said Araminta. "You will get
Sidbad down for me, wode you?"

"All right," said Jimmy ungraciously.

"Ad – Jibby."

"Yes?"

"Jibby, he's such a dasty boy. Will you put his 'quariub
up there 'stead of Sidbad?"

"His what?"

"His 'quariub. They let hib keep it id the garden. He
keeps fishes ad things id it. It's here."

Jimmy had approached the studio. Near the door was
a bucket full of water, water weed and small fishes.

"Oh, Jibby, you will, wode you?"

The sight of Araminta, desolate and Sinbadless,
touched Jimmy's tender heart.

"All right," he said. "We've g-got to be quick, though."

He set the ladder against the studio roof and took up
the bucket, glancing at one of the windows as he did so.

"What's all that steam?" he asked.

"They boil kettles ad things," said Araminta carelessly. "Go od, Jibby."

Jimmy went on. Slowly, moving it rung by rung, he carried the bucket up the ladder. Then he put it on the roof, secured Sinbad and threw him down to Araminta.

"Oh, thag you, Jibby," said Araminta. "Jibby . . ."

"Yes?"

"Will you put his bucket *just* where he put Sidbad? *Please*, Jibby."

Jimmy considered. Now that he'd got as far as this, he might as well do the thing in style.

"All right," he said.

He took up the bucket and staggered across the roof

SLOWLY HE CARRIED THE
BUCKET UP THE LADDER.

with it. But there was an open skylight in his way. He hesitated, stumbled, fell headlong, and the bucket emptied itself through the skylight into the room below. He heard a shout. People were running across the lawn. Terrified, he got up, scrambled down the ladder, through the hedge and back to the safe refuge of St Adrian's playground.

He passed the rest of the morning in a nightmare of apprehension, enduring the sarcasm of the history master and the reproaches of Miss Tressider with stony indifference.

At the end of the morning the school assembled in the hall to hear the Headmaster read the usual notices. When he had finished reading them he took a letter from an envelope.

"I have just received a note from Miss Truefit," he said.

Jimmy's heart stopped beating.

"She says," went on the Headmaster, "that she herself inadvertently left a half-smoked cigarette on a table in the studio this morning" – there was a lingering smile of enjoyment on the Headmaster's lips. He had always disliked Miss Truefit – "and that a small fire was started. One of the boys of St Adrian's noticed this, got through the hedge and, finding a bucket of water handy but the door of the studio locked, climbed a ladder and emptied the water through the skylight on to the fire. He disappeared as soon as he saw that regular help was forthcoming, and she does not know who the boy was, but she asks me to thank and congratulate him for her. Now which of you boys was it?"

"It was Jimmy Manning, sir," piped up a small boy at the back. "I saw him do it."

Jimmy looked blankly at the sea of faces round him. He

saw Roger's beaming with pride and pleasure. He blinked and gulped. He opened his mouth to speak, but no words came.

A burst of clapping arose . . .

## Chapter 33

# Christmas Eve

"It's g-getting jolly near Christmas," said Jimmy.

"Yes," agreed Bobby. "It's only about a week off now."

"D'you know . . ." said Jimmy thoughtfully.

"Yes?"

"I'd like to d-do something s-special for Christmas."

"Well, you're going to, aren't you?" said Bobby. "You're going to hang up your stocking an' have turkey."

"Yes, but I m-mean the sort of thing p-people do in b-books," said Jimmy.

"What sort of thing?"

"Well, c-curing misers," said Jimmy.

"What of?" said Bobby.

"Of b-being misers. There's a Shakespeare play about a man called Scrooge who was a m-miser an' he got c-cured by a ghost."

"I don't think it was Shakespeare," said Bobby.

"Well, whoever it w-was," said Jimmy vaguely.

"An' I don't see how you could do it," said Bobby, " 'cause you don't know any misers an' you don't know any ghosts."

"I could d-dress up as a ghost," said Jimmy.

Bobby considered this in silence for a few moments.

"Well, you'd have to get a miser, too," he said at last.

"There mus' be plenty of misers about," said Jimmy. "There are in b-books. Let's have a l-look round."

"All right," agreed Bobby.

The look round proved disappointing, and careful en-quiries in Jimmy's home circle brought no information.

"No, of course there aren't any misers about here, Jimmy," said his mother. "I don't know anyone with any money at all."

Jimmy had almost given up the search when, passing the Vicarage on his way to the village on Monday morn-ing, he saw a sight that made him open his eyes and mouth to their fullest extent. He crept through the hedge and furtively approached the Vicarage so as to have a nearer view of the incredible spectacle. Yes, there it was. He'd made no mistake. The Vicar sat at his desk near the window of his study and in front of him were ranged piles of coins – pennies, threepenny pieces, sixpences, shillings, florins, half-crowns. And the Vicar was count-ing them . . .

Jimmy ran back to impart the news to Bobby. He found him in the garden, sitting in a packing case being drawn by an imaginary team of dogs over an imaginary expanse of ice and snow and glacier.

"The V-Vicar's one," he said breathlessly.

"One what?" said Bobby, vaguely, his thoughts still occupied by the problems of the solitary explorer.

"A miser," said Jimmy. "I saw him c-counting his money same as they d-do, an' he'd got heaps an' heaps of it."

"Gosh!" said Bobby, getting out of his packing case, dismissing his team of dogs and his glacier and bringing his mind back to his immediate surroundings.

"Well, we can d-do that ghost thing now we've

f-found one," said Jimmy. "We'll do it on Christmas Eve."

"All right," agreed Bobby. "What sort of a ghost are you going to be?"

"Jus' a ghost," said Jimmy.

Bobby considered.

"It'd make it a bit more exciting if you could be the ghost of someone he's murdered," he said.

"Don't be s-silly," said Jimmy. "He hasn't m-murdered anyone."

"No," said Bobby with a note of regret in his voice, "I don't suppose he has."

So on the morning of Christmas Eve Jimmy got busy with his preparations. Finding a pillowcase in the ragbag that reached almost to his feet and had convenient holes for arms and head, he took it across to Bobby's and together they tried it on in the tool-shed.

"It's all right but your face," said Bobby, inspecting him critically. "You haven't got a ghost's face."

"Well, I can p-pull one," said Jimmy, contorting his small countenance into various fantastic shapes.

"No, they're none of them ghost's," said Bobby decisively. "We'll have to think of something."

And he thought of something. He appeared that evening with an old iron saucepan on to which he had painted in white paint a not very convincing skull with enormous eyes and a somewhat sheepish grin.

"My mother was throwing the saucepan away, 'cause it leaks," he explained, "an' I found the white paint in the garage."

The saucepan was rather a tight fit, and Jimmy was perhaps a little less enthusiastic than Bobby about his disguise.

"It's jolly uncomfortable," he complained in a muffled voice from inside it, "an' I can't speak prop'ly."

"Never mind that," said Bobby. "You've got to have a ghost's face if you're going to be a ghost."

"All right," agreed Jimmy, as he dragged off his saucepan. "We'll d-do it tonight, shall we?"

As dusk fell, the two set out for the Vicarage, and Jimmy donned his pillowslip and saucepan in the shelter of the hedge. Fate seemed to favour their enterprise. The side door was open. The Vicarage appeared to be empty. Feeling slightly disconcerted by the ease with which they had gained their entry, the two crept into the hall. There was a cupboard under the stairs, the door of which stood ajar.

"Come on," said Bobby. "Let's hide in here, then you can jump out at him when he comes."

They entered the cupboard and crouched among the brushes and brooms that filled it. Soon they heard the Vicar come in by the side door. But he was evidently not alone. They recognised the voice of Sir George Bellwater.

"They're always leaving this cupboard door open," said the Vicar, slamming the door of the cupboard as he passed. Then he went on into the study with his visitor.

"I'll open it again jus' a bit," whispered Bobby, "then we can hear when he goes an' the Vicar's alone. You've got to have a person alone to haunt them prop'ly."

He felt over the closed door with his fingers then gave a gasp of dismay.

"There isn't a handle," he said. "It's the sort you can't open from inside. We – we're imprisoned, Jimmy."

"What'll we d-do?" said Jimmy indistinctly from his saucepan.

"Dunno," said Bobby blankly, "but we've got to find a way out somehow. We'll starve to death if we don't."

"Help me g-get my saucepan off," said Jimmy, "then I can t-try."

In the semi-darkness of the cupboard, Bobby wrestled unavailingly with the saucepan. It was wedged immovably on Jimmy's solid head. In the study the Vicar stopped half-way through a sentence and listened.

"What's that noise?" he said.

"Someone in the kitchen?" suggested his visitor.

"There isn't anyone," said the Vicar. "My house-keeper's out."

"Seems to come from the hall," said the visitor.

They went into the hall. The sounds continued.

"It's in that cupboard," said the Vicar.

"Rats, probably," said Sir George.

"Sounds like something larger," said the Vicar. "I'll get my torch."

The door of the cupboard was opened and the light of the Vicar's torch revealed the strangest spectacle the two men had ever seen.

"He's a ghost," explained Bobby, "but his head's got stuck."

Together the Vicar and his visitor removed the saucepan, revealing the reddened and indignant face of Jimmy.

"I s-said it was better without the s-saucepan," he said.

During the explanations that followed the Vicar's visitor threw back his head and roared with laughter.

"I was checking up the collection, of course," said the Vicar mildly.

"Well, you've given me the best laugh I've had for

"HE'S A GHOST," EXPLAINED BOBBY, "BUT HIS HEAD'S GOT STUCK IN A SAUCEPAN."

years, Vicar," said Sir George, "and you can have the field on your own terms as a slight return for it."

"Thanks," said the Vicar.

With that the visitor took his leave, and the Vicar turned to Jimmy and Bobby.

"I'm very grateful to you," he said. "I've been trying to get that field of his for the Cricket Club for months, and the old skinflint has been holding out for the top market price." The vicar was a very young man and inclined to be indiscreet. "You'll stay and have a cup of cocoa with me, won't you?" he went on. "I'm sure you need it."

"Yes, please," said Bobby.

"Does skinflint m-mean miser?" said Jimmy.

"Yes," said the Vicar.

"Then I've c-cured a m-miser for Christmas, haven't I?" asked Jimmy.

"You seem to have," said the Vicar.

Jimmy drew a deep sigh of satisfaction.

"That's all right," he said. "That's what I w-w-wanted to do."

# *The William Stories*

1. Just – William
2. More – William
3. William – Again
4. William – The Fourth
5. Still – William
6. William – The Conqueror
7. William – The Outlaw
8. William – In Trouble
9. William – The Good
10. William
11. William the Bad
12. William's Happy Days
13. William's Crowded Hours
14. William – The Pirate
15. William – The Rebel
16. William – The Gangster
17. William – The Detective
18. Sweet William
19. William – The Showman
20. William – The Dictator
21. William and Air Raid Precautions
22. William and the Evacuees
23. William Does His Bit
24. William Carries On
25. William and the Brains Trust
26. Just William's Luck
27. William – The Bold
28. William and the Tramp
29. William and the Moon Rocket
30. William and the Space Animal
31. William's Television Show
32. William – The Explorer
33. William's Treasure Trove
34. William and the Witch
35. William and the Pop Singers
36. William and the Masked Ranger
37. William the Superman
38. William the Lawless

*Just William – a facsimile of the first (1922) edition*
*Just William – As Seen on TV*
*More Just William – As Seen on TV*
*William at War*
*Just William at Christmas*
*Just William on Holiday*
*Just William at School*